A Claire O'Shaunessy Mystery

Sue Myers

Badcat Literary Creations

Badcat Literary Creations

Copyright © 2013 by Sue Myers

All Rights Reserved

This novel is a work of fiction. Names, characters, places and incidents are either the product of the author's imagination, or, if real, used fictitiously. No part of this book may be reproduced, scanned, distributed or transmitted in any form or by any electronic or mechanical means, including, but not limited to, photocopying, recording or by any information storage retrieval system, without the express written permission of the publisher, except in the case of brief quotations embodied in critical articles or reviews or where permitted by law. To contact us with questions, please send your inquiry to authorsuemyers@gmail.com.

Cover Art by Julie Kukreja, Pen and Mouse Design

Printed in the United States of America

10 9 8 7 6 5 4 3 2

To my husband, Gene,
for his incredible support and love.

To Sally Sloan Christie,
my dearest friend since childhood.

And, to my dear friend Betty Koehler,
who is gone, but not forgotten.

Acknowledgements

My wonderful husband, Gene, has supported me through all my crazy adventures. And, if you don't think writing a book tops the list, think again. My adventure started long before *Deception* was born. I have met amazing people along the way who have been more than gracious with not only their time, but shared their experiences and knowledge with me. I couldn't have asked for more.

First, I need to thank the fabulous team who actually put *Deception* together. My editor, Brittiany Koren, Written Dreams, for all her support and encouragement, Julie Kukreja, Pen & Mouse Design House, Inc., for my incredible cover, and Lara Hunter, Book Technologies, for her tech skills which I will never understand!

A major thanks to Michele E. May, author of the Circle City Mystery series, for her constant support and guidance through the maze of computer editing—I couldn't have done *Deception* without you, along with our critique partner, Lisa Mork. And, my sister-in-law, Patty Schreck, who graciously took out her red pen to hunt for my grammatical and point of view errors. I'm sure I owe you several new red pens. To my NICU co-workers, Ruby, Robin, Cathy D. and Cathy V., for reading excerpts and listening to me babble on about my characters for more years than I can remember.

My undying gratitude to Christine Witthohn for her support and work. And to Karen Syed for giving me the push I needed.

To my old friends, Jean Barr, Margaret Briesch, Arlene Erlbach, Sherrill Bodine, Cheryl Jefferson, Cathy Andorka, Pat Pinianski, Rosemary Paulas and Jude Mandell. Your support and knowledge made all the difference.

Many thanks to my neighbor and walking partner, Norma Herrera, for being such a good friend and listener.

I want to include my friends in Sisters in Crime Chicagoland, Midwest Mystery Writers of America, and the Love Is Murder Board. And, a big thank you to Augie Aleksey, Centuries &

Sleuths Book Store, for his generous support of mystery writers.

And, the words 'Thank You', won't even cover all the support my husband, Gene, and my dearest friend, Sally Christie, gave me. The two of you kept me going when my writing career looked the bleakest. I love both of you!

As a closing note, I need to remind you that *Deception* is a work of fiction. This means I made it up! I've enjoyed including local sites and history. Any errors are mine. A belated thank you to my family and friends, whose names I borrowed for *Deception*. They were just perfect for the story, but none of the characters match the owners of the names. Have fun finding your name!

I worked on *Deception* for many years, so if I missed thanking anyone, please let me know. Hope you enjoy reading *Deception* as much as I did writing the story.

Chapter 1

Detective Patrick O'Shaunessy squatted next to the body, gazing at it in disgust. "What the hell?"

"I don't believe it," said Detective Jack Miller, as he stared at the dead man's shirt.

"I warned both of you. The jogger didn't realize he was whizzing on the dead guy until his stream splashed back on his legs," said Sergeant Perchowski as he swatted the flies swarming from the edge of Chicago's East Lagoon in Jackson Park.

Patrick shook his head. "Was the man blind? The victim's white tee shirt is a glaring flag. Of course now the undershirt has a nice yellow spot thanks to our early morning jogger." Just when Patrick had thought he'd seen it all, life dished him up another pile of crap. This was why he loved being a cop. No two days were ever the same.

"Talk about a contaminated crime scene." Jack watched as a patrolman corralled the area with yellow and black tape. "Perchowski, how many people would you guess have trampled over the crime scene already this morning?"

The sergeant scratched the back of his neck. "Let's see. There's the jogger," he pointed to the guy puking his guts out on the path, "his jogging buddy, two squatters, a couple of park maintenance men, and the older lady with her little, yapping dog. Apparently the jogger attracted quite a crowd before the old lady called 9-1-1."

"How did the media get here so fast?" Jack asked.

"They were covering a new exhibit at the Museum of Science and Industry by the east entrance. The minute they heard the screams, they were only too happy to send a cameraman and reporter over to see what was happening. It made the morning news before we could even get here."

"Hey, Sarge," called the patrolman who had hung the tape, "both the Coroner's office and the evidence techs are here."

"Send them down," Perchowski waved as he turned to Jack. "If you two don't need me, I'm heading back to the parking lot to see if I can make some order out of the chaos there. I have all the witnesses detained on the tennis court. I'll start getting statements, but I'm saving the puking jogger for you boys. Just holler if you need anything."

"Any chance you have bug spray on you?" Jack asked. "They seem to have taken a liking to my partner."

Patrick swatted at the bugs. "Word's out, we're serving fresh meat."

"Have some in the squad car. I'll send it back with one of the patrolmen." Perchowski said.

"Thanks." Patrick shook his pant legs and approached Jack. "What do you think?"

"Weird. Who dumps a body only clothed in underwear face down by a park lagoon?" his partner said.

"Did I hear somebody say 'weird'?" Craig O'Connor, a Death Investigator from the Cook County Morgue, asked. "Here's the bug spray." He tossed Patrick the can.

"Thanks."

"So what have you got for me?" O'Connor said. He placed his crime scene kit next to the victim.

"You're going to love this one, O'Connor." Patrick bent down to point out the yellow stain. "A jogger stepped off the path when nature called only to discover he was watering our victim and not the buckthorn bushes. Do you think a heart attack did our victim in?" He covered his mouth as he tried to suppress a grin.

"Right, O'Shaunessy," O'Connor said as he opened his kit and removed a camera. "I just don't know if our victim decided to have it *before* or *after* he bound his own hands and legs and fell face down. From the amount of mulch present, I doubt if bleach will be able to brighten his underwear or socks."

"How long do you think he's been dead?" Jack asked O'Connor.

O'Connor shot several angles of the body before stopping. "Well, my best guess at this point is a day or two. He was probably dumped last night; otherwise, the coyotes would have had him for dinner.

"Catch." O'Connor tossed Patrick and Jack each a pair of disposable gloves. "Let's roll him."

Chapter 2

"Claire, I want you to work up the case O'Connor just brought in from Jackson Park." Dr. Gregory Johnson said as he dropped the file on Claire's desk. Dr. Johnson was Chicago's Cook County Medical Examiner and Claire's friend and mentor, but at the moment, he was all business. "Because the media is all over this, the Police Department has asked me to move John Doe to the front of the line," Johnson continued.

"Okay," said Dr. Claire O'Shaunessy, a forensic pathologist. She opened the file and scanned the top sheet. "I see our John Doe was vacationing by a patch of buckthorn. Personally, I prefer a warm, sunny beach."

"Be forewarned the media is already barking at the back door. Please don't give them anything I'm going to hear about on the five o'clock news." He gave her a look that wouldn't bear discussing.

"Me?" She tried to feign innocence.

"Claire, you're killing me. Sometimes you don't think before you open your mouth. I'm still catching flak from the comment you made about the floater in Lake Calumet."

"I didn't know the reporter was disguised as a tech, honest? Okay, I'll keep a lid on it."

"Yeah, yeah, I know," Johnson said. "Anyway, the folks around here love their barbeques and picnics. They don't take too kindly to decomposing bodies showing up in their local parks."

"I don't suppose you wanted this yesterday?"

Dr. Johnson laughed. "How could I? He was only discovered at sunrise. Get back to me as soon as you've got something, okay?"

"I'll take care of it." In spite of her career, she couldn't imagine enjoying a picnic one minute, then chasing a stray baseball into the bushes only to discover a rotting corpse.

"Thanks." Johnson's cell phone rang. "This is Johnson. I understand." He flipped his phone closed. "Gotta run, Claire. I'll check in with you later."

Claire nodded to him as he walked out of the room, then took a long sip of her cappuccino. She laughed as she pictured Dr. Johnson running down the hall. The last time he ran at all was probably twenty-five years ago.

She savored the remains of her reheated morning cappuccino as she read the case file in her cramped office, if she could consider a worktable with a couple of file drawers stuck underneath, an office. With county and state budgets always teetering in the red, the coroner barely squeezed out funds for new equipment, let alone for ancillary spaces. Claire shared the crowded workspace with two other forensic pathologists. Since she was new, she got the worktable.

Claire didn't mind; it was the work that mattered, and being back in Chicago close to her siblings—an older brother and four sisters—was the important thing.

Reviewing the file, she noticed the police report was pretty straightforward. The report stated a jogger discovered the decomposing remains of a male adult. The victim was found lying face down by a heavily overgrown section of buckthorn. He was dressed in a white tee shirt, briefs and socks, and his ankles were bound with white tape. After the police rolled him over, they noted the same white tape binding his wrists. Age was undetermined, no identification present.

Claire reached for the phone to page Ian, her assistant.

"Rumor has it you pulled the John Doe case." Ian's voice came from the doorway.

Claire jumped at the unexpected voice. She had been deep in thought. Coffee splashed on the open file. The spike-haired, lanky, twenty-year old tech stood just inside her office doorway.

"Ian, how many times have I told you not to sneak up on me? One of these times you might find me with a scalpel in my hands," Claire said.

"Sorry, Dr. O'Shaunessy." Ian grabbed a box of tissues and helped her mop up the coffee.

"It's not your fault. Sometimes when I'm concentrating, I tune out everything around me. I was just about to page you anyway. Is there a room available for us to do the autopsy?"

"We're in room two and ready to go. The lab is downloading the x-rays. Also, we've shot the preliminary photographs of the body."

"Thanks, I'll meet you in the autopsy room in a few minutes."

"Okay, Dr. O'Shaunessy. Anything, else?" Ian asked.

She shook her head no, and Ian left as quickly as he had come in.

Claire liked her offbeat tech with his pierced eyebrow. He was conscientious and efficient. But most of all, he showed respect to all their patients. He was never rough when he handled them. Ian was new to the world of autopsies and started about the same time she had. But the morgue was short-handed and there hadn't been a trained diener, a morgue assistant, available to work with her on a regular basis, so they assigned Ian to work with her. Claire liked having Ian because he complemented her more hands-on approach with the cases. They made a solid team.

She picked up the spilled coffee container and tossed it over her shoulder. She smiled when the cup banged against the inside of the metal wastebasket.

"Hey, Sis, glad to see you haven't lost your touch." Patrick O'Shaunessy called out from her office doorway.

It was too late to duck. Her brother, with his devilish Irish eyes, grabbed her in one of his bear hugs, just like the good old days, and she knew he wouldn't let go.

"Okay, you win! Uncle!" she cried.

Patrick let go and straddled an office chair. "So, how's the new job?"

"Not bad. What brings you in here?"

"Miller and I have been assigned to the Jackson Park case. We're here for the autopsy."

"Well, you're in luck, detective. He's my case now. This will give me a chance to show you my stuff."

"Claire, you're so gross. Why couldn't you just get married and have babies like all of our sisters?" Patrick teased.

"You know I'm not the beauty shop, do lunch kind of gal. I could have followed the family tradition and been a cop." Claire saluted her brother .

"Excuse me, is this detective bothering you?"

Claire turned at the sound of the deep voice to see a tall, athletically built man standing behind her. His eyes were the color of rich espresso. His jaw line was firm. He was all business with his straight back and crisp white shirt. "No," she replied, jamming her elbow into Patrick's generous side.

"Ouch, that hurt," Patrick said.

"Tough! Hi, I'm Claire, Patrick's sister. You must be Detective Miller." So this was Jack, her brother's partner. Claire extended her hand to welcome the man. His large hand consumed hers and held it just a little too long for her comfort. It was a nice feeling, sending shivers up her spine, but she didn't need any distractions at the moment.

Patrick had mentioned Jack had a personnel jacket so clean it squeaked. When it came to justice, Patrick claimed Jack was driven, almost possessed. Her brother said it had something to do with his best friend's murder when they were in college.

Claire was focused on her new job and grateful to be living near her family. Her last relationship had soured, but that was behind her now. So why couldn't she stop feeling the power in Jack's grip even though they were no longer touching?

"We're heading down to autopsy. Care to join us?" Claire asked.

"Lead the way."

"Do you have a jar of Vick's with you?" Patrick asked his partner.

Jack took a small jar of Vick's from his pocket and offered it to Claire first.

"Thank you, but I'm fine," Claire said. She was used to the various smells in the morgue.

Jack held the jar for Patrick.

"Thanks. I know it won't kill the odor, but it sure helps. It reminds me of when I was sick as a kid, and my mother plastered it all over my chest." Patrick applied a generous layer over his upper lip.

Claire couldn't help smiling from behind her protective facemask. She remembered Patrick doing the same for her when she had a cold after their mother had died.

Before entering the room, gowns were a necessity. Claire watched as Patrick struggled to pull the shapeless gown over his oxford shirt and dark slacks. "Miller, don't even think about laughing."

"Trust me, I wasn't going to make any reference to the Pillsbury Dough Boy," Jack said.

Gowned and gloved, Claire pushed open the door with her backside for Patrick. "There are some seats by the desk or the back wall." She pointed to a couple of chairs. She took a quick glance at Patrick. Sweat formed on his forehead. The air conditioning was on full blast due to the warmer than usual fall. This was the first case they would be working together on since she had moved back to Chicago. She suspected Patrick wasn't comfortable watching her perform the autopsy.

Claire adjusted the protective head visor and looked to her assistant who had been waiting for her. "Ian, what do we have so far?"

"The x-ray of the left tibia is on the screen. The views of the full-body photographs should be available soon." Ian placed the surgical instruments on the small silver stand next to the victim.

Claire checked the x-ray of the lower leg bone on the computer. She pointed to a faint diagonal line. "Looks like an old fracture, perhaps late childhood accident, or a teenage sports injury."

"I collected samples of short, coarse fibers along with soil which appears to be yellow clay from the body. The lab is checking them right now." Ian hesitated a moment before going on. "I know you like to collect your own samples, but since there were so many of these fibers and pieces of soil, I thought you might not mind if the lab got a head start on identifying them."

"Thanks. Good thinking," Claire said. Because John Doe's death wasn't witnessed, Claire would be handling the autopsy like a crime scene. The slightest piece of trace evidence could lead the police to the victim's killer.

Overhead lights glared down on the bloated body. Claire stepped to the head of the table and spoke into a small recorder. "This is case 14-01165. John Doe was a Caucasian, 72 inches long and 165 pounds. A jogger found him face down in a wooded area, clothed only in underwear, no jewelry present, his hands and ankles bound. I will now begin the external examination."

Circling the body from the head of the table, Claire stated her findings. "The overall condition of the tissue suggests this man was dead approximately one to two days. Tissue damage to the calves and thighs was possibly from rodents or other wild animals. Noted are several abrasions to his face which may have occurred after death, since there is an absence of blood at the sites. His remaining skin appears intact except for a few areas at his waistband where his tee shirt is pulled up. The skin has split due to bloating. Hair and nails are loose."

Claire pulled the magnifying lens down to inspect his ears. With the pick-ups, she extracted blowfly larvae approximately the size of the second instar stage. "Ian, I believe these little guys will need one of your jars."

With a quick glance, she noticed her brother's flushed face. He was scratching his neck. She nodded towards the door, but he shook his head no. She knew this was difficult for him. A dead body on the street, even a dead apartment stinker in the heat of summer, didn't bother him, but Patrick's wife, Sylvia, had warned her he didn't handle autopsies well. Sylvia told her sometimes they even gave him nightmares.

"Any questions, Detective Miller?"

"I'm guessing the purplish discoloration on his abdomen and upper thighs means the body was face down most of the time."

"Correct," Claire said. "The areas you mentioned are considered the 'fixed' areas of lividity. But if you note the faint marks on his left arm and leg, they suggest, for a short time after death, he was positioned on his side."

"What would be the point to positioning him on his side?" Jack asked.

"Perhaps who ever transported him had something placed next to him and there wasn't enough room for the body to be flat," Claire answered.

Next, she examined the scalp for wounds, finding none. The abrasions on the left side of his forehead had the fibers and dirt stuck to them, but no blood.

"You'll note how white his nose, knees and the back of his right hand and forearm are; these areas were in direct contact with the ground and were supporting the weight of the body. The compressed tiny capillaries prevented lividity from forming. The swelling to his eyes and cheeks could make a visual identification difficult."

"Sis, what about the marks on his neck? O'Connor thought we might have a possible strangulation," Patrick said.

Claire pulled the tee shirt away from the dead man's neck. "There are bilateral darkened marks on each side of his neck. Once he is washed, we'll be able to assess the damage better." Her gloved fingers carefully palpated the victim's neck. "Ian, do we have a neck x-ray?"

"Yes. I'll pull the neck view up for you on the computer

screen."

"Thanks," Claire said.

Ian took a close look at the screen. "Wow, someone didn't like this guy."

Claire viewed the film. "Someone crushed our John Doe's trachea, and did a number on the hyoid bone as well."

"Could you show me the damage on the x-ray?" Miller stood looking directly over the top of her head at the computer screen.

Claire felt he was a little too close. Even though he was wearing a disposable gown over his clothing, she felt his chest graze her shoulder.

Quickly she pointed to the area just below the jaw, then steadied her voice. She could hear herself ramble into a full explanation on the purpose of the hyoid bone. This was her safety net, the science of the human body. No emotion, just facts. She learned this the hard way from her former fiancée's deception; don't mix business with pleasure.

"Miller," Patrick called from his chair, "if you don't stop her now, she'll go on for hours about this stuff."

"Hey, partner, remember this is an official investigation. We may need to know this. Dr. O'Shaunessy, does this hyoid bone serve any major function?"

"Only if you want to eat," Claire answered.

"Sis, please don't talk about food."

Claire ignored Patrick's comment and returned to the autopsy table. "Ian, let's cut and bag the adhesive tape from the wrists and ankles."

Removing the tape from the wrists was tricky because the skin was too decomposed. With a small suture removal scissors, Claire was able to cut the tape from the hairs on the victim's arms. The tape wrapped over the victim's socks made it easier to remove it from his ankles.

"Do you think we can trace the tape?" Patrick asked.

Claire dropped the last piece into the evidence bag. "I doubt if you'll have any luck. This is standard adhesive tape you'll find in hospitals, doctor's offices, even your local drug store. The best you can hope for is the lab pulls a fingerprint off the tape. And even if they get one, who knows how long the print has been there."

Slowly she examined the right arm, then the left. She stopped abruptly at the left forearm. "Ian, bring the camera over here. Can you get a close-up shot of both his wrists?"

Ian pulled the camera from the overhead mount down and aimed it at the left wrist.

"I'll hold the ruler for the picture. Detective Miller, do you see the slight changes in skin tone? It's faint, but note the shape."

Miller bent closer to the arm to examine the mark. Claire noticed how quickly he pulled back, as his gag reflex responded.

"How do you tolerate the stench?" Jack asked. "I don't know which is worse, the smell stuck in my nose or the taste when I open my mouth."

"Practice." Claire smiled, as she pointed to the wrist. "Do you see a faint circle, where the skin is lighter, approximately two inches in diameter, narrowing on each side? Check the right wrist."

Miller followed her to the other side of the table where Ian was photographing a comparison shot of the right wrist. "The only markings here are from the adhesive tape. Looks like our victim wore a watch, but we didn't find one at the scene," said Miller. "Why is this important?"

"Save that thought for a minute, detective. Look at the left ring finger. There is a deep gouge above the knuckle. First glance, you assume the cut is from the skin splitting as a result of the bloating from the release of gases. My guess is he wore a large ring on this finger. The killer removed the ring for fear it would help identify the victim. Also, I know it sounds thin, but the differences in skin tone tell me he spent time outside. What types of rings do men generally wear on their left ring finger which can be identifying?"

"Wedding bands or school rings," Ian answered.

"So, if it's a wedding band, there is a wife somewhere out there without a husband. If it's a college ring, then there's a chance he's employed and will be missed. If you pay attention, Detective Miller, the victim will tell you what happened."

Claire picked up the victim's left hand, clipped the fingernails and placed them in a brown envelope. "Other than recent dirt, these nails look like they were well cared for. I'll send the samples to see if the lab can find anything." She handed the sealed evidence bag to Ian for labeling.

Still, something wasn't right with the victim. "Other than the expected damage to the epidermis, the outer layer of skin, I don't see any defensive wounds, no bruising or abrasions to the arms. It doesn't appear as if he struggled," Claire stated. "Maybe he didn't see his attacker, or, it was someone he knew and he never anticipated a threat."

Miller circled the table. "Perhaps he was in his home when he was abducted. After all, he's wearing only underwear."

"If he was killed at home by someone he knew, then whoever was responsible might have thought he had to get rid of the body," Patrick said.

"Okay, we've got to get back to work." Claire knew it was easy for her to be sidetracked from the body on her table to the crime itself. It must be the three generations of policeman's blood running in her veins.

Using the large magnifying lens, she moved from the victim's head to his feet, thoroughly inspecting every inch of the body. Next, she collected the short, coarse fibers from different areas on the body and placed them on slides under the microscope, with the dual viewing eyepieces. All the samples appeared the same.

"May I?" asked Detective Miller.

"Sure, help yourself," said Claire.

"What's your take on them?" Miller said.

"The fibers look like they came from one of those cheap woven sisal rugs I had back in my college days. My guess is the rug is new and it hasn't been vacuumed. That's why there are so many fibers."

"We didn't find any drag marks on the ground. I wonder if he was wrapped in a sisal rug and carried to the dump site," Patrick said, as he stood up to stretch his legs before sitting back down. "And, another thing, O'Connor noticed the yellow clay on the victim, but he said the only yellow clay in the park was a good six inches down in the ground. The area around the body was covered with mulch from plant and tree debris."

"Where did this guy come from?" asked Jack.

Claire had the same questions. "Ian, I think it will be easier to remove the underwear if we cut along the seams. I don't see anything on the underwear giving us a clue to the cause of death." Together they removed the shirt, briefs and socks.

"Now here's an interesting piece of evidence," Ian said.

Claire and Miller walked over to where Ian had spread the

pieces on the work counter.

"I have a friend who works at a shelter. He mentioned the homeless often don't have underwear. Our John Doe was wearing an undershirt and briefs with the same label." Ian pointed to the labels with the pickups. "The manufacturer is mid-to-upper price."

"That doesn't buy us much help," said Detective Miller.

"You're right, but it does give credibility to Dr. O'Shaunessy's theory our victim was employed," Ian answered.

"Thank you, Ian." She always appreciated his skill for detail.

Claire watched Ian's eyes dance. She knew he had seen something else.

"Okay, I give," she said.

Ian carefully turned the victim's socks on the counter over with the pickups. "This is an interesting discovery."

"Socks? So he wore socks," Detective Miller said dismissively.

"Look closer," Ian said.

Detective Miller bent over the counter. Ian offered him the pickups. Carefully Jack turned the sock around so the back of the cuff was visible.

Claire watched as a smile spread over Detective Miller's face.

"What do you see?" Claire looked down at the insignia, a black stylized "R" on the cuff.

Even Patrick left the security of the desk chair to take a look at the sock.

"Ian my friend, I owe you an apology. Not only did the victim wear socks, he wore the top of the line," Detective Miller said.

"I thought you would be the right person to realize the importance of this find. I heard you ran in the Chicago marathon. How was your time?" Ian asked.

"Not bad," Detective Miller said.

Patrick shook his head as he inspected the socks with Claire. "Would someone tell me what you two are ogling over?"

"Ian, you made the discovery, you do the honors," Detective Miller motioned with his hand.

"I had a college roommate who ran marathons. He received the *Road Runner Sports Catalog*. Our victim is wearing socks with their insignia. They can only be purchased through the catalog," Ian said.

"Can you imagine how many people must receive that

catalogue?" Patrick asked. "Who knows when he bought them?"

"Running marathons is quite impressive, Detective Miller." Claire turned the sock around. Patrick hadn't mentioned this tidbit to her. "Other than being soiled from the elements, they don't look worn."

Ian and Detective Miller exchanged glances. Miller spoke first. "Both of you are missing the obvious. The Chicago Marathon was two weeks ago. Our victim probably wore out his other socks while training."

"Detective Miller, you're right. Patrick, look at his feet." Claire couldn't believe Patrick had followed her to the table. "Now look at the area just below his great toe." She pointed to the left foot. "See how the skin is torn in the shape of a rectangle. Ian, check inside the sock for a Band-Aid. It must have come off when we removed the sock. He was protecting his toe from blistering. The timing would be about right if he had run in the marathon. And, I would bet money he wore a watch while he was running, which would account for the mark on his left wrist."

"Dr. O'Shaunessy, I found the Band-Aid! I'll send it off to the lab."

"That's my sister." Patrick was beaming.

"No, Ian gets the credit for this one."

"Thank you, Dr. O'Shaunessy." Ian took a mock bow.

"Okay everyone, places, please," Claire said, "we still have the internal part of the autopsy to complete."

Chapter 3

Claire snapped off her protective gear in one fluid motion and dumped it in the receptacle marked for contaminated waste. Impatiently, she waited for the water to warm at the surgical sink before washing her hands. Claire realized it didn't matter where she worked, in an elite hospital or the county morgue, the water never got hot enough.

"Patrick went outside for some fresh air," said Detective Miller.

Claire wheeled around. *"Damn."* Soapy water ran down her arms onto her scrubs.

Detective Miller handed her several paper towels.

"Thanks," she said. Deciding to skip wiping the soap which was now inside her scrubs and running down her side, she faced the detective.

"Sorry. I didn't mean to interrupt you."

"You didn't. My mind was on something else." Patrick hadn't mentioned Jack competed in marathons.

"What made you take up running?" Claire asked.

"It's a long story," Miller said.

"Then give me the short version. Was it because of all the despicable things you see as a homicide detective?" Claire heard him sigh as he looked away from her.

"I lost a good friend through violence. Pounding the pavement helped me to clear my head and get back on track."

Claire could relate to the deep inner need for physical release. In high school, she'd been the top scorer for the girls' ice hockey team. Before her father died in the line of duty, she'd played for fun. After his death, she played for blood, and still did.

"How about I buy you a cup of coffee since you missed your lunch," Detective Miller offered.

"You missed yours, too." Claire dropped the towels in the waste receptacle. "You don't have to keep me distracted while Patrick burns a couple of cancer sticks," she answered while applying the lotion she kept in her pocket to her reddened fingers. Her sisters' hands never looked like this. They went for weekly manicures. Of course, they didn't need to wash them forty times a day either. "Did Patrick put you up to delaying me?" Claire asked.

Detective Miller grabbed another paper towel and offered it to Claire. "Here, I think you missed a few spots." He pointed to her right upper arm.

She wiped the missed drops and discarded the towels. "Thanks, Detective."

"Please, call me Jack. I think we go by our rank or last name to keep the work from becoming too personal."

"Sometimes it is. We've all had cases get under our skin that we can't let go." Claire remembered a child abuse case from two weeks ago. The little girl was the same age as one of Patrick's daughters. It had been sad to see the amount of physical abuse done to someone so small and innocent.

"What about that cup of coffee? I'd like to pick your brain about the autopsy," Jack said.

"Pick my brain? That's an interesting choice of words, considering my line of work."

"Sorry."

"You didn't answer my question." Claire headed back to her office without waiting to see if he would follow, which he did.

"What question?" he called from behind her.

Claire let out a quiet chuckle. Men. They never really listened.

"Did Patrick put you up to detaining me? He doesn't think I know he needs a couple of cigarettes to kill the odors from the autopsy. My sister-in-law told me he comes home after attending a procedure smelling like a furnace from smoking." She entered her office and dropped the case file on her worktable.

"Yeah, it was something like that," said Jack.

"He really hates attending them, especially when it's kids. When I was a resident, he told me about a case with a nine-year-old girl as the victim. That one really tore him up."

"I remember him mentioning the case," said Jack. "The killer had inserted intravenous catheters in the arteries of both her arms and basically let her bleed to death. Even in death, Patrick said he had never seen anyone so white. I don't know how we got on these other cases, but I do have a few questions regarding our current victim."

Claire nodded her understanding, then checked the time. It

was almost 3 p.m. She had missed lunch, and her stomach was complaining. "Give me a few minutes to change. There's a hot dog stand a couple of blocks away. It's a beautiful fall day, and I think we could all use some fresh air and lunch. By then Patrick shouldn't be so green."

***

Dressed in jeans and a knit top, with her unruly red hair pulled back with a clip, Claire took a bite from her Chicago-styled hot dog. She sat across from Patrick and Jack at a picnic table on the edge of the cramped parking lot. It seemed everyone else in the neighborhood had the same idea. A couple of kids played tag around the old, maple trees. The teens at the next table pretended to dance with their arms to the beat of a song played by a local radio station.

"Can you eat and talk business at the same time?" Jack asked.

Patrick almost choked on a greasy fry. "She probably could eat while slicing open some poor fool's gut and never have it bother her."

She kicked her big brother under the table. She bit down on a couple of fries to keep from smiling at her brother's declaration of pride, no matter how warped it would sound to most people.

"Ouch! Jack, tell her to stop kicking me." Patrick pretended to be in pain as he rubbed his shin.

"I don't think your sister likes to be told what to do." Jack bit off a French fry dripping in catsup then smiled.

Claire felt Jack's eyes burrowing right through her. She needed to change the direction of the conversation. "Jack, you had a few questions about the case?"

"I heard your assistant mention he thought the latent print lab might have some results soon." Jack washed the last of his hot dog down with a Coke.

"Yes. When they have a high profile case, specimens are often moved to the head of the line."

"I can't believe they made this such a high profile case." He stuffed the wrappers back in the greased stained bag and tossed it into a container on the edge of the cracked black top.

"You know we're getting pressure from the mayor's office and the Park District to solve the crime, so the citizens of Chicago will feel it's safe to use the parks again. And, of course, they want to eliminate negative media coverage."

"What about the fingerprints?" asked Jack.

"Ian was able to make a good set. Luckily, no animals gnawed on the fingers. Probably because the victim was found lying face down on his hands."

Patrick finished the last of his fries. "I've been thinking about the position he was found in. I bet he was rolled up in a sisal rug at the crime scene to make it easier for transporting. When he was unrolled in the park, he landed as we found him by chance."

"Patrick, you are a genius," said Claire. "The faint shade of lividity on his left side could be a result of his position in a vehicle. I can't be sure, but I don't think he was on his side more than two or three hours."

"If that's the case, then the time line could extend the perimeter from the dump site as far north as Wisconsin, out past Rockford and even around the southern tip of Lake Michigan into Indiana," Jack said.

Patrick leaned forward and rested his arms on the picnic table. Keeping his voice down so the young lovers who had replaced the music buffs at the next table didn't hear him, "We didn't find any drag marks near the body."

"You're kidding me?" Claire said.

"Let's say the suspect drove an SUV. First of all, sisal rugs are stiff. The rug could disguise the body if another vehicle drove too close. Second, the back end would be higher than a car trunk. If the driver had adequate physical strength, he could throw a wrapped body this size over his shoulder to carry, instead of dragging it. Besides, carrying the body would be quicker than dragging it."

Claire took a sip of her iced tea. "He had to have known the victim would be discovered sometime."

"Yeah, but he was gambling on later, not sooner," Jack answered.

"Then why not drive out to one of the collar counties? There are plenty of isolated areas out there. Why *this* park?" she asked.

"Perhaps the driver was scared to go any farther with the body?" Patrick offered. "Or he knew this area. He may not even be from Chicago."

"Wait a minute. Didn't they have trouble with wild dogs in one of the parks last year?" Claire rose from her side of the picnic table.

"Yes, but it was another park, which was close by. One jogger was killed and another was badly wounded." Patrick straightened up. "Maybe he thought the dogs would clean up his problem for him?"

"Perhaps something spooked our driver and he split before he could think about the position of the victim. Not a bright move on his part," said Jack. "Claire, when do you think you will have an official ruling on cause of death?"

"I can't render an official opinion until all the labs are back, but it's definitely a homicide. You just don't wrap your hands and feet in adhesive tape, fall face forward and cover yourself up with fall leaves after you crush your own trachea."

"You're right, Sis, how about a time of death?"

"Probably between one and two days ago. I wish I had more for you to go on right now."

"Thanks, Sis. Okay, Partner, guess we'd better radio in that we're back up. Come on, we'll drop you off Claire."

"No, thanks, I could use the walk."

"I don't think your brother was giving you an option." Jack opened the door to the back seat of the squad car they had driven to the hot dog stand from Cook County Morgue.

"Patrick still thinks I'm ten years old and he has to watch out for me." Claire didn't like other people making decisions for her. She decided to accept Patrick's offer because it would save her valuable minutes returning to work and she was already drained. Next time, she would stand her ground. But it sure was nice having her big brother back in her life.

Chapter 4

This case should be simple, Claire thought, tapping a pencil against the edge of her worktable. Jogger finds a body in a city park. Victim probably killed elsewhere. She autopsies the victim and sends fingerprints and routine samples to the labs. The lab identifies the victim.

Then why did she have such an unsettling feeling about the case? Why did she believe it was going to take a lot more to identify the victim?

She replayed the autopsy over in her mind. She and Ian had maintained the integrity of the crime scene, their body. They had followed procedures to the letter. She chewed on her conversation with Patrick and Jack at lunch. Something just didn't fit.

Claire dropped the pencil on the file and began pacing the small office. She had a deep gut feeling, the one her dad talked about; the one he claimed saved his ass numerous times as a beat cop. She could almost put her finger on it. Something was out of place. But what was it? She was definitely her father's daughter.

She had no problem listing the cause of death on the autopsy as asphyxia by ligature strangulation. But to clear it from her mind, she needed to know the how and the why, the complete picture.

Claire removed the photographs she had taken from the file. She spread them out on the worktable to study them. Nothing was jumping out at her, except the photographs of the ligature marks.

She picked up the group and placed them in order, as if she was circling the victim's neck. The poorly defined edges of the marks were a classic example of soft ligature insult, usually made by fingers. There appeared to be four lines on each side of the neck wrapping around to the front. The cuts on the trachea were probably from fingernails. Only the indentations from the thumb marks were present on the back of the neck. Unfortunately, too much tissue damage occurred for fingerprints to be recovered.

Claire took a closer look at the angle of the marks. They were practically parallel to the floor. She paged Ian and told him to bring any of the preliminary lab reports available.

"In ten minutes, I'm on overtime," Ian said as he entered her office with several sheets of paper.

"I'll sign your time card," Claire said, trying not to think about the budget. "You got lab results?"

"Only the prelims. I rushed them through on a promise you would buy pizza for lunch tomorrow."

"Let's see if the lab earned their pizzas." Food was the super glue holding the staff together. Eating was the one normal thing they did each day like any other business. Cross contamination of evidence as well as personnel, prevented the staff from eating in the lab or exam areas, so they ate together in the break area. Sometimes they discussed work, but mostly the conversations revolved around family, sports and the weather.

Ian handed Claire the results before sitting on the edge of one of the office desks.

"Okay," she said, talking mostly to herself as she reviewed them. "I expected toxicology to be negative. They didn't find anything under the fingernails. That's a bummer." She stopped after reading the next lab result and looked at Ian.

"The lab found a different blood type, O-negative, on the front of our victim's socks. Our John Doe is B-positive. I told you those were special socks, but whose blood is it?"

Claire shrugged. "I don't know, but you're going to help me figure this out."

"Me?" Ian ran his hands through his spiked hair.

"Hey, you're the one who noticed the socks. I'd say you're on a lucky roll."

Ian squinted at her over the top of his glasses. "Are you kidding me?"

A brilliant idea occurred to Claire. She dug through her backpack for some foot powder. Next, she pinned her hair on top of her head to expose her neck. "I want to walk through the murder. I'll be the victim, and you'll be the killer."

"I'm not sure I get what you mean." Ian raised an eyebrow.

Claire removed the lid from the container. "Open your hands over the waste basket so I can put powder on them."

"Okay, but I don't do kink." He held his hands out, palms up.

Claire laughed. "I'll go along with that." She sprinkled the powder over his fingers. "Now, come over here and look at the ligature pictures."

Ian didn't move.

"Come on, Ian. I know it sounds strange, but trust me. Maybe we'll find some answers."

"Okay," said Ian as he approached the pictures.

"First of all, our victim was strangled," Claire explained.

"Right," he answered.

"The ligature marks in the photo almost look like even rings around his neck. I want you to come up behind me and place your hands around my neck exactly where the marks are in the photos. Then press just hard enough to leave a powder imprint."

Ian followed her directions.

Claire felt his fingers tremble as he pressed on her neck. These weren't the painful, crushing fingers her victim had felt. How frightening, she thought.

"Look at the marks on my neck. Are they parallel to the floor or on a slant?"

He circled Claire. "They're parallel to the floor."

"How tall are you?" she asked.

"About five feet ten inches, I guess."

"I'm five feet six inches. That's a four-inch difference. Ian, did it seem natural for you to place your hands where you did, or did you have to bend your arms up or down?"

"Can I try it again?"

Claire heard his earlier discomfort replaced by a steady, inquisitive voice. "Sure, Ian, give it another try."

She felt his fingers over their original marks. "What do you think?" she asked.

Ian kept them in place just a moment longer before speaking. "Easy. Like, this is where they should be if I wanted to strangle you."

"Our victim is about your height. I'm guessing the attacker is approximately four inches taller. We didn't find postmortem contusions on his arms or hips during the external autopsy, so I don't believe he fell."

"Why would our victim stand there and let the killer strangle him?" Ian asked.

Claire kept her back to him, so not to break the spell. She felt her heart skip a beat. "I thought I was safe." She could feel the tension in her voice. "You eased me to the floor after you killed me. Then you bound my wrists and ankles."

"But *why* didn't you fight me? There weren't any defensive wounds on your arms?"

Claire heard the tension in Ian's voice rise. The same question had played over and over in her head. Why *didn't* the victim fight back? A chill ran through her blood colder than ice on a winter day.

"Because you were so quick I didn't have time." Claire turned to face Ian. Her voice was barely above a whisper. She could hear him suck in a deep breath.

She pointed to the autopsy photo. "This must be it, see his crushed trachea? Our victim never thought his safety was an issue. He never saw it coming. Perhaps he saw something he shouldn't have. Something so horrible, so bad," she continued, "that he couldn't be allowed to live. The killer couldn't afford to leave a witness."

Ian's voice quivered. "What about the blood on the sock? Was it mine?"

"No." She could feel the adrenalin rush as they got closer to the answer she sought.

"How can you be sure?"

"You were behind me. The blood was on the front of my socks."

"But, whose blood is it?"

She stared directly into his eyes. Her heart pounded. "It belongs to the other victim."

"Other victim? Oh…my…God!" Ian sat down on the closest chair.

Claire leaned against the worktable. Neither spoke for several minutes.

"Now what?" Ian brushed the remaining powder off his hands before wiping them on the back of his scrubs. "And, where's the other body?"

"I don't know. I'll page Dr. Johnson and my brother, Patrick. Can you check with latent and see if they have anything on the fingerprints?"

"No problem." Standing, Ian shifted from one foot to the other. "Dr. O'Shaunessy, did the lab earn their pizzas?"

Claire stopped paging in mid-dial and smiled. "You bet!" She reached in her backpack and handed him several bills.

"Thanks." Ian flashed a smile as he started to leave. "I'm sure the lab will be at your complete disposal."

Nice to know the lab can be bought off so cheaply, Claire thought as she finished the page to Dr. Johnson. Next, she hit Patrick's name on her speed dial.

"Detective O'Shaunessy," he answered.

"Patrick, it's Claire."

"Everything okay?" his voice was full of concern.

"No. I think there's a second body…"

Chapter 5

Jack and Patrick drove back to headquarters. Jack felt more frustrated than enlightened. Until they identified the fingerprints, it limited the leads they had. He couldn't even look for another body. He would check with Missing Persons. If there was any chance their victim was either employed or married then he might just luck out.

Claire's call to Patrick had said it all. "He must have thought he was in a safe environment."

Jack racked his brain for answers. Their John Doe had possibly lost his life through no fault of his own other than being in the wrong place at the wrong time. His best friend, Tad had lost his life the same way. Jack knew there was a good chance this victim might not be identified. The victim could have come from three states away. Maybe no one even missed him. And, what if there was another victim out there? Would they ever find that person? The one thing he did believe was this victim wasn't homeless.

"Hello, Jack? You just missed our turn-off."

"Oh, sorry." Jack said, his mind on other things.

"Mind telling me where you have been since we dropped Claire off at the morgue?"

Jack took the next left turn. "Just thinking. Hopefully we'll get a hit on the fingerprints. I'll give Missing Persons a shot. But if there really is a second victim out there, and he *is* alive, we're signing his death warrant if we can't find him."

"She got to you."

"What are you talking about?"

"Claire. She got to you," Patrick said, with a smirk.

"I don't know what you mean."

"She's good. She has a sixth sense, or something, when it comes to figuring out possible scenarios for a crime."

"Yeah, you're right. It's almost as if she was there when the guy was killed. *Weird*. Please don't tell me she's on one of those psychic networks."

"Actually," Patrick's voice softened, "she's a carbon copy of my old man. After dinner, they would make a game of it. My dad would give her clues about a crime, and she'd try to solve the case. Thank heavens Claire went to medical school. At least I know she's safe in the morgue."

"Admit it, Patrick," Jack said, "the idea of Claire packing a gun and chasing the bad guys scares you to death."

"Okay, you got me, but the bad guys are probably the ones who should be scared."

***

The late afternoon sun was dipping in the west as Jack rounded the block and parked in the end space behind the station while Patrick checked in with Perchowski. The wind swept up, putting a chill in the air sending dried leaves scurrying across the pavement.

"Okay, Perchowski. Thanks for the update. We appreciate your efforts," Patrick said.

"No news?" Jack asked.

"Not much. The evidence techs found scattered broken pieces of yellow clay in the road close to the trailhead, but the majority of northern Illinois is yellow clay. There wasn't enough to identify a tire tread pattern. However, some of the pieces were tall, which might mean a more expensive tire. Also, the body was in an area covered by mulch. No clay." Patrick zipped up his jacket against the fierce Chicago wind.

Jack could hear his partner's labored breathing as they climbed the stairs to their second floor office. He worried Patrick's weight and smoking would catch up with him. *Then what?* He winced at the thought of losing a partner he enjoyed working with, especially after the death of a close friend.

Captain Joe Ramos, the Area 1 Homicide Commander, stood at his desk motioning them to his office as they cleared the entrance to the homicide division.

"Captain, you wanted to see us?" Patrick asked.

"Any luck?" The Captain turned, hiked up his pants slightly at the knee, and sat down.

Jack smiled at the maneuver. It was an unconscious move police officers in uniform did to preserve the crease in their pants. Jack wondered if Captain Ramos did it to maintain the crease or to impress the brass upstairs.

"Yes and no," Patrick answered. "No ID, but the coroner retrieved a decent set of prints. Now we just have to wait to see if the victim is in AFIS."

"The forensic pathologist offered a theory based on the victim's lack of defensive wounds. She raised the question of why would the victim stand there and allow someone to crush his trachea without fighting back. The lab discovered a second blood type on the front of his sock. Perhaps he was murdered because of what he witnessed," said Jack. "I'll see if Missing Persons has anything."

"Good," the Captain answered. "Keep me posted. It must be a slow news day. The media has been hounding the desk sergeant."

"Okay, Captain. We'll let you know as soon as we get a bite." Jack nodded to the Captain and followed Patrick out to their desks. He tossed his jacket over the back of his chair, loosened his tie and rolled up his sleeves.

"Nice of you to give Claire credit for her theory, but you could have used her name." Patrick sat down, pulled open the bottom drawer of the standard issue gray metal desk and propped his feet up. Next, he grabbed a pad of paper and started scribbling down notes.

Jack looked across the two desks which faced each other. "I wasn't sure if the Captain would consider it a conflict of interest since this is your case and family autopsied our John Doe."

Patrick's Irish grin covered his face. "Are you kidding me? I used to box the ears off Ramos at the neighborhood gym during my high school days. He knows I don't pull punches."

"You did?" Jack raised an eyebrow. He was amazed at hearing that, considering Ramos was now Patrick's superior.

Patrick motioned for him to lean forward on his desk. "I had my other sisters stand behind me outside the ring in their short skirts and tight sweaters. Never lost a match."

Jack was intrigued. "Where was Claire?"

"She was just a kid then. I had a friend, Frankie Biaggi, stuffed her in my locker so she wouldn't tell. She thought the whole episode was disgusting."

Jack laughed. "Why am I not surprised?"

Patrick tossed his note pad across the desk to Jack.

Jack read his partner's notes. "White male, approximately five feet ten inches, weight 165 pounds, B positive blood type, lean build, possible runner, possibly wore either a school ring or a wedding band, buys medium plus priced name brand underwear, orders socks from a specialty catalog, strangled, no defensive wounds, found with both hands and feet bound with surgical tape, yellow clay particles and sisal fibers present on body, moved from place of death, deceased approximately one to two days, and had someone else's blood type on the front of both socks."

"Don't forget Claire gave me the blood type, O-negative, for the second victim," Patrick said.

Jack added that to the notes then stretched his arms and clasped his hands behind his back. He always enjoyed tossing ideas back and forth with his partner. They'd been a team for only two years, but it seemed like forever. "We have more on the killer. We assume it was a man because he would have to be strong enough to carry the body, but it could be a larger woman. Also, remember Claire thinks the killer is at least four inches taller than the victim because of the placement of the ligature marks on his neck."

"Wait." Patrick removed his propped up feet from the drawer and leaned on his elbows. "Maybe our victim was the second body carried in the rug? The type O-negative person was in the rug first. The clay was from another site. Maybe he never saw anything at all."

"It can't be. The blood had to be wet enough to transfer and how was it on only the top part of the socks? He must have had his shoes on when the blood was transferred."

Patrick reached across to Jack's desk for his notes. "Let's go back to the underwear. If Claire's theory is correct, the victim had no idea his safety was an issue. So where would you find someone in his underwear?"

"For starters, I would pick a bedroom at the vic's home or a friend's home. After that, my guess would be a hotel, or some places of employment."

Patrick shoved the small notebook into his jacket pocket. "I hear some CEO's and pricy attorneys have private bathrooms in their office suites."

Jack glanced around at the tired office décor. About all he could say was the squad room was functional. "We're in the wrong business. Let's go back to the bedroom or home as a possibility. Both places seem logical." He rolled his pencil between his hands. "We're missing something. If this is a case of a cheating wife, I can see the lover dumping the partially clothed husband to make the murder look like it took place elsewhere. However, if the husband kills the lover in his own home, the stakes are higher. He's either in a state of panic or rage or both. He's not thinking about the lover's state of dress."

"What about the other blood type?" Patrick threw the case file in his desk drawer and locked it.

"He hit his wife across her face. It's her blood."

"Nah, it makes it more complicated. The crazed husband has to get rid of the victim's car. The wife has a bloody nose or a black eye to explain away. Also, there is a possibility the victim would be missed. If he has been a reliable employee, his boss might question his absence." Patrick took off his tie and stuffed it in his jacket pocket.

"But the employer might have the police do a well-being check at his place of residence. If his car is gone, then the police might suggest a missing person's report be completed if he doesn't show up in a couple of days. I'll check upstairs, but I don't have a gut feeling for the cheating spouse scenario."

"I'd rule out hotels because if there's blood, the maids would have noticed it unless the place was a dive with brown shag carpeting. We're back to my sister's theory. No defensive wounds, which leads to the element of surprise and the possibility of a second victim."

"I could go along with that." Jack stood up and shoved his chair under his desk.

"What if we look at this from a different angle? Let's put clothes on him, such as a work uniform of some type," Patrick said.

"If we go along with the work uniform idea, what did our victim see that cost him his life? Would the uniform give him away? We don't even know if the murder happened at work. If his boss is involved, he probably won't be filing a missing person's report, unless he is confident no one will suspect him. We're not getting anywhere with this tonight. Let's get out of here. I need some fresh air," Jack said.

"I thought that's what we had at the park this morning."

"No, I mean fresh air without swarming bugs and crime scene tape." Jack ran his hands through his hair in frustration.

"Why don't you take what we have to Missing Persons while I check for recent wife abuse reports and call Sylvia? I don't want my wife thinking we're ignoring her promise of lasagna and homemade bread. Try not to find anything which can't wait until after dinner?"

"I'll do my best." Jack chuckled as he slung his jacket over his shoulder and headed for the stairs. Dinner with Patrick's family was like coming home for him.

Chapter 6

"Hey Agnes, Charlie, we're over here," Bill Peterson called out from under the brilliant red maple tree. As he watched his friends enter the gate of the rural cemetery, he thought what a glorious day it was to record the history on the old headstones. The weather couldn't have been more perfect for their last outing of the year.

Their wives had joined them later, mostly out of curiosity after listening to Bill and Charlie discuss their adventures. Now the girls had their outings down to a science which included a wonderful lunch with all the trimmings. Bill's wife, June, had already set up the portable picnic table and decorated it with a colorful fall cloth and a pot of mums. A thermos of steaming coffee with mugs was ready for their morning break, while a bottle of white zinfandel chilled in the cooler for lunch. Life just doesn't get better than this, he thought. Good friends, good food, and good weather.

"Agnes, let me give you a hand." Bill noticed her face was flushed from pulling the old, red wagon up the slight incline. Charlie followed, carrying four webbed folding chairs. "June has the table all set up over by the red maple. By the way, is my favorite chicken salad in your cooler?"

"Yes," Agnes panted. "And I bet Charlie's favorite cran-apple pie is under the green cloth in June's pie basket."

"Nothing gets by you, Agnes. Hi, Charlie."

"Hey, I noticed you parked down by the road. Glad I followed suit after I dodged all those potholes. Boy, they would have done a number on the car's suspension system. Where's June?" Charlie asked.

"You know June; she couldn't wait to get started. She just went up the road a bit. I made each of us copies of the cemetery map." Bill passed out the maps. "This is the section June is working in now." He pointed to the far right corner. "Agnes, I assigned you to the next section to the west, which is right in this area, and Charlie and I will take…"

A scream interrupted Bill's directions.

"What was that?" Charlie asked as they all looked toward the direction June had gone.

"June!" they said in unison.

The next scream intensified. They dropped their maps and ran towards June. Bill knew his wife was not the squeamish type. She had survived growing up in a house with five older brothers and had raised their three sons.

Bill reached her first. "Are you all right, honey?"

June pointed down at a newly dug gravesite with her clipboard clutched tight against her chest. "I'm fine."

Bill looked at the fresh grave on the backside of the old stone marker. A dirty left hand with gnawed digits was exposed.

"Oh my goodness," Agnes exclaimed, approaching the grave.

"Stop. Don't go any closer," Charlie said. "This could be a potential crime scene. I'll call it in. This sure seems like old times."

Bill watched as Charlie pulled out his cell phone and dialed the number he and his partner had dialed for more years than he cared to count.

"Hey, Dave, is that you on dispatch?" asked Charlie.

"Yeah, it's me. How's retirement treating you?" Dave's voice echoed over the cell phone.

"Retirement's great, but that's not why I called. Bill and I have a dead body on our hands."

"Okay, Charlie, what are you two up to?" Dave said.

Charlie looked at Bill grimly. "I'm not trying to be funny, Dave, I'm serious. This is official business. We found a dead body in the old cemetery just off Routes 71 and 15."

Bill knew by the look on Charlie's face that Dave thought they were joking. Charlie handed him the phone. "Dave, Charlie, our wives, and I were doing volunteer work out here when we came across a body someone tried burying to skip the funeral costs."

"Sorry," said Dave. "I thought you were just giving me a hard time since this is such great golf weather. I'll be out there pronto."

Ten minutes later, the foursome could hear the sirens in the distance as they drank their morning coffee. Bill noticed his wife's knuckles were white from clenching her mug so tight. Even though their wives had heard them talk about tough cases when they were on the force, June and Agnes had never seen actual bodies. He was amazed they were as calm as they were. Minutes later he saw Sheriff Dave Wilson and several others hike the old dirt road up to the cemetery.

"Hey, Bill, Charlie, where's this body you called in?" Sheriff Dave Wilson reached over and shook their hands. "And, what are you doing out here?"

"Good to see you again, Dave," Bill returned the shake. "We are researching old cemetery headstones for the LaSalle County Genealogical Society. June was working in the east section, up around the bend, when she discovered a recent grave with the remains of a hand exposed." Bill pointed to the area on the map.

"I thought this cemetery was closed. Now, which one of you beautiful ladies is June?" Dave pulled out his notebook. He had started on the force shortly before Bill and Charlie retired.

"I am. I'm Bill's wife. May I offer you some coffee?" June stood with her mug in one hand, clipboard under the other arm, and several sharpened pencils sticking out of the bun on top of her head.

"No thank you, Mrs. Peterson. I have my travel mug in the squad car. Could you tell me what happened?"

"Well, I was up around the bend in the east section just like Bill said, recording the Bristol family graves." June pointed to the area on the map for Sheriff Wilson. "Then I started on the Sanders family. I was just finishing their eleventh grave. It was so sad. Those poor people lost six babies before they were even a year old. That's when I noticed the fresh grave dug to the backside of Ruth Sanders' headstone. I couldn't believe my eyes when I saw that horrible looking hand reaching out as if it were asking for help." June finished in one breath.

Bill just stood behind his wife and smiled at Sheriff Wilson. He remembered the days of interviewing witnesses. They often told you more than what you needed.

"What happened next?" Sheriff Wilson turned his attention back to his notes.

"Why, I screamed of course. An unexpected hand reaching out as a final act in death does catch one off guard."

"I agree, June," Agnes said.

"And you are?" The sheriff sounded like he was afraid to ask.

"Agnes Bee McGuire. And Bee is spelled with two e's, not B e a. My mother loved honey."

"Where were you when Mrs. Peterson screamed?" Dave asked.

"Why I was back here at our command center with my husband, Charlie, receiving instructions from Bill."

Bill noticed June and Agnes standing a little taller. "Dave, would you like Charlie or me to walk you to the site, and then take our wives home?"

"I know I can't work over by Ruth Sander's grave, Bill, but couldn't Agnes and I work on one of the other sections?" June asked. "This is our last outing of the season and we have so much to do."

"Mrs. Peterson, I can't have you wandering through the crime scene. Perhaps if you could give me a moment, I will have a couple officers check the west and south sections for signs of foul play. If the areas look clean, then I have no problem with you working over there."

"Thanks, Dave," Bill said. "We'll wait at our command center," pointing to the picnic table with its pot of mums.

"Thank you, Sheriff Wilson. I do hope you will join us later for lunch. Agnes makes the best chicken salad this side of the Illinois River. And my cran-apple pie took first place at the county fair last year."

"It sounds delicious. I'll see if I have time."

"Bill, why don't you take Dave up to the crime scene, and I'll wait with the girls until the other sections are cleared, then I can join you."

"How does that work for you, Dave?" Bill asked.

"Okay, let's get to work." Sheriff Wilson assigned two officers to check the other areas and called the Coroner's office. The crime scene investigators were already unloading their equipment. "Any suggestions before we move forward?" he asked his old colleagues.

"We walked on the grass along the edge of the road on account of the deep ruts, but I did notice tire tracks in the clay. My guess is they belong to whoever buried the body," Charlie answered.

"Okay, everyone, let's stay off the road from this area to the crime scene until the investigators make tire impressions," Sheriff Wilson ordered.

Chapter 7

A half-hour later, Bill and Dave stood aside while the team photographed every inch of the grave and surrounding area. They collected soil samples, a cigarette butt and paper wrappers which probably landed there after last week's storm. The other sections had been cleared, and June and Agnes were back to recording the headstones.

"Hey, Sheriff Wilson," a young officer called from the cemetery road. "I have two different sets of tire tracks." Bill and Dave immediately went over to investigate.

"The crazy thing is," the officer went on, "one stops here and the other continues around the bend."

"Officer O'Rourke, take your partner and check out how far the tracks go." Dave asked the rookie.

"What do you make of the second set of tire tracks?" Bill asked.

"Probably the same thing as you." Dave scratched his chin.

"Yeah, I figure the second set will stop at Old Man Wallace's grave, and your officer will be collecting a dozen or so empty beer cans. Nice to know the legend lives on."

"When did it even start? I'm from southern Illinois. I've heard a few rumors, but never knew the whole story," Dave said.

"The story goes back before I was born. Mr. Wallace, who liked his beer, died in a farm accident. His aging wife was admitted to what was then the county's old folks' home. The new owners of his farm reported all sorts of strange happenings over a period of the next ten years. Within six months of Mrs. Wallace's death, everything stopped, but the rumors in town never did."

"What kind of strange happenings?"

"Nothing really bad," Bill said. "Farm equipment wouldn't be where it was left the night before. Hay stored in the barn wound up behind the barn. Laundry left on the line overnight lay on a fence in the pastures in the morning. They say Old Man Wallace missed his wife. In later years, anything happening in the area we couldn't explain was blamed on him."

"Why do the kids go to his grave?"

"Mostly to put hexes on teachers, other kids, and to drink

beer. I'll never forget the first time Charlie and I biked up here when we were about twelve to prove how tough we were. Charlie had overheard his older brother and friends talking about how they had put a hex on their history teacher, and when he came out of school the next day, he had a flat tire."

"And how does one put a hex on his history teacher?" Dave asked. He stood with his feet part and his hands on his hips.

"Actually, it's pretty easy. You and your friends grab a six-pack and go up to the grave after dark. You light a few candles, drink a beer, make your request, and most importantly, leave an opened, untouched beer for Old Man Wallace to show respect. You come back the next night, and if the beer is empty, it meant he would honor your request. Usually the beer can is found empty."

"You mean they believe he drinks the beer from the grave?" Dave was shaking his head with a smile on his face.

"I think there is one happy raccoon out here, but why spoil the legend?"

"What happened to you and Charlie when you biked out here?"

It was Bill's turn to smile. "It almost killed our legs to bike up the last part of the road. After we searched about an hour, we found the grave. As we stood there staring at the old headstone, the wind kicked up as the sky turned black. You never saw Charlie and me move so fast. By the time we hit Charlie's house, everyone was in the cellar. A tornado hit close by. We figured Old Man Wallace was mad because we didn't bring him a beer. We never went back until we were seniors in high school with our girlfriends and a six pack."

"Looks like the coroner's here." Dave pointed to the black van driving up the first leg of the road.

"Hi Dave, I hear you've got a body rising from the grave for me." Dr. Henry Sage, a retired Cook County forensic pathologist, waved as he approached the crime scene. Dr. Sage still enjoyed filling in back in his home county. His tweed jacket and nondescript bowtie made him look like a professor, rather than a scientist.

"Nope," Dave chuckled. "Only one badly gnawed left hand so far. What brings you out here from Will County?"

"Your lucky elected coroner is on vacation. I'm covering the north end of LaSalle County for him for the time being," Dr. Sage answered. "Are you done photographing the area?"

"Yes. You're on deck, Henry." Dave pointed behind Ruth Sander's headstone, while introducing Bill and Charlie, who had joined them at the grave.

Henry snapped on a pair of disposable gloves, pulled a soft brush out of his case and bent down to clear the loose soil from around the hand.

"What do you think?" asked Charlie.

"My guess is we have a female, but can't be sure until the team uncovers the body. It will be slow going at best."

The three members of the county crime scene team, under Henry's watchful eye, began the tedious task of clearing the soil off the body. While two techs carefully brushed dirt off the skin, the third sifted for possible evidence. As sections appeared, more photographs were taken.

As the day wore on, Bill and Charlie took turns having lunch with their wives. June sent lunch up to the site for Dave and Henry. At first, Dave declined, but Bill reminded him the refusal may not be worth having to deal with June and Agnes. The rest of the team took turns feasting on the chicken salad and pie under the maple tree.

***

Cold soberness replaced the morning's tone of lightheartedness and excitement as the sun dropped. The soft westerly breeze blew colorful leaves over the body of the naked young woman. Removing his tweed hat, Henry spoke. "Over the years, I've seen a great deal of tragedy in my line of work, but this one especially saddens me. Someone didn't want her found. Her family must be terribly worried."

"I wonder if her family even knows she's missing?" said Bill.

While Henry and his team finished their investigation, Charlie helped the wives pack up and took them home. Bill stayed to offer Dave any last minute assistance.

"What cemeteries do you plan on visiting next year?" Dave asked Bill.

"Why?"

"I think I'll plan to be away at a conference, or fishing."

"Not a bad idea. This never happened to Charlie or me when we were in the department," Bill said.

"I'll check missing persons for our area, but I doubt if she's from around here. Most of my missing persons are either canine or feline. As soon as Henry can give us a decent head shot and description, I'll start posting her on all the appropriate web sites and pray for a hit."

"Maybe her fingerprints will show up on one of the data bases. And we can always hope Henry finds something during the autopsy." Bill unrolled his sleeves as the cool night air settled over the cemetery.

As Bill and Dave walked down to their cars, they could hear Henry's voice in the background directing the team to be gentle with the body as they placed the victim on the gurney.

Bill looked back up the incline. "I hope Dr. Sage can identify her. She deserves her own grave and marker at the very least."

Chapter 8

Ever since the news slipped out about the body buried behind Ruth Sander's grave, Sheriff Dave Wilson's office in Ottawa, Illinois and the cemetery just north of town, were besieged with television crews and reporters. This was why Dave was holding this meeting at his home and not in his office. He didn't want his daughter or her friends on the five o'clock news for their own safety. There was someone out there to be feared, and he wasn't giving the killer another target.

A couple of days before the discovery, Dave noticed Stacy, his daughter, was a bit jumpy. The slightest sound sent her to the ceiling. After speaking with the parents of her four friends from a recent slumber party, they reported the same behavior.

So here he sat, in jeans and a tee shirt, no uniform, over a cup of coffee at his dining room table. Before him on the table were six beer cans. Each one individually sealed in an evidence bag.

"How about everyone sit down and get comfortable," Dave suggested. He ignored the five pairs of eyes glued to the beer cans.

"Now, all of you know we recently discovered a body at the old Calvary Cemetery. In addition, you all know about the burial site for Old Man Wallace, whose legend has been handed down for generations. Just by chance, we discovered these beer cans at Wallace's grave the other day. Thanks to the pilot program for missing children which we started in our schools last spring, we were able to identify the fingerprints on these cans. This isn't a lecture about the pitfalls of under-age drinking, or drinking and driving. No, what I need to talk to you girls about is possibly murder." Dave watched the five pairs of young eyes widen. This was exactly the reaction he wanted.

He leaned forward with his elbows resting just inches from the beer cans. "Here's what really concerns me. Reporters will discover who has been to Old Man Wallace's grave recently. Even if the visitors were underage, their names and pictures might appear on television or in the newspaper. We're dealing with a very scary suspect, one who doesn't care if he kills young women.

Now, if I can be assured Old Man Wallace's visitors were there on another night, I can squelch the rumors."

"Dad," Stacy spoke up first which didn't surprise him. His daughter was known for taking the lead and always doing the right thing. "We had a meeting and decided to tell you what happened that night."

Dave knew his worse fear was about to come true. *Shit,* he thought, as he exchanged glances with his wife who was standing by the hutch.

"Okay, go, on," he said, his hands gripping his thighs.

Stacy looked to her friends for support. "On the night of our slumber party, at about two in the morning, we drove out to the cemetery to ask Old Man Wallace to help us."

Dave noticed his wife tried to hide her smile with a sudden cough.

"What did you need him to help you with?" Dave couldn't believe he was asking this question. This wasn't a school counselor or a minister; it was a guy who died in the late 1920's!

Jessica suddenly blurted out, "This is all my fault. I'm so sorry." She wiped the tears gathering on her cheeks.

"No, it's not," said Jennifer. "We all thought it was just what Danny deserved."

"How did Danny, and I assume we're talking about your boyfriend, fit into the picture?" Dave didn't know whether to laugh or scream. Instead, he took a few sips of his coffee in an effort to regain his self-control.

"Oh, Dad!" Stacy said with the flair for drama only a teenager could display. "Danny was seen by Jennifer and Erica kissing that new girl Lisa, the one with the tight top and low cut jeans, behind the field house. So, we borrowed one of your six packs and went to the cemetery to ask Old Man Wallace to put a hex on Danny. And, it worked. The next day Danny sprained his ankle during football practice."

"You *borrowed* a six-pack? How do you *borrow* a six-pack?" Dave realized he had just changed from the respected county sheriff into a stunned parent in less than three seconds. Quickly he recomposed himself. "We'll talk about this later, Stacy."

"But, Dad, we were going to replace it."

Dave didn't want to know how the under-aged girls planned to replace the six-pack. He could read empathy on his wife's face.

She just rolled her eyes and shook her head at him.

"Okay, let's get back to the real issue at hand, which is your safety. Now, who else knows about this adventure?"

No one moved. Dave could almost taste the deafening silence. He looked at his daughter for an answer. "Stacy?"

"No one, just us," she answered as she drew her clasped hands up to her closed mouth.

Dave found it hard to believe five teenage girls had kept the secret to themselves.

"What about you, Jennifer?" he asked his daughter's best friend.

"I didn't tell anyone, honest, Sheriff Wilson." She crossed her heart.

"Okay, what about you, Jessica?" Dave continued around the table.

"I saw him bury the body," Brianne said, her voice barely above a whisper.

No one said a word.

"It's okay, Dad." Stacy tried to sound reassuring. "He didn't see us."

No, the killer didn't, and that's why you are still alive. He hoped the deep breath he just took would slow his pounding heart. "Okay, girls, we need to back up and start with what happened right after you arrived at the cemetery. Stacy, I'll begin with you."

"We had to drive slowly up the road because it was in bad shape. We hid Jennifer's dad's car behind the tool shed. Once we were at Old Man Wallace's grave, we lit the candles and opened the beers, and we remembered to put one opened can by his headstone to show respect. Next, we joined hands and told him our story. Then, we asked him to put a hex on Danny."

Bill Peterson was right, Dave thought to himself, the legend lives on.

"What happened next, Jennifer?" he asked.

"We were just about to toast Old Man Wallace when we saw a pair of headlights come up the road. Actually, I think we heard the car first. We blew out the candles, laid down flat behind the headstones and hid our faces like Stacy told us to do. I think I heard him get something out of the car, like a shovel because then I heard him digging. He was swearing about some damn stupid doctor."

"How long did this go on?" Dave asked the girls.

"It seemed like forever before he stopped shoveling," answered Erica. "I remember hearing a scraping sound and then a loud thump."

"I saw him drag something that looked like a rolled up rug," said Brianne.

"Brianne, you were supposed to keep your face down," all the girls said at the same time.

"I'm sorry. I just had to see what he was doing. I wanted to make sure he didn't sneak up on us." Tears spilled from the teenager's eyes.

"We're not mad at you." The girls were out of their chairs and hugging their friend.

"Okay, back in your chairs," Dave said.

The girls complied.

"What else did you see, Brianne?" Dave continued. He knew they were scared, but they might hold the key to the identity of the killer. He also knew Brianne was a good student in school. He prayed she remembered something he could use.

"Well, I watched him roll the body of the woman, except I didn't know it was a woman at the time, into the grave and cover her with the dirt. He was talking to himself. He said something about this one wasn't as heavy."

Dave was no longer leaning forward with his elbows on the table. He was almost out of his seat when he caught himself. Another body? His men had checked the entire cemetery, and there was only one body found, besides the ones that were six feet under. Why didn't this guy just bury both bodies in the same place?

"Did he say anything else you can think of?"

All five girls shook their heads.

"Brianne, can you describe this man or his car for me?"

"His car was a big dark SUV, but I'm not sure of the make of the vehicle it was."

"I'll worry about that," he reassured her. "So he was driving a sports utility vehicle. Good. Now what do you remember about the man? Close your eyes and play the scene back slowly." This was a technique he had found very helpful when questioning witnesses.

Brianne paced her hands flat on the dining room table and

closed her eyes as requested. The room grew quiet. Dave could feel everyone willing her to remember.

With her eyes still closed, she spoke. "He was big, really big. His hair must have been cut short because I remember thinking his head looked square. His clothes were dark. When he was done, he turned the car around and left."

The girls started talking all at once about how frightened they had been when Brianne asked, "Don't you want to know about the license plate? I brought my camera, so I used the telephoto lens to see it. I didn't take a picture because I was terrified he would hear me."

Stunned, everyone stopped talking.

Gently Dave inquired, "What did you see?" He would take anything this girl could recall.

"When he turned the car around, the light over the license plate showed a little red barn."

"Wisconsin plates?" His wife asked.

"Could you read any number or letters?" Dave could hear the girls suck in a breath in anticipation.

"It was sort of strange. It had just two words, THE FEW."

"…the proud, the Marines." Dave finished the slogan. He still had his old uniform in the back of his bedroom closet.

Dave stood to get the girls attention. "Has anyone here told anyone else about this incident? Have you discussed this anywhere someone could have overheard you?"

All the girls answered no.

"Did anyone else know you planned this adventure? Your siblings? Your parents? Other friends?" Dave asked.

Their answer remained the same, no.

"I can't emphasize how important it is for this information not to leave this room. Your safety depends on it. Keep to the buddy system and let your parents know where you are at all times. If you can't reach your parents and you need a ride home, you know where to find me."

Dave had purposely not invited the girls' parents. He was sure the girls would have clammed up, but now he had to do his job. "I know none of you will like what I'm about to say, but I have to contact your parents. You're all minors and they have a right to know what happened." He watched the five faces in front of him stare down at the table.

"I'm toast," one of the girls whispered.

"However, about these beer cans in front of me," he stated, "under normal circumstances, I would recommend the owners of the fingerprints be grounded for a week or so. However, due to this special situation, I'm going to forget about them this time. Next time, I assume there won't be a next time."

The momentary panic on the girls' face passed as they promised.

"Dad, we didn't even get to drink the beer," Stacy said.

Dave smiled. There is one very, very happy raccoon, he thought.

Chapter 9

Jack's eyes burned from lack of sleep. He rubbed them as he leaned back and stretched while talking on the phone with the DuPage County Sheriff's office. He downed the last of the bitter liquid passing for coffee. This was sea scum compared to the rich brew Sylvia made.

"Thanks for checking your records," said Jack. "If anything shows up, please give us a call."

"Any luck?" Patrick asked, throwing his jacket over the back of his chair.

"Nope. I came up empty-handed after checking with all the collar counties around Chicago. Lake County has had a leg for over a year, and Kane County found a head in the Fox River seven months ago. Nobody has any unidentified bodies or parts with B positive or O negative blood covered in sisal fibers and yellow clay."

Jack couldn't sit still any longer. He was up and pacing. Sometimes he could think better on his feet. If only he had time for a run right now. It had been two days since Claire autopsied the man found by the Jackson Park lagoon. She had called earlier this morning to let him know the Latent Print Department hoped to have a reading on the partial prints later today. Even if they can submit them to AFIS, the Automated Fingerprint Identification System, it didn't mean they would get a hit. Meanwhile, the lab had sent DNA samples of both the blood types collected from their victim through CODIS, the Combined DNA Index System.

Jack couldn't sit still or wait any longer for new evidence to surface. He headed towards the stairs.

"Where do you think you're going?" Patrick called from across the room. "If you go up to Missing Persons one more time today, Finch is going to kill you."

Jack stopped short of the stairs. "All right then, you go. Finch likes you."

"Right." Patrick took his feet off his makeshift footstool, the bottom drawer of his desk, shook out his wrinkled pant legs and shifted his shoulder harness. "Okay, I'll go, but this is the last time until we get an answer back on the fingerprints."

Jack followed Patrick up the stairs to Finch's cubicle.

"What gives, O'Shaunessy?" Finch asked without taking his eyes off his computer screen.

Jack noticed him drop his smile the minute Finch saw him standing behind Patrick.

"Are you still looking for a lead on your Jackson Park case?" He directed the question to Patrick.

"Yeah. Would you mind running your magic fingers over the keyboard one more time and we *both* promise to stay out of your hair for the rest of the day. If Miller tries to make a break for the third floor, I promise to cuff him to his desk."

"Fair enough." Finch set his fingers in motion.

Patrick and Jack crammed behind Finch. The walls of his space were covered with many years of missing persons' photos, some dating from the last guy who sat in Finch's chair.

Jack knew thousands of individuals went missing every year. Many simply chose to disappear for a variety of reasons, but turning up dead was a big difference from deciding to get lost in the crowd.

"Only a few more," Finch announced after several minutes.

Patrick winced as he rolled his shoulders. "Wait. Stop. Flip back a couple of photos to the morgue shot of the woman."

"I thought you said your victim was a man."

"Correct." Patrick leaned on Finch's desk to get a better view.

"Is this the one?" Finch asked.

"Yes. Can you print the photo and report?" Patrick asked.

"Consider it done." The printer spit out the pages.

"Who is she?" Jack asked. He noticed Patrick's jovial expression was gone.

"I'm sure it's Claire's friend from the old neighborhood."

"How did we miss this before?" Jack said. Both he and his partner had bugged Finch several times today.

"Look at the date and time. It was just put online." Patrick skimmed through the report. "Oh, shit. Let's get this to Claire. I think we just found our O negative victim."

Chapter 10

Thirty minutes later, Patrick placed a morgue photo in front of Claire. She ran her fingers over the grainy photocopy.

Claire gasped. "This can't be. It's Sarah Morgan. What happened to her, Patrick?"

"She was found in an old cemetery in LaSalle County, just outside Ottawa."

"What was she doing out in LaSalle County? She lives on the north side of Chicago." Claire turned the photo face down. She couldn't look at Sarah's pale face.

"According to the pre-lim, she died of hemorrhage resulting from a puncture to the iliac artery after a surgical procedure. What's a transvaginal aspiration of ovarian follicles?" Patrick handed the report to his sister.

Claire read the report, and then reread it. "This doesn't make any sense. Why would Sarah have a procedure done to harvest her eggs? She's not married, and if she wanted to get pregnant without involving a man, why didn't she have it done in Chicago? There are certainly enough reputable clinics here."

"I know, Sis, can you explain this trans procedure?"

Claire ran her fingers over the back side of the picture. "Sure, it's one of the options for women having difficulty conceiving. First, the woman takes medication, usually by injection to elevate certain hormone levels. This results in the ovarian follicles filling with fluid. Next, the physician removes the eggs in surgery by using a long needle attached to a probe with a camera on the tip. The surgical procedure involves inserting the probe in the vagina, and the camera reads out on a screen the location of the enlarged follicles. Then he can pierce them and aspirate the egg-filled fluid. Next the embryologist fertilizes the eggs in the lab with the donor sperm."

"Is this a difficult procedure?" Patrick asked.

"No. Actually it's pretty straightforward." Claire walked to the window overlooking the vacant parking lot. She felt as empty as the view in front of her. The tears she'd kept in check a few minutes ago streamed down her face.

Jack crossed the small office in a few steps and handed her his handkerchief. "Then, how did Sarah die?"

"Thanks." Claire wiped her cheeks hoping she didn't leave a smudge of her mascara on the white linen. "Because someone was either damn careless or didn't know what he was doing and punctured the iliac artery."

"Claire," Jack's voice softened. "The story gets worse."

"How can it get any worse? Sarah's dead." Sarah was the first of her old gang to die. The old neighborhood as she knew it took one more hit. First, her mom died when Claire was young, then her father was shot down when she was in high school. Now, Sarah was gone.

Jack pulled a chair over. "You better sit down; the story is a bit bizarre."

Claire sat, her normally high energy level drained.

"I contacted the LaSalle County Sheriff's Office and spoke with a Sheriff Wilson. Sarah's body was discovered in a shallow grave at an old cemetery by members of the local genealogical society. To top it off, several high school girls witnessed the burial, which included the sheriff's daughter. They were practicing some local tradition of asking a deceased Mr. Wallace to put a hex on one of their boyfriends for cheating.

"Apparently, they heard the suspect make two comments. One referred to 'that damn stupid doctor'. And, the second comment, 'this one wasn't as heavy as the other one', referred to Sarah," Jack said.

"Luckily for the girls, they weren't discovered," Patrick said. "For their continued safety, the LaSalle County Sheriff's Office is not releasing the fact that they were present in the cemetery. One of the girls got the plate number on her camera and that was pending at the time Sarah was entered into the database.

"This is only the half of it," Patrick went on. "Not only does Sarah have O-negative blood, but she was buried in an area which is mostly yellow clay. The real kicker is the coroner found a large amount of sisal like fibers on her body."

"You have got to be kidding me." She stared from Patrick to Jack and back to Patrick again.

"Yep, we're thinking the same thing. There has to be some link between Sarah and your victim," Patrick said. "Think of the comment about the other one being heavier? Maybe your victim is the one the suspect was talking about."

Claire was already out of her chair and grabbing her phone. "I need a sample of her blood to see if we can get a match with the O-negative we found on the Jackson Park victim's sock."

"Wait," Jack said, "first I need to contact Sheriff Wilson and set up a meeting. Does Sarah have any family who can make a positive ID?"

"No. At her parents' funeral, there were only folks from the old neighborhood and a distant cousin from the west coast."

"I could drive out to make the ID," Patrick offered.

"Not without me." Claire grabbed her backpack. She wouldn't consider putting this type of stress on her brother.

"Slow down." Jack blocked her office doorway. "I'll make the call to set up the identification for tomorrow. Claire, you check with Dr. Johnson to make sure you can still work the case. The last thing any of us wants to happen is to catch the suspect and have him get off on a technicality. We want to get him for not only Sarah, but your victim, too."

Claire leaned back against her desk. "As much as I hate to admit it, you're right. I'll do everything by the book. Sarah deserves at least that much."

Patrick raised an eyebrow and whispered under his breath, "That'll be a first."

"How well did you know her?" Jack asked.

"She sat in front of me all through school until she moved to Barrington during our junior year of high school. Her home backed up to ours across the alley. We smoked our first cigarettes together and shared all the usual rites of passage. Boy did we have some good times together. I remember she was going to make her first billion by the time she was forty, and I was going to heal the sick. Guess neither one of us quite made it."

"I would say you did." Patrick gave Claire a hug.

"When was the last time you had contact with her?" Jack asked.

"We lost touch right after college, but I ran into Sarah at Starbucks last month. We exchanged phone numbers, but never had time to get together."

Claire touched the backside of Sarah's morgue photo. She should still be here, but she wasn't. Sarah was always so full of life. That girl could wear a bikini like no one else. The guys would literally trip over each other to get a look. Now she was lying in a cold drawer in LaSalle County with a white drape hiding the classical 'Y' incision made with the coroner's scalpel across her torso.

Questions raced through Claire's mind. If Sarah died during a procedure, then where, why and by whom? This procedure needed a surgical setting, an infertility specialist, an anesthesiologist, and an embryologist at the very least. A patient doesn't usually end up in a make shift grave in a rural cemetery after the procedure is completed. Privately, Claire vowed to find out how this had happened.

Claire looked at her brother and sighed. "Okay, guys, we'd better get back to work. We've got a killer to catch."

Chapter 11

Claire was surprised it hadn't taken much effort on her part to convince her supervisor, Dr. Johnson, to allow her to assist Patrick with Sarah's ID. Apparently, Dr. Harry Sage was Dr. Johnson's mentor when Johnson first arrived at the Cook County Morgue. Claire planned to meet Patrick and Jack at the Sheriff's Office.

As much as she enjoyed her work, nothing beat a drive out of the city on an incredibly beautiful day. Besides, she wanted the time alone to think about Sarah and simply absorb the beauty of the fall colors. They would peak in the next few days. A sign the shorter days and colder nights were soon to follow. In spite of the reason for the road trip to Ottawa, Illinois, she was going to make the most of it. The last few months had been rewarding and draining at the same time. She felt her new job was a perfect fit, but a few hours away from work was good for her well-being.

By the time Claire had made the decision to quit her job at a prestigious east coast hospital and leave her fiancée, her nerves were frayed. Dr. Greg Stratford was from old money, and with it came a certain level of understood power. That power included Claire having to go against her own code of ethics for what Greg explained as the 'greater good'. It turned out the greater good was filling the administration and physicians' personal pockets. Greg was from this elite group, like his father and grandfather. In Lyons Ridge, Pennsylvania, their last name was synonymous with Clinton General Hospital.

She had met Greg while they were completing fellowships at the University of Chicago. Afterwards, he had put a diamond on her left hand. She took this for love, but eventually learned it really meant control.

Claire had thought she and Greg were on equal footing since they were both physicians. Nothing could have been farther from the truth.

When she first voiced concerns over decisions made by the head of pathology, Greg took her in his arms, kissed the top of her head and told her she must have misunderstood. Next, he would insist on taking her out for a romantic dinner. However, after several incidents, she believed her gut reaction was right.

Greg made it very clear she needed to keep her mouth shut or her job could be in jeopardy. After one of her autopsies, she discovered a crucial specimen missing. She knew she hadn't thrown it out or mislabeled it, but had no way of proving it. She could read the writing on the wall when the director of pathology reprimanded her for her carelessness and for embarrassing Greg.

She took the warning as a threat. This case had nothing to do with Greg. There was no reason for the pathologist to even mention his name during the reprimand, unless the old boys' network was in play. Would they take it to the next level, which could cost her the job or even worse, her license? To add to her paranoia, the rumor mill fanned the flames Greg was only faithful to Greg, another part of family tradition. His mother had even gone so far as to take her aside and reiterate the old saying, *boys will be boys.* In so many words, she told Claire to look the other way and think about what she was gaining, meaning old money and a standing in the community.

Greg's mother had no idea what it meant to be an Irishwoman from the Bridgeport neighborhood on the South Side of Chicago. Her South Side Irish upbringing was in her blood. Nobody told her to look the other way, or lie down like a rug for Greg to wipe his feet on. Mrs. Stratford had done this her entire marriage, but Claire wouldn't.

The next day following her last autopsy, she emptied her locker, left her lab keys and hospital identification along with her resignation on the director's desk and walked out. Back at the apartment she shared with Greg, she packed her clothes, books and the few personal items she had brought with her into her old Ford Taurus. As her last act, she left her engagement ring on the kitchen counter with a note which read, 'Thanks, but no thanks,' and left.

The next morning, Chevoun, her oldest sister, found Claire sitting on her Bridgeport stoop, sipping a cappuccino, watching the sunrise over Chicago. One week later, she had an apartment and a job. Greg never called. She was an O'Shaunessy, a survivor, and it felt damn good to be back home.

Claire drained the last drops of cappuccino as she pulled up to the LaSalle County Sheriff's Office. Patrick and Jack's unmarked car wasn't in sight. Good, she thought, she could use these last few moments to steel herself for what the day would bring. She was used to dead bodies. Actually, she didn't think of them that way. They were her patients and often victims of violent crimes. While she believed their souls had gone on to their just reward, their bodies had not passed on to their final resting place. Their bodies stopped at her morgue for a reason. She tried to find truthful answers to their families' painful questions. She dug deep into her cases to give the police everything she could to help them find her victims' killers. But this time was different. Sarah wasn't her patient; she was a friend.

Chapter 12

"Hey, what took you so long?" Patrick's voice boomed as he pulled up next to her.

"Excuse me, it seems like I beat you here. Besides, you're still in the car."

"Jack, I told you she has a lead foot. Never let her drive."

"I'll try to remember that," Jack said as he climbed out of the unmarked squad and stretched his legs.

Claire thought she saw a twinkle in Patrick's eye, or was it a tear.

"Ready?" Patrick asked Claire.

"Lead the way, big brother."

As they walked into the station, they found Sheriff Wilson waiting for them. "Hi, I'm Sheriff Dave Wilson. How was your drive?" He extended his hand to each one of them.

"Other than road construction, a piece of cake. I'm Detective Patrick O'Shaunessy, this is my partner Detective Jack Miller, and this is Dr. Claire O'Shaunessy, a Cook County forensic pathologist and my kid sister." Patrick smiled.

Claire felt the tips of her ears redden. She shook Dave's hand.

The sheriff let out a laugh cutting the tension in half. "The cells in the county jail are bigger than my office, but come on in and we'll get started. Please give Gladys your coffee orders. She baked one of her famous sticky bun cakes when she heard we were having company. Her recipe can't be beat at the county fair."

"That sounds like my kind of woman," Patrick said.

Claire elbowed her brother as the gray-haired woman the Sheriff referred to as Gladys turned three shades of red. Claire hoped someone could make her blush when she was Gladys' age.

"Sorry Patrick, Gladys is spoken for, and you don't want to have to duel it out with her husband, Hank."

The sheriff waited for Gladys to place the refreshments on the side table and then close the door before he spoke. "I understand the deceased happens to be an old neighborhood friend of yours. This has to be tough on you." Dave looked directly at Claire. "If there is anything I can do to make this easier on all of you, please speak up."

"Thank you," Claire said. "To start with, I don't understand why Sarah was having an infertility procedure in LaSalle County. I checked with the American Fertility Association, and I couldn't find a listing for this area. Joliet appears to be the closest."

"You're right. I've faxed her picture to all infertility specialists outside of Chicago within a three hour driving range from here, and nobody said they took care of her. Most replied they were on staff at a hospital which could have handled Sarah's problem."

"What about private clinics?" Jack asked.

"I checked with the state, and none are listed for the immediate area. I hate to mention this, but could she have been selling her eggs through a backdoor operation for money?"

Patrick grabbed Claire's arm before she could respond. "We haven't had time to do a background search on Sarah since I saw her picture on the police web site last night. Because it's someone from the old neighborhood, we wanted to make the official identification first."

"What about family?" the sheriff asked.

"No siblings; parents died a few years back in a small plane accident while on vacation," Patrick said.

"Then this is a difficult case for all of you on more than one level."

"Also, I have a man back in my morgue who died about the same time Sarah did." Claire swallowed hard. She squeezed the coffee cup even harder. It was too much to comprehend.

"The police found him in Jackson Park covered in sisal fibers. His death might be linked to Sarah's. I was hoping to get a sample of Sarah's blood to match against the O-negative blood found on the front of his sock. His blood type is B-positive." In spite of her chosen career, she doubted if dealing with Sarah's death would ever get easier?

Jack opened a large yellow envelope and handed papers to Dave. "We found yellow clay on his body and in the parking lot. We didn't have enough to match a partial tire tread."

Dave pulled out a photo of tire treads found at the cemetery. "While the lab guys are working on identification of the tire prints found at the scene, I checked with my neighbor, who owns a tire business in town. He said the depth of the pattern and the width of the tire indicates a high end priced tire. Did you bring a sample of the yellow clay?"

Jack produced a small sealed evidence envelope from his pocket. "I even have a sample of the fibers."

"Good." Dave spread out a map on his desk. "I circled the area where Sarah was found. Could you mark the area where your victim was located?"

Patrick marked the area in the park. He ran his finger from the park to the Dan Ryan Expressway, down the Dan Ryan to Interstate 57, and then to Interstate 80 west. It was a direct shot to LaSalle County.

"What if we are looking at this the wrong way?" Patrick suggested. "We are assuming Sarah died out here. What if she actually had the procedure done in Chicago, and the guy with the SUV dropped our victim off first in the park, and then he drove out here to bury Sarah. Jackson Park is close to the expressway."

"That's not possible," injected Dave. "You found the yellow clay at the crime scene. He had to have stopped at the cemetery first."

"Well that shoots a hole in this theory," Patrick said as he took another bite of Gladys' cake..

"Why would he dump the bodies in two different counties? This was extra work and double the risk of being caught," Claire asked.

"Simple," Dave said. "If you dispose of the two bodies in two different counties, you have less of a chance of them being traced back to the killer. Perhaps he picked LaSalle County because he lives out this way. He had to have prior knowledge of the cemetery location because it's been closed for many years and is off a rural county road.

"Let's work up a list of all the facts matching these two victims and a couple scenarios," Dave said.

For the next hour, they shared the information they had collected. Claire did not have a good feeling about the outcome. There were so many unanswered questions. What had Sarah gotten herself into? Was she selling her eggs? She didn't need the money. Her parents had left her a sizeable estate. However, there was no mistaking the cause of death. The procedure couldn't have happened in a licensed facility; otherwise, the medical staff would have called for help if they weren't in a position to perform emergency surgery to save her life. *And, why didn't someone call for help?* Somebody had to have seen what happened.

"Oh my God." The words slipped out before Claire could hold them back. She could almost taste the fear the man in her morgue had experienced.

The three men stopped talking and looked at her in unison.

"Claire, are you all right?" Jack grabbed her icy hands. "What's wrong?"

She heard the concern in his voice. "He saw her die," was all she could get out.

"*Shit*. She was right about this case from the beginning." Patrick shook his head.

"What's she talking about? Who saw who die?" Dave's voice commanded their attention.

For a moment, Claire thought her heart had stopped then broke loose at a break neck speed with her respirations trying to catch up. Her stomach turned as bile rose in her throat. Yes, she could definitely taste her dead patient's fear in her mouth. A sense of cold washed over her. Not like a cold blast when someone opens an outside door during a Chicago winter, but a cold you never come back from, like death.

She zipped up the collar on her fleece pullover. She remembered how Ian's fingers felt around her neck during their reconstruction of the victim's death. Her eyes closed for a brief moment. When she opened them, again three pairs of eyes burned right through her.

"You see, Sheriff Wilson," her voice was slow but deliberate. "It has been bothering me why the man back in my morgue died from strangulation with no defensive wounds on him. From the marks on his neck, it looks like the killer came from behind. This would add credence to my theory he was unaware of the impending threat to his life. I believe he was in an environment where he felt totally safe when he saw something that altered that level of safety. His blood type is B-positive. We found O-negative blood splattered on the front of his socks. He must have seen Sarah die."

"And you think he was killed because of what he saw." Dave finished Claire's line of thinking. "Unbelievable. You may have just given us the motive for this case."

"That's my sister. She takes after our old man." Patrick

beamed.

"We don't have an ID on Claire's victim. I called before we got here, and the tech was running the fingerprints through AFIS," Jack said.

Gladys knocked on the door as she entered the crowded office. "Thought you would like to know I tracked down that license plate from the cemetery. The Wisconsin plates belong to a ten-year-old red Dodge pickup. The owner is a marine stationed in the Middle East for the last year. Talked with his sister who hasn't had the heart to tell him the plates were stolen." She handed Dave the report and left.

"Gladys is good," Jack said with a sound of appreciation in his voice.

"Yes," Dave answered. "And I'm dead meat if she ever retires. She can get state secrets out of a dried turnip. People give her information they never intended to without even realizing it."

"What line of work is her husband Hank in?" Patrick asked.

"Hank's retired, but I don't think one ever really leaves the FBI."

"Well, then I guess I *had* better watch myself around Miss Gladys," said Patrick.

Dave chuckled. "I think we've done as much as we can here. How about I take you all to lunch at Turner's Café? Best chili in the state of Illinois."

"Sounds good," said Jack.

Claire was in no mood for lunch right now. "I'd rather wait until we've made the ID. I'd also like to see the crime scene."

Dave stood and opened the office door. "Well then, let's go see Dr. Sage."

Chapter 13

Claire could feel an empty, sick sensation in the pit of her stomach. This was the moment she had been dreading, identifying Sarah's body. Sheriff Wilson offered to drive them. Claire wanted the privacy of her own vehicle, but Patrick overruled her. This was the second time in a matter of a few days she had let him win. Next time, as she had promised herself before, she wouldn't back down.

Finally, she agreed to ride with them, grateful Jack had insisted on driving. Sarah's death had to be affecting Patrick, too.

As Jack drove, Claire barely noticed the golden maple trees on the drive to the coroner's office, but then this was not one of life's golden moments she wanted to remember. For Sarah, there would never be another special moment, either personal or professional.

Claire knew how lucky she and her sisters had been to have Patrick after losing their parents. He had made their precious moments wonderful. He was in the stands cheering for her ice hockey team when she made the winning shot taking her high school team to state finals. When she graduated from medical school, he made sure their entire family had front row seats. It warmed her heart how he smiled every time he introduced his kid sister, the doctor.

Meeting Dr. Harry Sage was the only bright spot in the day, Claire decided. She couldn't help but love Dr. Johnson's mentor. His mild, gentle manner was comforting. Over his worn corduroy pants, he wore a tweed blazer with suede elbow patches, and a soft, yellow oxford shirt accompanied by a red, paisley bow tie. Sage's gray hair and spectacles completed the picture.

"Good afternoon, Sheriff Wilson, why don't you have everyone take a seat in the waiting room." Sage's calm voice soothed them.

No one sat down.

"Please, sit down," he encouraged them. "I want to go over the autopsy report first before you see Sarah. I understand you have no question about the identification."

"That's correct." Patrick cleared his throat. "I'm Detective O'Shaunessy." He extended his hand to Sage. "This is my partner, Detective Miller, and my sister, Dr. O'Shaunessy."

After handshakes were exchanged, they took seats opposite the viewing window. Jack sat protectively next to Claire on the small sofa, his suit jacket unbuttoned.

After introductions, Dr. Sage spoke. "May I extend my deepest sympathy for your loss. My autopsy findings show the cause of death was hemorrhage from perforation of the left iliac artery. The deceased was under general anesthesia and didn't suffer any pain. Because of the severity of the injury to the artery, it was impossible for her to survive unless she had received immediate attention."

Claire clutched the facial tissue in her hands. She willed herself mentally to separate her personal feelings from her professional side, but it was more difficult than she thought it would be. When Jack placed his hand over hers, she willingly accepted his support. His hand warmed a chill she just couldn't shake. She noticed Patrick grab the arms of his chair so hard his knuckles turned white.

"So, Dr. Sage, if I understand you correctly, Sarah Morgan didn't stand a chance?" Jack interrupted.

"Correct, Detective Miller." Dr. Sage nodded. "Let me continue, then I'll answer any questions you have."

Claire could visualize in her mind every word of the autopsy report as Dr. Sage spoke right down to how Sarah's gnawed left hand looked. She wanted to throw up. The man who buried her didn't even care enough to make sure she was safe from the wild life, but if he had, none of them would have known Sarah's fate.

Dr. Sage placed the report on the side table and folded his hands as he looked into their eyes. "Unfortunately, I don't have the answers you are seeking. Who did this to Sarah? What pushed her to make this decision? Why did she agree to have this procedure done outside a medical facility? Where did it happen? I can only answer the question, how she died."

"How are you going to rule, accidental, manslaughter, or homicide?" Jack asked, now sitting forward with both hands on his knees.

"I've not decided on the official rhetoric for the moment. The puncturing of the artery I assume was accidental, but negligent just the same. The fact remains, no one even tried to get help for Sarah. Someone buried her in a shallow grave as a means of disposing her body proving this was clearly not performed in a licensed facility. This goes beyond simple negligence. Someone not only needs to be held accountable for Sarah's death, but be prevented from harming anyone else."

"Can we see her now?" Patrick shifted his weight in the small waiting room chair.

"Of course, but I have to warn you, the photo copy picture looks better than she does. Even though she was protected from insects for the most part, I'm afraid the burial took a toll on her skin." Dr. Sage directed them to the viewing window where Dave stood. He phoned his tech to open the curtains. A white sheet draped Sarah's body up to her shoulders.

Claire approached the window first. Jack was right behind her. She knew Patrick would stay a couple of steps behind them. Viewing a friend was never easy for him.

She studied the young woman before her. It was Sarah, only it wasn't the beautiful vibrant Sarah she knew. "Do you need me to sign anything, Dr. Sage?" Claire asked, not able to take her eyes off the still body before her.

"No, that won't be necessary."

"When can you release the body?" Patrick asked.

"Probably in a few days. I want to make sure I have crossed all my T's so the DA's office can hang the people responsible." Dr. Sage nodded to the assistant to close the curtain. "Do you have any questions?"

Claire turned from the viewing window. "I do. I have plenty of them, but as you said, none you can answer. I do have one favor though, could I get a sample of Sarah's blood?"

"Of course my dear, I'll have my tech get it for you."

"Thank you," was all she could say. She fought to keep her tears at bay and stay professional.

"If there is anything else, please do not hesitate to call. I'll send you a copy of the final autopsy report." Dr. Sage pressed his business card into her hand. "By the way, Dr. O'Shaunessy," he said, addressing Claire on a more professional level, "how is my old protégé, Dr. Johnson? I do hope you are driving him crazy."

Claire noticed there was a devilish twinkle in Sage's eye. "I do my best," she said, wondering how much Dr. Johnson had revealed about her impulsive behavior.

Claire turned to Sheriff Wilson. "I'd like to see the cemetery."

"No problem," Sheriff Wilson responded. "I have to warn you though; the road running through the cemetery is in rough shape. I'd advise leaving your car on the main road. Thanks for your time, Harry."

The pathologist nodded his head in return. "Wish I could have been of more help. The tech will have the sample for you in a minute. Have a safe trip home."

Chapter 14

Jack followed the sheriff's suggestion and parked behind him near the cemetery entrance. The sun was hot, and he could taste the dust as the wind stirred it up. As he got out of the car, he opened one of the water bottles Dr. Sage had sent along with them. The cool water eased his parched throat. Dave, Patrick and Claire were quenching their thirsts, too.

Glancing around the area, Jack was impressed how well the old cemetery was maintained. The grass was cut, bushes trimmed and leaves raked. He read the dates on the headstones. Some dated back before the Civil War into the 1830s. A few of the headstones had sunk over time, while others tended to lean towards one side. Several graves had no markings at all other than simple white limestone squares.

He noticed an aged bronze plaque near one section listing fallen soldiers for several wars as he followed Dave to the site. Yellow and black tape still roped the crime scene.

"The shallow grave is just up on your left behind Ruth Sanders's headstone. The crime scene techs shifted through all the soil covering Sarah as well as around the area. I see they leveled the ground after they finished."

Everyone stepped gingerly behind Ruth's grave. Quiet silence filled the air. The freshly turned soil reminded them of the horrific final act Sarah had suffered.

Jack kept a close watch on Patrick and his sister. He knew they were hurting. All he could do was be there for them. He knew firsthand the cutting pain of standing over an old friend's grave. Tad had been gone for many years, but moments like this stung like salt in a fresh wound. Both Sarah and Tad died much too young at the hands of another by acts which were totally incomprehensible.

Jack knew the only solace left for Claire and Patrick was the knowledge that Sarah felt no pain. She had slept through her death. Without question, Tad had felt the searing pain of the two bullets he took. But, had he known he was dying? The question still pained Jack.

"Could you show us the other grave?" Claire asked Dave.

"Do you mean Old Man Wallace?"

"Yes, I think so. The one where the hexing ritual took place," Claire said.

"Our dear friend Mr. Wallace is buried up just a ways," he replied and pointed up a slight incline.

On the short walk up the hill to the gravesite, Dave filled them in on the history of Mr. Wallace.

"So this scenario has been passed on for some eighty to ninety years?" Patrick removed his jacket and slung it over his shoulder.

"It looks that way." Dave stepped off the path and walked about two rows in. "Here he is," he said, pointing to Mr. Wallace's headstone.

Jack smiled as he rubbed his hand over the rough headstone. "I hope eighty years after I'm gone, someone puts a beer on my grave and believes I have some mythical powers from the other side. Could they leave me some of Sylvia's lasagna, too?"

Patrick shot Jack a look, and then turned to Dave. "How are the girls who witnessed the burial?" he asked, loosening his tie. "They had to have been scared to death. I've two daughters myself."

"Still shaken up, but okay," Dave said. "We have kept their names off the report. I don't want to worry about some crazed person coming after them or their families, especially when one of them is my own daughter. Besides, I don't have enough staff to protect the girls and do everything else around here."

"I understand. That was a good idea. Once the press gets wind of a story this intense, they'll run with it. They don't seem to care who gets hurt along the way," Patrick said.

Claire took out her camera and adjusted the dials. "Dave, where was the girl lying down when she looked at the suspect through her camera lens?"

Dave walked over to another row of headstones in back of Mr. Wallace's. He checked the name. "Right here, behind this one."

"Could you walk down the road to approximately where the suspect would have been standing at the back of his vehicle?" she said.

"What are you thinking, Claire?" Patrick asked.

"I need to see what the girl saw." Claire got down on her stomach by the headstone in a patch of dried leaves. She watched Sheriff Wilson walk back towards the crime scene, turn and wave. Steadying her digital camera with the telescopic lens which she always traveled with, Claire refocused and shot the frame.

"What are you looking for?" Patrick asked.

"I want a better handle on the man's size," she said.

"Aren't you a little old to be rolling in the leaves?" Jack offered her a hand, but she refused.

"I hope I'm never too old to roll in the leaves. It's a shame you think you are." Annoyed, she brushed the remaining leaves from her clothes and left to join the sheriff.

"You don't have the hots for my sister, do you?" Patrick gulped down the last of his water.

Even though Claire was out of earshot, Jack's ears burned. "Not a chance. We better catch up with them," Jack said, nodding towards the sheriff and Claire.

"Okay, I thought I would warn you she can make you eat nails."

"Who needs nails when I can have Sylvia's lasagna?" Jack grinned.

"Smart boy," Patrick said, "but I have a gut feeling one, or both of you, is going to give me a lot of heart burn."

Chapter 15

The worst was over. Everyone breathed a little easier by the time they'd returned to the sheriff's office. Emotions were back in check. Patrick and Jack were going over police business while a seed which had started to germinate in the cemetery began to bloom for Claire. By refusing their offer to drive out with them to Ottawa, she had the independence she needed to do some investigating on her own. Dr. Johnson had given her the rest of the day off, so nothing was standing in her way.

"Claire, how about some lunch?" Patrick asked. "*Hello, Claire?*" He repeated the question when she didn't answer.

"Sorry, I was thinking about the work I need to catch up on back at the morgue," Claire lied. "I'm not hungry right now. I'll grab something on the way back." She hoped her growling stomach didn't give her away. She hated to lie to Patrick, but what other options did she have?

"If it's because of something I said back at the cemetery..." Jack started to apologize.

"No. Don't even think that. It's been a rough day for all of us. I just have to get back to work, okay?" She didn't think Patrick was buying her explanation, but figured Jack would. She thanked the sheriff for all of his assistance and promised to keep in touch with any new information she discovered. "I'm going to see if Gladys will part with her recipe before I go."

"I doubt it," replied Dave, "but give it a try."

"We should be on our way, too. Dave, couldn't we at least buy you lunch before we go? It's on the department," Patrick asked.

"Thanks, but it's getting late and I have a ton of reports to fill out. Every year I have to justify why I need the manpower I request. The government thinks we are a quiet, sleepy county. Nothing ever happens here."

"Thanks again." The men exchanged handshakes.

Claire stopped at Gladys' desk and waved when her brother looked back at her. Her intentions were more than just collecting a recipe. She needed information.

"Did everything go okay?" Gladys asked Claire.

"As well as could be expected," she answered. "I told my brother I wanted to ask you for your sticky bun recipe, but I really need some other information."

"I wouldn't have given it to you anyway. My recipe is top secret, dear, otherwise I know a few ladies who would be daring enough to make a slight change just to beat me at the county fair but I'm glad you liked it," she said. "What can I help you with?"

"I want to check out stores between here and let's say Joliet, which carry fiber mats or rugs. Dr. Sage and I found the same fibers on our victims. The mats had to be purchased somewhere. I know the stores and shopping centers closer to Chicago, but not out this way. And, I would like to keep this from my brother until I have something positive to report."

"A little sibling competition is good at any age." Gladys smiled. "Let me get the phone book, and we'll make a list."

"Did Gladys give you the recipe?" Dave asked, as he came up behind Claire.

"Now sheriff, you know my recipe is classified information. If I gave it to Claire, then I would have to kill her. She was asking about quilt shops. We have a darling one here in Ottawa and there is a lovely one over in Morris."

Claire winked at Gladys. What a save, she thought.

"I didn't know you were a quilter. If I had known, I would have hooked you up with my wife. She has enough fabric at home to start a shop. I know she has her eye on Stacy's room when she heads to college next year."

"Yes, it's my passion," Claire said. *When did I get so good at lying*? I can't even hem a skirt, Claire thought. Sarah had always covered for her. In high school, Sarah had finished Claire's home economics' projects. She knew Sarah's death was a hole that would never be filled.

"Well if you ladies will excuse me, I have work to do. I'm sure Gladys can help you."

"Thanks again for your time today," Claire said.

"No problem." Dave quietly closed his office door behind him.

"That was close." Claire let out a deep breath.

"I knew the sheriff would buy the quilt shop idea. Now let me make a list for you."

Chapter 16

Twenty minutes later with Gladys' list and directions to the closest fast food chain, Claire was on her way. Her spirits were a little lighter as she drove to the first shop after devouring a juicy burger with all her favorite trimmings. She hadn't realized how hungry she really was.

At the first shop, the sales clerk showed her what she had in stock, but nothing matched the fibers found on the victims. Claire was slightly disappointed, but realized the chances of finding the right shop on her first stop wasn't likely. By the fifth shop, she was discouraged but still determined.

Her cell phone rang several times. She had stopped checking to see who had called. Patrick was persistent. By now, he knew she wasn't back at her desk or in the autopsy room. The sun was setting lower, right along with her energy level. She had one last shop on her list. Claire was tempted to skip it, but she was already there. Well, if Gladys could take the time to make her the list, the least she could do was make the effort to check out every shop on it.

She pulled her faithful Ford Taurus into the empty space right in front of Bali Imports. The shop, at the end of a strip mall, was hardly even noticeable. Bells jingled as she opened the door to the small shop bulging with everything not made in the USA. Items not piled to the ceiling were hanging from it. Fashionable displays were not the shop's forte.

"Can I help you?" said a young voice from behind some multi-colored hanging beads which divided the short aisle.

"Yes, I'm looking for fiber floor mats," Claire answered.

The teenager broke through the beads with her arms swinging, trying not to get her green streaked hair tangled in them. Earrings completely decorated the outer ridges of both ears and her naval. One sneeze and she would lose her very low riding jeans. Flip-flops slapped her feet under the torn edges of the jeans. Her eyes looked like they ran into a jumbo magic marker.

"Hi, I'm Nikki. That's Nikki with an 'i'. There are some in the next aisle over. What size were you interested in?"

"How large do they come?" Claire followed the teenager down the narrow aisle, around the corner to a stand full of the rolled up mats.

The teen bent down and checked a sticker on the stand. "Our largest is five feet by seven feet." She stood up as Claire extracted a small clear plastic bag from her purse and a roll of clear tape. Claire collected fibers from the rug with the tape and compared them to the ones in the plastic bag.

"Are you trying to match them with another mat?"

Claire's heart pounded as she answered the girl, "Yes." She removed her Office of the Medical Examiner picture ID from her purse and showed it to the girl. "I'm Dr. Claire O'Shaunessy. Right now there is a man lying in the Cook County Morgue with these fibers all over his body. There is also a woman in the LaSalle County morgue with them on her body. We believe they were murdered at the same place and wrapped in mats like these before their bodies were dumped in different counties." The words spilled out of her mouth before she could even think about the effect they might have on the young teenager.

"Cool!" The girl said.

"Do you remember selling any of the large ones to a buyer in the last month or so?"

"No, but let me ask Zenna." She disappeared through the stock and was back in seconds with a girl almost her double, only dressed in a micro-mini skirt hanging off her hips and pink mixed in her black dyed hair.

Claire introduced herself to Zenna and repeated her story. "The police and I are looking for a large framed man, possibly dressed in dark clothes, with short hair, who would have purchased two of the mats about the same size you carry. Do you remember any one fitting that description?" Her cell phone vibrated again. She ignored it.

"I waited on him about four weeks ago when we were having all that rain. He said he kept his car in a barn with dirt floors and was looking for something to cover the dirt. I guess his tires and hub caps must get muddy." Zenna beamed with importance. Her body automatically moved with the overhead music.

"By any chance did he pay by check or a credit or debit card?" Claire held her breath.

"No, he paid by cash. He had a big roll of cash in his pocket."

Zenna's eyes widened with her last remark.

Claire had lost on that score, but she wasn't about to let go. "Zenna, do you think you could describe him to a police sketch artist?"

"Do you mean one of those artists you tell them to make the nose larger or smaller?" She twisted the hair dangling at her neckline.

"Yes." She crossed her fingers praying Zenna could do this.

"Zenna never forgets a face," Nikki bragged. Nikki's hips followed her friend's to the music.

"First of all, Zenna, how old are you?" Claire put on her serious professional face hoping to pull the girls back in from radio land. Her cell phone vibrated in her pocket again.

"I'm seventeen." Zenna stood as tall as her moving body would permit.

Claire took out her vibrating cell phone and flipped through caller ID. This was Patrick's sixth call. She would ignore his messages for now. "I would like to call one of the lead Chicago detectives on this case to set up a session for you with a police sketch artist. Because of your age, it may require your parents' approval first."

"It's just my mom and me, but I know she'll say yes. This is so exciting, Nikki! Can you believe it; we may help find a real killer."

"I can't wait to call Justin." Nikki was bouncing up and down.

"Whoa!" Claire had to contain their newfound excitement. She wasn't about to add their names to the killer's list. "Before we go any further, the two of you need to understand the seriousness of the situation. This man has killed twice that we know of, and he would have no problem doing it again. If he thought someone was in his way, he would dispose of the person without a thought. Not getting caught is his primary objective." She watched the reality sink in and sober them. Both girls were still. Neither moved to the beat of the overhead music.

Nikki grabbed Zenna's arm. "I'm scared. We'd better not do this. He might come back for us."

"Oh my God," Zenna responded, hanging on to Nikki. "You're right!" Her voice was two levels higher.

Claire's last words had just the right effect. Now, she would pull them back in with a safety net. "This can be done safely, and the suspect will never know where the information came from unless you tell your friends. You can't tell anyone but your parents. You can't even talk about it when you are together, for fear someone else will overhear. The police will tell the news media the suspect was seen by a man in Chicago." She watched them slowly let go of each other. She couldn't beg them for fear they would refuse. They were young and justifiably scared. She needed them to resolve their terror on their own terms and come to her.

Zenna spoke first. "Are you sure he won't know my name? I want to help you catch this guy, but I don't want to die."

"You won't say anything about the floor mats, will you, or he'll know it was us for sure." Nikki's face was white under her creative makeup.

"Give me a minute to check it out." Claire pulled out her cell phone and dialed Jack's number.

"Claire, where are you? Patrick is ready to skin you alive." Jack said on the other line.

There was no doubt in her mind Patrick would ground her like a thirteen-year-old child if he could, and Jack sounded more concerned than he should have. Before Jack could say another word, she addressed him. "Detective Miller, this is Dr. O'Shaunessy calling. I would like to set up an appointment with the police sketch artist as soon as possible. I believe I have someone who can identify our suspect. There are two issues; first, the person is a minor, and I want it made perfectly clear the media believes this information came from a man in Chicago, not a seventeen-year-old girl from the Joliet area. The second issue is that she needs a guarantee the news media will not know about the floor mats. Do you think you can arrange this?"

Claire imagined Jack was picking his jaw off the floor about now. "Detective Miller, is there a problem?"

"No, not at all, you just caught me off guard for a moment, Dr. O'Shaunessy. I can arrange it. Would the young woman in question and one of her parents like us to have an unmarked car pick them up at eight tomorrow morning?"

Claire had thrown Jack a curve ball. "I'll check with her mother and give you a call back. In the meantime, I'll have Zenna…

Zenna tugged on her arm. "My real name is Sally Thomas, after my grandmother. My friends call me Zenna."

The day was truly full of surprises. "Detective Miller, her given name is Sally Thomas, but her friends call her Zenna. She can give you the address." Claire handed the phone to Zenna. Under the colored hair, heavy makeup, pounds of cheap jewelry and outlandish clothes, Claire could see a seventeen-year-old girl asserting her independence.

No sooner had Claire spoken with Zenna's mother, when Jack called back confirming tomorrow's plans. He included Captain Ramos' promise that their identity would be protected. After reminding both girls of their responsibility to remain silent, Claire drove back to the morgue.

***

Two hours and several thousand cars later on I55, Claire parked her Ford behind the Office of the Medical Examiner for Cook County. Grabbing her cup of cappuccino, she dashed for the back entrance to the county morgue building as rain pelleted her. The forecasted storm had arrived. She swiped her ID and quickly pushed the heavy door open.

Most people would be spooked by the morgue's eerie silence, but Claire welcomed the peace. She could think clearer when it was quiet. Besides, she wasn't really alone. The day staff may have gone home, but the evening maintenance crew was cleaning the autopsy rooms. And, in the cooler, a couple hundred patients waited for final disposition.

Since the labs were closed, Claire went directly to her office to view the fibers she collected at Bali Imports. At the shop she had officially bagged some of the fibers for evidence, but had collected a few samples for her own research. After unlocking her office, Claire rushed in and turned on her microscope. Her hands were shaking as she placed the fibers on a glass slide and focused the lens. If they matched the fibers on Sarah's body, this would be a major break in the case. This would link Sarah's death and Claire's other case back to the sketch of the man who had purchased the mats. Carefully she adjusted the lens until she got her answer.

Chapter 17

Dr. Arthur Rothschild glanced out the expansive windows of his Lake Point Towers penthouse overlooking Chicago's most expensive view. As the sun set behind the Chicago skyline, the city lights rose. This moment was worth everything it cost him to live here. He chose the same chair to watch the power of the universe go from daylight to complete darkness every evening. He had studied it for years. He knew when the precise, finite moment occurred, when the sun pulled a blanket of stars over the city with each changing sunset.

Without looking, his fingers gently wrapped around the Waterford crystal stemware filled with a world-class champagne. Arthur lifted it to his lips and breathed in its essence before allowing it to roll over his tongue. He considered champagne one of man's greatest creations. The effervescence warmed his throat, flowed to his fingertips and caressed every cell of his being.

Next, his manicured fingers selected one of the preeminent private brand cigarettes, Treasurer, from the brushed metal packet on the table next to him. He liked to roll it between his fingers to read the watermarked corporate logo on the tipping paper. He inhaled the richness of the 100% Virginia leaf tobacco, culled of the seeds and stems, blended to a strict, all natural formula. The cost for its luxury was immaterial to him, even though he knew it was four times that of commodity cigarettes. He held to the concept if you had to ask the price, you were out of your league. For him, luxury was his birthright.

With deliberation, he placed the cigarette between his lips, snapped open the 1933 antique Zippo lighter and pulled in the heat of the flame. The rich aroma permeated the air. He exhaled and pulled in another breath over his educated palate.

No one knew he smoked except his maid, and she was paid enough to forget whatever she saw. People looked at smoking as a weak, dirty habit. This was because they lit up on street corners, huddled in allies, and under the downtown 'L' tracks. They had no class. They littered the streets with their dirty cigarette butts. They didn't understand elegance. His mother had never smoked in public.

May Rothschild was a classy lady. In the evening, she enjoyed a splash of cream sherry in a crystal brandy sniffer, along with a premium cigarette in an antique, hand-carved ivory cigarette holder. She used to say no true lady ever let tobacco touch her lips. He never met a woman who could compare to her. He still missed her.

As the sun flashed its last colors across the sky, Dr. Rothschild raised his glass in a salute to his mother's memory. Then, with his other hand, he flicked the ashes off his cigarette. Relaxed, he pulled in another breath of the rich aroma as the phone rang.

He read the caller ID. It was Renata, his assistant. "Yes" was all he said.

"Do you have the news on?" she asked.

"No." He reached for the channel changer, and flipped through the three major networks. The lead story was the same.

A reporter was saying, "If you have any information regarding the sketch of the man believed to have killed and dumped the body of a man by the Jackson Park lagoon, please call the number at the bottom of your screen."

Dr. Rothschild stared at the near perfect sketch of Edwards. He dropped the luxury cigarette into the ashtray, unaware some of the ashes floated down to the Oriental rug.

"Renata, fax the clinic schedule *now*."

Within seconds, the schedule printed out on his fax machine. Only one couple was scheduled to arrive from Virginia and needed to be seen immediately. Timing for the in vitro fertilization procedure depended on the recipient's cycle.

"What do you want me to do?" Renata asked.

"Nothing until I talk with Edwards." He disconnected and immediately pressed Edwards' number on speed dial.

He spoke before Edwards could respond.

"Why is there a police sketch of you on every channel? The police are looking for you as a person of interest regarding the body found in a Chicago park. You said no one saw you. Obviously, someone did!" His voice grew tighter and louder. Thank heavens he had had the presence of mind never to allow Edwards at his penthouse, or the Michigan Avenue office. They were never seen together, except once at the clinic, the night when stupid Dr. Logan caused Sarah Morgan's death.

"There wasn't anyone in the park. The parking lot was empty," Edwards said.

Dr. Rothschild listened to Edwards' curt response. He didn't doubt Edwards had been careful. But this time, it hadn't been enough.

"Obviously someone saw you! Did you empty the apartment in question?"

"Done."

"What did you do with the items?"

"Burned them."

"All right. Get back to the estate and take care of Logan."

"What about Chun, the embryologist?"

"He won't talk if he wants the rest of his Chinese relatives to see this side of the Pacific Ocean."

Dr. Rothschild snapped his cell phone shut. He had no tolerance for incompetence. Until now, he could trust Edwards to follow his instructions explicitly. The ex-marine had proven he could make critical decisions without hesitation. However, that had all changed. Now he was a liability. He would have to deal with Edwards, but for the moment, he needed him to clean up a few more loose ends. Then he would call in a favor, and there would be no more Edwards.

His mother had told him always to have a handful of IOU's in his back pocket. She had taught him well.

He pressed Renata's number on the speed dial. He knew she would be waiting. He expected his employees to be available at a minute's notice.

"Yes," she said before the cell phone could ring a second time.

"This might be a good time to break in the new infertility specialist and anesthesiologist you hired. I want them ready to handle the couple from Virginia."

"Consider it done. I assume this means we won't be using Logan's services any longer?"

"Edwards will handle the exit interview. I'll phone you in the morning." He had invested a great deal of his energy into the success of his clinic. There had been huge risks involved, but no one was going to crush his dream.

Rothschild stood in front of the expansive windows. At the

final moment of darkness, he briefly wondered if there was any correlation between the sunset and the phone call, but his ego wouldn't let him go there.

Chapter 18

Edwards shoved the cell phone into the pocket of his black leather jacket. He was sick and tired of Rothschild's high and mighty attitude. Who in the *hell* did he think he was? He may come from money, but he was a damn poor excuse for a man. Edwards didn't trust a man who was afraid to get his fingernails dirty, and Rothschild never soiled those damn sissy nails. A real man wouldn't have his nails manicured. This was just one of Rothschild's disgusting habits.

With a quick turn of the wheel of his SUV, Edwards pulled out of the fast food restaurant. Within minutes, he was back on Interstate 80 heading west. He made a point to stop at different fast food restaurants just off the interstate. Even though Rothschild's estate was well hidden in a rural farming area which backed up to the woods edging the Vermilion River, he altered his drive. Today he would exit at Utica. Tomorrow he might choose the LaSalle-Peru exit. His military training had taught him never to be predictable.

In the three years he had been with Rothschild, he went from being the security force to Rothschild's death squad. This wasn't what he had signed up for. Rothschild never said to "kill" someone. He just ordered you to "take care" of the problem. The insinuation was clear. In addition, Edwards wasn't getting paid enough for the risks involved. Perhaps he would call Dirk and let him know he wanted back into the game. After living ten years of never sleeping in the same place for more than two nights, he needed a break. This was too steep a price to pay for the luxury of owning a mattress. At least as a mercenary, he understood the ground rules and the risk.

The killing didn't bother him; otherwise, he could never have become a mercenary. Edwards hated the degrading way Rothschild told him to clean up his messes. Now he had Logan to take care of. Rothschild didn't have to explain the damage Logan could cause if he opened his mouth in a local bar after too many scotches. *Damn it!* When had he turned into a damn babysitter?

Edwards had several choices as he saw it. He could walk

now, but Dirk might not have a job for him. Having money was a crucial element for getting lost in the crowd.

He could pump Logan up with alcohol, remove his identification and dump him in a questionable area of Peoria or Springfield. The local bums would take care of him. But the chances of being seen or some do-gooder calling the cops was high.

Or, he could finish him off like he had Parks. It would be easy enough to do. Since the mess in the clinic, Logan stayed in his quarters with enough scotch to keep him unconscious. With the help of a little kerosene, Logan would have a very inexpensive cremation in the rubbish pit behind the barn.

Edwards turned off the interstate at the Utica exit, and pulled into a convenience store parking lot. An ice cold six pack would be nice to have as he watched the fire and spread the ashes in the corn field. He liked the plan. No body to find accidentally. No bullets or wounds for some eager medical examiner to rule on, only ashes and a few bone chips to fertilize the fields. Maybe he should pick up some marshmallows to roast while he watched the flames erase Logan's existence.

He parked the SUV in a darker section of the parking lot. There was no sense having anyone associate his car and plates with his face. He had ditched the Wisconsin plates after dumping Parks' and Morgan's bodies. Currently Iowa plates were on his car. And, thanks to Dirk, his driver's license and insurance matched a Frank Snyder.

In a hidden locked compartment in the back seat was a selection of papers and license plates. The yearly fee to update them through an associate of Dirk's was worth every dollar. Occasionally, when he was on the road, he would add to his plate collection.

The convenience store was empty except for the obese female clerk behind the counter with dirty blonde hair pulled into a thin ponytail. She didn't look up from her gossip magazine until Edwards dropped the six-pack on the counter.

"Anything else?" she asked.

"Gum?"

"To your right, next to the newspapers."

Edwards reached for the gum when his eyes caught the headlines on the local paper.

Female Hand Reaches Out From the Grave

Edwards grabbed the paper and threw it on the counter with the gum. "I'll take the paper, too."

"You aren't from these parts, are you?" The woman bagged the items.

"Nope, Iowa." This was more conversation than Edwards found comfortable with a stranger.

"Drive safely. You'll have to read the story about the gal buried in the cemetery on your next road break."

Edwards nodded then strolled to his car. He fought every muscle in his body that screamed, "Run." He couldn't waste any time reading the article now in case the clerk decided to watch him for lack of anything better to do.

He returned to the interstate. When the LaSalle-Peru exit appeared in a couple of minutes, he slipped off the highway, unnoticed, into the dark of the night.

Edwards enjoyed having the black top all to himself. The full moon provided plenty of illumination. The tight muscles in the back of his neck eased as his SUV rolled down the county road towards Rothschild's estate. What lay ahead really pissed him off, but for now he would breathe in the cool night air and let it cleanse him.

He made up his mind to call Dirk. If Dirk didn't have any work for him, he would head to Mexico where living was cheaper, if not easier. Dirk would have something for him eventually. After he collected his next check from Rothschild, he'd be gone. This wasn't exactly the type of career requiring a two-week notice. Edwards almost had to chuckle at the thought. He would go out for the paper one morning, as they would say, and never return.

He'd secured everything he needed in the secret compartments he had built into his car. The young mother of three who accidentally bumped his car door at the Walmart last week had no idea how much ammunition was stored in it. Because it would be an issue crossing the border, he would store his car in a locker in Dallas before flying to Mexico.

Ten minutes later Edwards turned down an unmarked road, the entrance swallowed by tall pines at night. Even during the day, it was hardly noticeable. After the first curve, he stopped at a security gate and punched in his code. The black, iron gate rolled to the right and he entered. Seconds later, he drove behind the main house and pulled into the area separating it from the out buildings.

Something wasn't right. The hair on the back of his neck stood on end.

The first thing he noticed was there were too many lights on. Automatically he released the safety strap on his shoulder harness and removed is gun. He was approaching the tackle barn when Renata appeared looking slightly disheveled.

"Thanks a lot," she yelled. "You left me with Logan and I had to do the exit interview. He's in the tackle barn. Make sure everything is disposed of."

"What happened?" Edwards had never seen Renata this furious.

"Well, he finished off the last bottle of scotch you left him and then thought I would welcome his affections." Renata stormed off to the main house.

"Not bad," Edwards thought. Renata had done half his work.

Inside the tackle barn, he found Logan in a pile. From his awkward position, Edwards wondered how many bones Renata had broken before snapping his neck. The drunk probably felt no pain by then. He almost felt sorry for the doctor, but he truly resented him. What a waste of an education.

Logan should have had Edwards' life growing up. Edwards didn't know the men his mother slept with. Prostitution was the only skill she had. But, she saw to it he never went to bed hungry. She never ate until he was finished eating. Her body wore out before she reached forty.

Edwards grabbed the fiber rug out of the storage room and wrapped Logan up. He threw the load over a large wheelbarrow and pushed it out into the night. An owl hooted. The only other sound came from the crunching of the leaves and twigs as Edwards rounded the barn. He returned for Logan's personal items, and threw them in the rubbish pit on top of Logan's crumbled body.

After a quick trip to his SUV for the beer and newspaper, Edwards found himself a comfortable spot and opened a can. In the moonlight, he read the story of the unidentified female found in the local cemetery, then tossed the paper on top of Logan. He doubted if Rothschild would see the local paper. Right now Rothschild was too busy worrying about Parks. *Damn*, Edwards thought, those wild dogs should have finished Parks off.

In the early morning mist, Edwards lit the fire in the rubbish pit. If anyone spotted the smoke, they would assume another farmer had cleaned up a field. A few hours later, Edwards distributed the cooled ashes and bone fragments in the cornfield.

Now, it would just be a matter of time before he was in Mexico, soaking up the rays.

Chapter 19

From the enclosed visitors' area above the open floor of the Chicago Board of Trade, the security guard pointed out Kelly Davis to Patrick. The young woman with a French braid manned the phones in her cubicle. Patrick viewed the chaos below as madness. Why a bunch of grown men in brightly colored jackets would wave their arms in the air and scream was beyond him. Two minutes later the bell rang and the same men disbursed within seconds.

After the bell, Patrick and Jack followed the security guard down to Kelly's cubicle. Few employees remained on the trading floor. A maintenance crew swept up the snowstorm of shredded paper.

"Kelly Davis?" Patrick asked.

Kelly looked up. "Yes, that's me."

The young woman before him shouldn't have had such dark circles under her eyes after eight hours of work. Perhaps the darkened areas were from lack of sleep or worry. He had a feeling he wasn't going to make her day any better.

"I'm Detective O'Shaunessy and this is my partner, Detective Miller." Patrick watched her eyes catch their badges clipped to their jacket pockets. "Are you the Kelly who filled out a Missing Person's Report on Sarah Morgan?" Finch had found Kelly's report while searching the internet for another name.

"You found Sarah?" the woman asked.

Patrick heard the hopefulness in her voice. His gut tightened. After over twenty years on the force, this part of the job never got easier. "Would you be able to look at a photograph of a woman matching Sarah's description?"

She nodded.

Jack held out the photograph taken by Dr. Sage's tech. "Take your time," he offered.

Patrick stood next to Kelly. She wouldn't be the first person to have her knees buckle from the shock of losing a friend.

Kelly glanced at the photograph in Jack's hands. "She's dead, isn't she?" Tears streamed down her cheeks as she looked from

Patrick to Jack before handing the photograph back to Jack.

"Yes, she is. I'm sorry for your loss. Were you friends?" Patrick probed.

"I guess so. I mean..." The tears fell harder down onto her yellow jacket with the bright blue breast pocket.

Jack pulled up a stool for Kelly to sit on. She accepted the stool and grabbed tissues from a box on the counter.

"What happened to her?"

Patrick answered, "We believe Sarah was murdered."

"Where did you find Sarah?" Kelly balled up the damp tissue in her hands.

Patrick continued to dole out the bare facts of the case. He didn't want to overwhelm her. "She was found partially buried in a rural cemetery."

"In Chicago?"

Patrick had her. His years of experience told him her first question should have been, "What do you mean murdered?" But she didn't ask that question. Instead, Kelly expressed more concern over where they buried Sarah, as if there was more than one choice. Why?

Patrick measured his words carefully. "No, in LaSalle County." Kelly raised her eyes and peered beyond him. The reaction was slight, but the inference was there. She knew something, but what? He watched Kelly wrap her arms around herself, a classic sign of fear. She was pulling into herself, shutting down.

Kelly rubbed her arms as if she was trying to warm up. "How did she die?" she finally asked.

Patrick gave Jack a quick glance. From Jack's expression, he had heard the cool tone of Kelly's last question too. Was it possible she wasn't surprised about the news of Sarah's death? Could she be relieved it wasn't her, or scared she was next?

With a slight nod only Jack would recognize, Patrick passed the questioning over to him. They had done this a thousand times. It wasn't a case of good cop versus bad cop. Sometimes it was the older cop versus the younger cop. One witness might be more comfortable with the older, fatherly type. The next one would respond to someone looking more with it. Or maybe it wasn't either. If one of them felt it wasn't working with a potential lead, he would pass it off to the other. It didn't matter to them who asked the questions as long as they got answers.

"We are waiting for the final autopsy report," Jack said. "Anything you could tell us might help. How long did you work for her?"

Kelly shifted on the stool. Her shoulders sagged. "I've worked for Sarah for two years. This was her father's seat, you know."

Jack threw a look to Patrick, who shrugged. "Were you her assistant?" Jack asked.

"I guess you could say that."

Patrick took notes as Jack continued. "Did anyone else work for her?"

"No. I was the last one," she answered.

"What do you mean you were the last one?" Jack asked.

Patrick watched as Kelly looked away, as if to pull her thoughts together.

"When I started with her, there were three others."

Jack raised his eyebrows. "Do you have their names?"

"I can't remember their last names. They quit about a week after I started. I don't have the information here, but I could probably find it. Their first names were Jake, Theo and Kim."

"Why did they leave?" Jack pushed.

"I don't... I don't know." She shook her head.

"You don't know, or you don't want to say?" Jack asked.

Kelly stood up. "I would only be speculating if I said anything. What's going to happen to Sarah now?"

Patrick noticed the abrupt change in Kelly's temperament. "Her body will be released to her family in a couple of days," he lied.

"She doesn't have anyone. I'm probably it." Kelly sat back down. The tears poured this time. She took the tissues Jack offered and tried to compose herself, but it didn't work.

"Why would you say that?" Jack asked.

"Her parents died a number of years ago and she didn't have any siblings. She should at least be buried with her parents."

"What about friends?" Patrick knew Claire had only run into her old friend at Starbucks recently, but surely Sarah had kept in touch with others from the old neighborhood.

Kelly moved to let the maintenance crew come in and sweep out her area. "I don't think she had any."

This didn't sound like the Sarah Morgan Patrick had known. The guys were always falling at her feet. She loved a good time. What had changed her? What choices had she made which led her to that rural cemetery? "Why do you say that?" Patrick asked.

Kelly removed her jacket and stuffed it in the locked cabinet which held her purse. "She had some issues."

Jack stood right in front of Kelly as she slipped the purse strap over her shoulder. "What kind of issues?"

"It's not my place to..." Kelly tried to walk around Jack, only Patrick stopped her.

"Don't give me that *shit*. Those issues could have been what got her killed." Jack wouldn't give up.

Patrick waited for her to answer. If Jack couldn't reach her in the next few minutes, they were screwed.

"I have to go," was all she said as she headed toward the exit.

Jack walked right in front of her again. His tall frame towered over her. "Was it drugs or alcohol? If it was either of those, the information will appear on the autopsy's toxicology report."

Kelly couldn't get past Jack. She closed her eyes and sighed. "It was gambling. Now *can* I go?"

Patrick heard the frustration in her voice. "No," he answered, using a softer tone. "At this moment, you are our only link to Sarah. We need you to come with us to the station to answer more questions."

"Do I have to go to the police station?"

Patrick saw her eyes widen like a scared animal. "How about the coffee shop around the corner?"

Several minutes later the three sat in a booth waiting for the waitress to bring their order. Patrick had his notebook out. After scribbling down a few things, he looked at Kelly. She looked like a drowned rat. Her shoulders were bent. Tears seeped from her swollen eyelids. Tissues had removed her smeared makeup.

The waitress delivered three hot chocolates and Kelly sighed in relief. Good, Patrick thought, comfort food. After a sip, he put down his mug.

"Kelly, I know this is a lot for you to take in at once, but we are losing ground each day with the investigation. Sheriff Wilson from LaSalle County is working the case from his end, but since Sarah is from Chicago, we are hoping we can find out something about her which will lead us to her killer before the trail goes cold.

Do you think you could help us out?"

Kelly nodded her head yes.

Jack leaned forward, wrapping both hands around his steaming mug. "When was the last time you saw Sarah?"

Kelly straightened up in the booth. "Last Friday, when the market closed."

Jack continued, "Did she tell you where she was going after work, or if she had plans for the weekend?"

"No."

Patrick cut in. "You mentioned gambling. What type of gambling? The casino boats? Off track betting?"

"No," she answered. "Vegas. Sarah liked to roll the dice."

Jack let out a low whistle. "That could be expensive."

Kelly scooped up the marshmallow melting in her cup with a spoon and ate it. "She loved to fly to Vegas on those weekend junkets and take the red eye back in time before the market opened on Monday."

"Where did she get that type of money?" Patrick knew about Sarah's inheritance but he wasn't sure how much she had shared with her employees.

"Her parents left her everything. I understand they had a home in Barrington and a condo in Boca Raton, Florida."

"Not bad." Patrick emptied his mug. "How was she holding up with her gambling?"

"She wasn't. She seemed desperate. Recently, I heard through the rumor mills, she had gone through her inheritance, lost her Beamer and condo. Actually, I've been waiting for my paychecks to bounce. I already have my resume out."

Patrick went fishing. "What's her seat on the Board of Trade worth?"

"Probably, $600,000.00. I know she had an offer for less than half of that recently. Word is out that she needs money. I've been afraid if she sold it, she would end up penniless. I guess it's a mute point now."

Patrick eased back against the booth. "Well, if she had lost basically everything before you started two years ago, what was she doing for cash?"

Kelly played with the spoon in her mug. "You know how the credit card companies send you their cards in the mail pre-approved? She cashed them out. Each time she got a new one, she would cash out the maximum allowed. Then she would make minimum payments on the outstanding bills to keep the collection companies off her back. With the rest of the money, she would fly to Vegas. She told me all she needed was one good roll of the dice. But I don't think it ever happened."

Patrick twirled his pen between his fingers. Collection companies generally don't bury their debtors in rural cemeteries. The road between debt and death was getting longer. Sarah was definitely mixed up in some scam, and it had cost her her life.

Jack looked at the tab and threw a few bills on the Formica table. Casually he asked, "Could Sarah have used a loan shark?"

Kelly immediately let go of the spoon. "No."

That was the shortest *no* Patrick had ever heard. There was definitely some piece of information behind her quick response. He picked up the questioning. "So, you don't think she ever used a loan shark? Did you see anyone waiting for her after work or following her?" He purposely ran the questions together hoping to find a crack in her response.

"No, I don't know." Kelly's breathing quickened.

"Look, Kelly," Jack said, "we're not the bad guys. We only want to find Sarah's killer. Let's back up for a moment. Do you think she owed a loan shark?"

"I never heard Sarah say anything about owing money to a loan shark, but she could have. She didn't share much."

"Okay," Jack went on, "what about seeing anyone lingering around work, who looked out of place?"

Kelly pushed the empty mug aside. "Other than a few of the regular homeless guys begging out front, I didn't see anyone."

"Did the two of you leave work together?" Patrick asked.

"Most of the time we hopped the 'L' together, but I get off at Belmont and wait to hitch a ride home with my dad. Sarah would transfer to the Ravenswood Line which ran near her apartment."

"Since we held you up, we'll give you a ride to where your dad works," Patrick offered as they got up. He stared into Kelly's eyes. "I have one last question, what do you think Sarah was doing out in LaSalle County?"

What color was left in Kelly's face was gone. She shook her head. "I don't know."

Chapter 20

"I don't know? Right?" Jack slammed his fist on the dashboard of their unmarked car after Kelly had gotten out. "Kelly knows something; I'm sure of it. What is she holding back?" He turned to Patrick. "I wonder if Sarah was selling her eggs illegally to pay her credit card debt."

"Women usually share female stuff with each other," Patrick remarked. "Growing up with five sisters was an eye opener. If they weren't complaining someone took the last mini or maxi pad, they were in deep discussion about who was doing what, and with whom. If that wasn't enough, our next-door neighbor was a recovery room nurse. She would tell the girls how the nurses would have contests to see which male patient was the most endowed."

"You're kidding me? The nurses looked?"

Patrick laughed so hard he almost hit a parked car as he pulled into the space in front of Sarah's apartment. "Sure they look. You're not scared you would lose the contest, are you?"

Jack ignored the comment. "So, what you're saying is Sarah probably told Kelly she found a way to make some extra money."

"Yup. I bet Kelly knows where. Remember she reacted more to Sarah being found in LaSalle County than being buried in a rural cemetery? She never asked who found Sarah either, or how she died."

As Patrick got out of the car, his eyes scanned the dilapidated framed structure before him. This was not Sarah's style. The outside stairs were swept, but the brown evergreens on either side should have been pulled out a lifetime ago. All Patrick could think was, Sarah, what happened? He knew gambling could do this to a person, but why did it have to be someone from the old neighborhood who he had pushed on the playground swing with his kid sister?

Patrick rang the manager's bell. It took several minutes for Sarah's landlady to answer the door. "Good afternoon. I hope we aren't disturbing you. I'm Detective O'Shaunessy, and this is my partner, Detective Miller. May we talk with you for a few minutes? This is about Sarah Morgan." They showed the gray haired woman their badges.

"Oh dear, please do come in," the elderly woman with the cracking voice said. "You're not bothering me. My soaps are over, and a talk show was putting me to sleep."

"Thank you," Patrick replied as they entered the dingy hallway. "I'm sorry to inform you, but Sarah has died."

"Oh yes, I know," the voice croaked. "That nice brother of hers was here yesterday, or maybe it was the day before. Can't remember like I used to."

Patrick exchanged looks with Jack. *Bingo!* She doesn't know Sarah was an only child!

"I'm sorry," Patrick said. "I missed getting your name."

"Did I forget to introduce myself? Oh, well, it doesn't matter. My name is Audrey Gardner."

"Miss Gardner, may I call you that?"

"I would prefer Audrey. It makes me feel younger." She reached up and patted Patrick on the cheek. "I was born in this house. Never married. Was having too much fun with all those sailors stationed at Navy Pier during the big war. So many of them didn't come home you know." Her smile faded as her voice drifted away.

"Ma'am," Jack asked, bringing her back to the present, "could you tell us what you know about Sarah and her brother?"

"Come in and sit down. These old legs don't last very long."

Patrick nodded to Jack as they followed Audrey into the musty sitting room. She was dressed in a cotton day dress like the ones his mother use to wear. Patrick wondered how long it had been since she'd opened the windows and let fresh air fill the room. He had seen this many times. The elderly were afraid they wouldn't be able to secure the windows so they never risked opening them.

"Now where were we?" Audrey had lost her line of thinking between the hallway and the sitting room.

"You were going to tell us about Sarah and her brother," Jack replied.

"Ah, yes." Audrey's wrinkled hands smoothed her dress over her lap. "Sarah was such a wonderful tenant. She was quiet, never had visitors late at night, and never left garbage in the hallway."

Jack stretched his legs out in front of him before resting his elbows back on his knees. "Did Sarah have visitors during the day?"

"Why, I don't believe so, now that you mention it."

Patrick thought if Audrey didn't pick up speed soon he would fall asleep. "What about her brother? Did he visit often?"

Audrey rocked back and forth in the chair. "No, he only came after she died in a terrible car accident. I can't remember if he said it happened in Iowa or Ohio."

"Don't worry we can look it up," Patrick reassured her even though he knew no such accident had occurred.

"Wait a minute I remember now, it was Iowa." Audrey smiled. "The same state as his license plates."

Patrick asked, "Do you remember what type of car he drove?"

"Heavens, no. I haven't paid attention since my yellow Vega gave out. He drove one of those big black boxes."

"An SUV," replied Jack.

"A what?" Audrey asked.

Patrick felt like he was in a time warp. He could have painted the guest bedroom for his wife in the time it was going to take to pull the answers out of Audrey. He couldn't chance rushing her and having her forget the one detail which might help them. "Audrey, how did you know it was Sarah's brother?"

"Why he showed me his driver's license, except he explained they had different last names because they had different fathers. The picture looked just like him, too." Audrey sat up a little straighter after relaying the information.

Patrick knew this imposter had scammed Audrey, but there was no point in upsetting her. "If I showed you a sketch a friend gave me, do you think you could tell me if it looks like Sarah's brother?"

"I bet I could," Audrey bragged.

"Good," Jack replied. He handed Audrey the sketch made from Zenna's description of the man who bought the fiber rugs from Bali Imports.

Audrey fingered the sketch. "Yes, this is Sarah's brother, Frank Snyder, such a nice man, so polite. He even packed up all Sarah's belongings. He said he didn't want to trouble me, and they would bring closure for him."

I bet it brought closure for him. Patrick wanted to pace the floor. Sitting this long was driving him crazy. "By any chance did you get his address?"

"No, I didn't. Oh dear, Sarah got mail today. How will I get it to Frank?" Audrey clutched her dress.

"We'll get it to her brother for you," Jack offered. "And, if it isn't too much trouble, could we see her apartment?"

"You go ahead while I look for her mail. Sarah's apartment is the second door on the left at the top of the stairs. The door isn't locked. Can't see no reason since there are only a few pieces of furniture. I rent most of my apartments furnished. Everyone shares the same bathroom on the second floor."

"Thank you," Jack answered. He beat Patrick up the stairs.

A minute later Patrick joined him in the room Audrey called an apartment. She was right about the furniture. Besides the bed and night stand, there was a dresser missing most of the drawer handles, an old chair and ottoman with the stuffing coming out between the well-worn threads, and a small dinette set with a hot plate. The only item reasonably new was a college dorm size refrigerator humming in the corner. This was a far cry from Sarah's home in Barrington where her bedroom closet was larger than this room.

Jack stood in the center of the room with his hands on his hips. "Bet you lunch that brother Frank wiped the place clean. There's probably no point in calling the crime scene guys other than to follow protocol."

"Give Ramos a call and see what he wants done. I'm going to see if we have any luck with Sarah's mail; if our dear Audrey can even find it."

"Okay," Jack said as he dialed Captain Ramos' cell.

Patrick called out from the doorway to Audrey's apartment, so as not to scare her. "Did you find Sarah's mail?"

Audrey stood with a pile of envelopes and sale flyers in her arms. "Do you think you could sort this? My eyes aren't what they used to be."

Patrick took the pile to the dining room table. "Not a problem." He sorted out two stacks. "This one is yours." He handed the larger stack, mostly sale flyers, to Audrey.

"Thank you so much Detective," she answered. "You will get Sarah's mail to her brother Frank, won't you?"

"Not a problem." Patrick shoved the mail into his jacket

pocket as he heard Jack come down the stairs and head out the front door. "Thank you, Audrey, for your help. Don't forget to lock the front door."

Audrey followed Patrick to the door. "You can drop by any time you have questions." She smiled and waved.

Patrick handed the stack of mail to Jack as he climbed behind the wheel and pulled away from the curb with one last wave to Audrey. "I gather Ramos took a pass on the apartment?"

Jack looked through the flyers. "He figures the guy probably wore gloves and wiped it down. However, he is having Finch run a trace on Frank Snyder. It'll probably be a dead end."

Patrick hadn't driven but a block when his partner held out a cream-colored postcard.

"Well, what do you know?" Jack held up the card.

Patrick hit the brakes as a mid-size sedan started to pull into his lane without looking. "What did you find?"

"Dr. Arthur Rothschild sent Sarah a reminder for her yearly pap smear test."

"So?" Patrick hated driving down Western Avenue during rush hour.

Jack read the card. "The return address is for Premier OB, GYN and Infertility Specialists on north Michigan Avenue."

"This day just keeps getting better," Patrick said.

Chapter 21

Twenty minutes later Patrick and Jack found Claire sitting on Patrick's desk talking with Finch. She twirled a brown envelope between her fingers.

"You two aren't trading state secrets, are you?" Patrick asked.

Claire spoke first. "I have something you want and so does Finch. The issue is do I get to hear what Finch has?"

Jack stepped forward. "Claire, you know Patrick can't divulge any information we collect on this case."

Claire hopped off Patrick's desk. "Okay, I get it. Patrick, I'll see you later. Sylvia invited me for dinner. Nice talking with you, Finch. Goodnight Detective Miller." She walked towards the door, envelope in hand, wondering how long it would take Patrick to make the trade. She had him right where she wanted him, and it was killing him. Power to the women, she thought.

"Claire, come on back. Jack, you and Finch take her to the conference room. I'll let Captain Ramos know what we found out and meet you there. And Jack, don't let my sister slip away with that envelope."

Claire smiled all the way to the conference room. Finally, she had won a round. She took a chair on the opposite side of the table just to let Jack think he had the upper hand. His day would come, too.

A few minutes later Patrick joined them. "Okay, which of you two power mongrels would like to go first?"

Finch sat back and said, "Ladies first."

"Now how do you know if I'm a lady," Claire challenged Finch.

Patrick threw up his hands. "After the afternoon I had with Audrey, I need a break. Claire, you go first, and if you behave, I'll let you stay."

"Who's Audrey?" Claire asked.

"We're not going there right now," answered Jack. He stretched his legs under the table.

Claire opened the envelope and slid a sheet of paper across the table to Patrick. "What the report basically says is the O negative blood found on the front of my victim's sock does belong to Sarah. And, as a sidebar, the fiber I collected at the Bali Imports shop matches the fibers on Sarah and the body back in my morgue."

Jack let out a low whistle. "These two cases *are* tied together. It wasn't just wishful thinking when we found the fibers and clay."

Claire nodded, then continued. "The lab was able to get a decent set of prints, but because my victim isn't local, it took a little longer to hunt Dr. Parks down through AFIS." Claire pulled a mug shot out of the envelope and handed it over to Patrick and Jack. "This is Dr. Steven Parks from Lexington, Kentucky. He was arrested for driving under the influence of narcotics in his home state. He is, correction, he was an anesthesiologist at Lexington Memorial. He quit working for them almost two years ago. The hospital has no idea where Dr. Parks is currently practicing. He's licensed only for the state of Kentucky. The Lexington Police are looking for next of kin. Patrick, I gave the Lexington police yours and Jack's names and cell numbers."

Jack leaned back in his chair and ran his hands through his hair. "Wow. Claire, are you saying Dr. Parks was there when Sarah died from the puncture to the iliac artery?"

"Right now, the blood on Parks' sock only proves he came in contact with Sarah's blood sometime after she hemorrhaged to death and before she was buried." Claire slid the lab results and photo back in the envelope.

"I can't prove my theory, but my gut tells me Parks died because he saw Sarah die" Claire tapped the envelope on the table. "My personal opinion is that Parks requested help, but someone stopped him. This has to be an illegal operation. Once Parks went into doctor mode, like trying to save Sarah when she got into trouble, he became a liability. Someone couldn't afford to have him call 9-1-1."

"That would make sense," replied Jack. "If they called for help, their operation would be exposed. Parks must have asked for help."

"Like if he tried to dial 9-1-1," Patrick said. "What bothers me is his license only covers Kentucky, and he is in our morgue. I wonder how his arrest for driving under the influence of narcotics affected his job. I'll call Lexington Memorial tomorrow. For now let's move on, or we'll be here all night." Patrick scribbled in his notebook. "Now, tell me about the fiber match."

"As you know, on my way back from LaSalle County, I hit pay dirt at Bali Imports. That's where I met Zenna and she provided the information for the police sketch. I collected samples of the sisal fibers and sent them to the lab. They came back a match."

"A defense attorney could argue that the mat is sold all over the U.S.," Jack said. "However, it's a link to the man who possibly buried Sarah. Not bad investigative skills, Claire."

"Jack, don't encourage her," Patrick said, rubbing the bridge of his nose.

"Claire, this afternoon, Jack and I met with Kelly Davis, Sarah's assistant. I don't know how to break this to you, but according to Kelly, Sarah had a major gambling problem. Kelly told us Sarah had lost everything in the last couple of years, and was gambling with cash withdrawals from credit cards."

"You're joking, aren't you?" Claire said as she stared at Patrick. "She never even bet on the Bears or the Sox."

"Apparently she liked Vegas and the dice, an expensive combo," Patrick explained, as he leaned forward on the table. "Kelly appeared to be scared to death. She didn't seem shocked to hear Sarah was dead. She never even asked who had found Sarah. And, when we mentioned she was found in LaSalle County, she didn't question it. We didn't tell Kelly we knew how Sarah died."

Jack picked up the conversation. "It gets better. Next on our list was Sarah's landlady, Audrey Gardner. She was pretty batty, but she told us Frank Snyder, Sarah's *brother*, picked up her personal items."

"But Sarah doesn't have a brother," Claire said, clearly shocked. "Who is this Frank Snyder?"

Finch leaned forward. "Jack, I ran Frank Snyder's name through the Iowa Department of Motor Vehicles and Department of State Licensure. They showed a Frank Snyder in his late sixties. I called him at home. He claims he's never been to Chicago, and he drives a Buick. He reported his plates stolen about four months ago. He thinks they were taken at a local Walmart."

Finch continued. "I didn't see the fake Frank Snyder driver's license, but I hear the ID picture matched your sketch. So, I have a couple thoughts. We could have an identification theft going on. It may not be for financial reasons, only identification purposes. Someone is buying this information, and someone else has the ability to produce the fake ID's. It could be a state employee. Perhaps the plates are stolen first, and then the ID's are made to match."

"That's a good idea, Finch," Jack said. "Claire, I showed Audrey the sketch made from the information Zenna gave the artist, and the landlady said it was Frank Snyder."

"Now for the frosting on the cake," Patrick added. "Jack found a reminder card in Sarah's mail for her yearly pap smear. The return address was for Premier OB, GYN and Infertility Specialist on north Michigan Avenue. Her appointment was with a Dr. Arthur Rothschild."

Finch rose. "Hmm. If you don't need me, I'll head upstairs to see what I can come up with on this Dr. Arthur Rothschild."

"Thanks, Finch, we're about done here," Patrick answered as he waited for the door to close behind Finch. "Claire, you can head over to the house. Tell Sylvia we'll be home in an hour. Jack and I want to work on our plan."

"You're not getting rid of me that easily, Patrick. Sarah was my friend, too."

"But this is where your job ends. It's up to Patrick and me to take it from here," said Jack.

Claire leaned over the table and stared into his eyes. She could feel her Irish blood boiling. She had had just about enough of men telling her what she could and couldn't do. Greg hadn't been able to handle her, and now Jack Miller was about to find out the same thing.

"Detective Miller, you don't tell me what I can and can't do. This is between my brother, Patrick, and me."

"Oh Christ!" Patrick rubbed his eyes. "There better be a good strong red wine to go along with Sylvia's lasagna, or I'll stomp my own grapes. Claire, sit down and shut your mouth for once. In case you haven't noticed, we have a couple of really dead bodies, and I don't want to add you to the pile."

"But, Patrick..."

Jack got up. "I'm going for coffee or whiskey, whichever I can find first," he said as he left the conference room. At the door, he turned back. "You're right Patrick, she is a handful."

"You said *I* was a handful?" Claire's voice was still operating on loud.

"*Claire, stop!*" Patrick broke the pencil in his hands in half. "And, sit down."

Claire did as she was told. She knew she had pushed her brother too far. He was still trying to protect her, only he didn't see her as all grown up and quite capable of taking care of herself.

"You are an outstanding forensic pathologist. You and your lab gave us some invaluable information. But you don't work for the police department. If I let you help, Ramos will have my ass, if not my job. Look, I'll let you know what's going on. You can always offer suggestions, but you can't work this case. Understood?" Patrick got up and put his arm around Claire. "Please go quietly for once. I'm too exhausted to argue with you."

Claire knew Patrick was right, but this didn't mean she agreed with him. "Okay, I'll behave. But if I find out you're not keeping me in the loop, then all bets are off, okay?"

"Thanks, Claire. I'll catch up with you at the house."

"I think I'll take a pass for tonight. I'm behind on reports for Dr. Johnson, and I think Jack will enjoy his dinner more if I'm not there." Claire stood up and squeezed her brother's shoulder. "Give my love to Sylvia and the kids. I'll stop by and see them tomorrow."

Patrick gave her another hug. "I think you owe Jack an apology."

Claire laughed. "Don't push your luck, big brother."

Chapter 22

Claire shivered in the cool fall air as she ran to her car. Her adrenaline was working overtime. What a day! It had started with the positive identification of Sarah's blood on the socks then followed with the discovery that her victim was Dr. Parks, an anesthesiologist from Kentucky. She still couldn't quite grasp the revelation of Sarah's gambling. And how did the man in the sketch know to pose as Sarah's brother? She almost forgot about Dr. Rothschild's reminder postcard. Was *he* responsible for Sarah's death?

"Okay, Claire," she said to herself, "think!" The only answer she could come up with was 'Frankie'. Patrick would tan her hide if he knew she still had Frankie Biaggi's cell number on speed dial. Frankie may not have the answers to all her problems, but he would have the connections she needed. Besides, she needed to tell Frankie about Sarah's death. She didn't want him to hear the news some other way. She pressed his number. It only took two rings.

"Is that you, O'Shaunessy?" Frankie hadn't lost any of his Chicago-style Italian charm.

"It's me." Her heart almost skipped a beat thinking of his trademark dark wavy hair and tight jeans. How the girls from the neighborhood had swooned over him.

"I heard you were back in town. You should have called me sooner. My heart has been breaking. Say, is it really true, do you cut up dead people?"

Claire laughed. Actually, it felt good to laugh after the day she'd had. "Yeah, I cut up dead people Frankie."

"So, is this a social call? I thought you got yourself some tight ass doc for a fiancée. You miss your wild Italian?"

"You know I always miss you. As for the tight ass doc, I kicked his butt. But to answer your question, this isn't a social call. I need your help. Can you meet me at Jimbo's?"

"Let me check my social calendar. You're in luck; I have an opening in fifteen minutes."

"I'll be there."

***

The sports bar was only half-packed. Claire had no trouble finding Frankie near the back in his usual spot. He gave her a welcoming kiss smack on her lips as he copped a squeeze of her butt. It was comforting to know some things never changed.

"Sit down, Gorgeous. I ordered you your favorite beer." Frankie leaned his chair back on two legs. "Now what kind of service can Frankie provide for you?"

On the drive over, Claire had thought about how she was going to tell Frankie about Sarah, but in the end she just blurted it out. "Sarah's gone."

Frankie and Sarah had been a hot item even after her family moved to Barrington. Sarah's parents thought the move would break them up, but it didn't. Frankie was pure blue collar. Sarah's education did them in. Her degree scared him, and he walked. But he never forgot her.

"Gone where?" He tipped the chair back on all four legs.

"Frankie, she's dead." Claire could feel her eyes filling with unshed tears. She blotted them with the table napkin.

"What do you mean, *dead*?" Frankie grabbed her wrist.

Claire let him hold on. "I'm so sorry."

"What happened?" Anguish spread across his face. His smile was gone. His deep dimples which had broken many a heart vanished. "Tell me what happened!" He pounded his fist on the table so hard the beer sloshed over the edges of the glasses.

"Shhh, we need to keep this quiet so Patrick and his partner can get the ones responsible, do you understand?" Claire realized she had to obtain his silence if her plan was to work. "Are you in?"

"You don't have to ask, I'm in. What happened to Sarah? What do you want me to do?" His hands clasped both of hers.

Claire gave Frankie a run down on everything. She knew she could trust him to keep his word. "News of her death has managed to stay out of the Chicago papers. We're hoping this gives those responsible a false sense of security. Frankie, I need a real big favor."

"Anything," Frankie responded. "I'll do anything to help you and Patrick get this piece of scum. How could someone do this to our Sarah?"

She shook her head. "I wish I knew. Can you help me? I need

a set of fake ID's. I think an Illinois driver's license and a Chicago library card should do it. I thought I would use my mother's maiden name, O'Reilly. Let me know how much I owe you." Claire relaxed a little now the deed was done.

"Does Patrick know what you are up to?" Frankie asked. He released her hands and took a sip of beer before leaning the chair back on two legs.

"No, and you're not going to tell him." Claire swallowed a mouthful of the locally brewed beer for fortification. "I figure if he knew I was going to schedule a routine appointment with this Dr. Rothschild, using a false name, he would lock me in my bedroom like in the old days."

"Yeah, but Patrick always forgot about the window. You're not going to do anything stupid, are you?"

"No. I'm just going to have an appointment and see if I can get a feel for anything. If I find out something, I'll tell Patrick. Once it's over, he won't be too mad."

"Okay. Do you want me to go as your husband?"

"No. I think being single will work better, but thank you for offering."

"Just part of the Biaggi charm."

She didn't tell Frankie she might have to play the part of a desperate single female, or how far she was considering taking the scam if she had to.

"I don't like it, but I want Patrick to catch the creep who did this to our Sarah. Maybe I could have a few minutes alone with him."

"I'll ask Patrick." Claire crossed her fingers already knowing her brother's answer.

"Can you bring a new passport photo to me tomorrow evening? It should take only a day or two after that. By the way, this is on the house for old-time's sake." Frankie winked at her.

Claire finished her beer and answered all Frankie's questions about her job. For some reason he seemed mesmerized by the idea of a woman doing autopsies, or as he referred to it, cutting up dead people. Maybe it was easier for him than thinking about Sarah. Claire could appreciate the sentiment. Any reprieve from the pain of Sarah's death, even for a brief moment, was welcomed.

"What are we going to do about Sarah?" Frankie's smile was

still missing. "We're her only family since her parents died."

"I know she would want to be buried next to her parents. Can we talk about this in a few days?"

Once again he took her hands in his, but this time he bent his head down. Claire watched Frankie's tears spill onto the table. She couldn't think of any words that would make this better.

Chapter 23

Patrick was still shaking the rain off when he entered the squad room. "I know I look drenched. Do you think it is asking too much of my family to leave me at least one umbrella when Sylvia takes my raincoat to the dry cleaners? Take my advice, don't get married and have any kids, especially daughters."

"I don't have to," Jack replied. "I've got Sylvia as my very own personal chef. Coffee is fresh, if that helps."

Patrick headed straight for the coffee pot. "Sorry I'm late. I had to drop my daughters off at school. The girls missed their bus because of the usual battle for the bathroom mirror. Where are we at with the calls?"

Jack finished his coffee and tossed the paper cup into the wastebasket. "Since Lexington is an hour ahead of us, I was able to reach the medical director. Apparently, Lexington Memorial's policy is to offer their physicians two to six months of rehabilitation at a private facility in North Carolina. Off the record, the director told me the hospital usually cut the physician a severance check unless the physician had brought in a lot of money for the hospital. If the physician falls into that category, and insists on coming back, they would downgrade him to a benign research project. Then if the physician slips back into his old habits, he could be easily removed from staff without interfering with patient care."

Patrick hung his damp sports jacket on the back of his chair before sitting down. "Since Dr. Parks was an anesthesiologist, he probably was handed his severance check. Any word on his family?"

Jack tapped his pencil on the edge of his desk. "Off the record of course, the medical director told me Mrs. Parks took the severance check and headed to her divorce attorney. She left the area with their two sons."

"Guess I can't blame her. The arrest probably made the crime report in the local paper. That's hard to swallow, let alone the grief the kids probably got at school. Did he tell you anything on the record besides spitting out the hospital policy?"

"No, but off the record, he dropped the name of Dr. Parks' attorney and the name of the medical facility in North Carolina."

"What would we ever do if we didn't have any off the record conversations?" Patrick said. "Okay, which one do you want to run down?"

Jack got up for a second cup of coffee. "Want a refill?" he asked his partner.

"No, thanks."

"Since you're the one who had to go without an umbrella, I think you should have first choice." Jack poured his coffee and laughed.

"That's it, take pity on the old married guy. Someday it'll be your turn," Patrick said. "All right, give me the attorney since you seem to be on a roll with medical directors."

Patrick was on hold five minutes before the receptionist with the perky voice came back on the line and told him she was putting him through to Mr. Barron.

"This is Mr. Barron, Detective O'Shaunessy, how can I help you? I understand you are calling from Chicago." The voice at the other end of the line was politely cold.

"Yes sir, I am. I was wondering if you have a client by the name of Dr. Steven Parks?" Patrick waited for the standard line that Mr. Barron couldn't divulge client information.

"What happened to Steve?"

Patrick sat up straight in his chair. He wadded up a sheet of paper and threw it at Jack to get his attention. "Before I start, if you would like to verify my call, I can give you my Captain's number."

"No, that won't be necessary. My secretary already did before she put your call through," Mr. Barron replied.

Well that accounts for the five minutes of taxpayers' money he spent. "How well do you know Dr. Parks?"

"I'm his attorney, we were college roommates, I was his best man at his wedding, and I'm godfather to his oldest son. That's how well I know him. Is he in trouble?" Mr. Barron asked.

Shoot, Patrick thought, this would be much easier if he was only Parks' attorney. "Mr. Barron, I'm sorry to tell you, but Dr. Parks is deceased." Patrick gave him a minute to digest what he had just said before continuing. "His body was found by the Jackson Park lagoon Sunday morning. We just confirmed his fingerprints though AFIS. Can you tell us why Dr. Parks was in Chicago?"

Barron snapped, "What happened?"

Now it was Patrick who couldn't divulge information instead of the lawyer. "I regret I can't share the details with you at this point in the investigation, but the official cause of death is strangulation." He looked over at Jack who was on the other line listening. He saw Jack taking notes so Patrick could concentrate on the conversation.

"Strangulation? How did it happen? Who did it?" Barron fired off his questions like a seasoned attorney.

Patrick took in a deep breath and let it out. He understood Dr. Parks' friend wanting all the answers, but it wasn't going to happen. "Mr. Barron, I'm sorry for your loss. I can understand how frustrating this must be for you to have to wait for all the details. At this time, we believe Dr. Parks' case is related to another pending death investigation. We don't want the public to get wind of this and connect them."

"Was someone else strangled?" Mr. Barron asked.

Patrick replied, "No, the manner of death was different."

"Then why do you think the cases are connected?" Barron wasn't going to let it go.

"Let's say, if we can't stop the person or persons responsible, I'm going to have to make more calls like this."

"Are we talking serial killer?" Mr. Barron barely got the question out.

"No, but he is just as dangerous," Patrick explained. He wondered if the killer had no problem eliminating anyone who was a threat to him or got in his way. "Please let us do our job. If you go on-line, you can read what we have released to the press. The medical examiner believes Dr. Parks was killed elsewhere and his body dumped in the city park."

"He was found on Sunday, and this is all you have?"

Patrick pictured Mr. Barron loosening the perfect knot on his tie. His professional demeanor was gone for the day. "I have one more piece of information which we released to the news service, a sketch of the suspect. I can't tell you how the police obtained this information, but we believe this man either killed Dr. Parks or knows who did. The copy I'll fax you is better than what you can get on-line."

"Detective, may I ask what information AFIS had on him?"

"Sure," replied Patrick. "They showed Dr. Parks was arrested for driving under the influence of narcotics in Lexington, Kentucky. I assume you already know that?"

"Yes. I handled the legal problem for him."

"Mr. Barron, do you know why Dr. Parks was in Chicago? Do you have a current home address or place of employment for him?" Patrick waited for the answers.

"Mr. Barron?" asked Patrick responding to the long silence. "Mr. Barron, are you still there?"

"Yes. I'm still here. I'm having a hard time processing the information. I don't have the answers you want," he said.

Patrick pushed. He didn't think Mr. Barron was playing games. There had been a radical change in the tone of his voice after Patrick broke the news. Right now he sounded human. You could hear the pain in his voice with every word he spoke. "Do you mean you don't know the answers, or you won't tell me?"

"I honestly don't have the answers. If you are calling me from Chicago, then I guess that's where he was working." His sigh was audible.

"Let me see if I have this right. You're his attorney, college roommate, best man at his wedding, and godfather to one of his sons, yet you don't have any current personal information on him?" Patrick exchanged glances with Jack.

"Correct," Mr. Barron answered.

Patrick continued. "Were you aware Dr. Parks only had a license to practice in Kentucky?"

"Yes. He was Board Certified in Anesthesiology. If Steve had applied in another state, they would have run a background check on him. I imagine he would have let me know."

"When you needed to, how did you reach him?" Patrick asked, pulling out his bottom desk drawer which he often used as a foot stool.

"Steve had a long range pager. I know this whole thing sounds bizarre, but it is how he wanted it."

"No cell phone number or e-mail address?" All Patrick could think was this guy had become a recluse, possibly suffering from depression. Not a surprise. Parks had literally thrown away his career and family.

"No. I think he knew I would have had them traced," Barron

replied. "I think he needed space."

"How soon after you would page Dr. Parks did he return your call? And how did he reach you?" Patrick questioned.

"He usually called within a couple of hours. He probably used a pre-paid disposable phone or a phone card. One time the caller ID would read Georgia, the next time it would be Colorado. It was always different."

"What if you wanted to send him mail?" Patrick was not getting a good feeling about Parks' new job.

"Steve would have me send it in care of general delivery. Each time it was a different town, usually in Indiana."

"When was the last time you saw him?" Patrick was starting to believe Parks might have accepted a position at an illegal clinic, like the type Sarah possibly died in.

"About sixteen months ago. He stopped by my office."

Patrick stood up to stretch then sat down. His shoulders ached. "What shape was he in?"

"Surprisingly, he seemed relaxed. After he finished his time in rehab he was devastated by the loss of his position at Lexington Memorial. Sandy, his wife, took their two sons and moved back to her parents' home in Virginia. I thought for sure he was going to have a relapse. I let him stay at a condo I own. He applied everywhere, but the grapevine beat him to every job.

"Then one day, he walked into my office and dropped a ten thousand dollar cashier's check on my desk. He said a job he had heard about while in rehab came through, and this was his sign-on bonus. I asked him the obvious questions, but he just said he wasn't ready to talk about it. He asked to sign the divorce papers Sandy's attorney had sent over. He gave Sandy full custody of the boys. All he asked for in exchange was she send him pictures and an occasional letter on how the boys were doing. And he wanted to give me power of attorney for himself should I ever need it. He said he might be out of the area for a while."

"When was the last time you paged him?"

"Sunday, I had pictures of the boys for him. I tried him several times that day, and every day this week. I was hoping he was just out of range. However, I had a bad feeling about Steve not returning my page. This was the first time he failed to call me."

"Mr. Barron..."

"Please, call me Charlie," he interrupted. "At the moment, I don't feel very much like Mr. Barron, the attorney."

Patrick was starting to like the guy, which was unusual since too many attorneys had screwed up his cases in court. The guy was really upset about losing his friend. Patrick had several more tough questions to ask. "Charlie, I appreciate your help. Are you up to a few more questions?"

"Do you need me to fly up there to identify Steve?"

Patrick could hear the apprehension in his voice. Dr. Parks wasn't in great shape when the jogger found him. There really wasn't any reason for his friend to see him that way. "I don't think that will be necessary. We were able to ID him by his fingerprints. But, if you could put us in contact with Dr. Parks' dentist, it would provide a double check for us."

"No problem. I'll have him call you today. What else can I do for you?"

Now this was a first, thought Patrick, an attorney offering to help a detective. "What did he want done with the check he brought you?"

"He asked me to set up a college fund for his boys," Barron replied.

"How about alimony or child support?"

"He sent a cashier's check the fifteenth of every month to me. Then I wrote a check to Sandy."

Patrick guessed Barron would continue to write her a check every month, or at least for a while. "Would you like me to contact the local police to tell his ex-wife?"

"No, I'll fly out this morning. I should be the one to tell her."

"Does he have any other family?" Patrick figured when someone died, usually it was like a ripple effect. The family tells one person then they discover they have three more to call. With Sarah, there would be only her old friends, maybe a few business acquaintances, and a distant cousin.

"He has a dad and brother over in Louisville. His dad disowned Steve after he lost his position, but his brother keeps in touch with me. I'll let them know. When will the body be released?"

Patrick would have to call Claire, but he didn't think she needed the body anymore. "I'll check with the medical examiner and let you know."

"Is there anything else?" Mr. Barron sounded depleted.

One thought popped into Patrick's mind. "Yes, I have one last question. What did he like to do in his spare time?"

"The sad thing was Steve didn't have any free time until he was in treatment. His dream of becoming a doctor consumed his life. He could barely squeeze out time for Sandy and the boys. But physical activity was encouraged in treatment. He took up running. He used to say pounding the pavement helped to kill his demons. Why do you ask?"

"No special reason except to know Dr. Parks a little bit better. Thank you for your time." Patrick wondered if Mr. Barron was as spent as he was, and it wasn't even lunchtime.

"You'll be in touch with any further developments?"

"Of course. You can count on it, Charlie." Patrick meant what he said. In spite of Dr. Parks' fall from grace, the man had a good friend in Charlie.

Patrick hung up the phone and looked at Jack. "So, what do you make of that?"

"Sounds like the family had no clue what he was up to. Back to the drawing board," Jack sighed.

Chapter 24

Claire stood in the same enclosed visitors' area of the Board of Trade as she had on her junior year business class trip. Not much had changed. She had been careful not to arouse Patrick's suspicions when she tried to find out what Kelly Davis looked like. The yellow jacket with the bright blue breast pocket and the French braid helped Claire spot her.

Claire ran down to the door where Kelly would exit the trading floor. Within minutes Kelly emerged.

"Kelly, Kelly Davis?" Claire called out, but the young woman kept walking at a good pace. Claire pushed through the early rush hour crowd until she was right next to her. "Kelly," she tried again as she gently touched her arm.

Kelly turned, "You must have me confused with someone else." She kept walking towards the 'L' staircase.

Claire stopped in front of her. Kelly jumped like a scared rabbit. Softly Claire said, "No Kelly, I don't. Please listen to me. Sarah and I were best friends growing up."

"Why can't you people leave me alone?" She didn't even try to move. Tears spilled down her cheeks. "I'm sorry. I just can't hold myself together." She blew her nose with a tissue Claire handed her.

"There's a Starbucks a block north of here on LaSalle Street," Claire said. "I haven't had my cappuccino fix for the day. Come on, I'll buy you a cup. You look like you could use one."

Kelly seemed to weigh her decision before she answered. "I don't know you. How do you know me?"

"That's a fair question. My name is Claire O'Shaunessy."

Kelly stepped back. "You're the police."

"No, I'm not. You're thinking of my brother, Patrick. He spoke with you yesterday."

"I don't want to talk to the police." She stepped back even further.

"Please, just hear me out. I'm not on the police force, but Patrick and I grew up with Sarah. Look what her death is doing to you? Can you imagine how Patrick and I feel?" Claire pulled out the guilt card. Being raised Catholic gave her a whole deck.

"I don't know." Her tears stopped, but she kept scanning the people on the street.

Claire used her first name again hoping the familiarity of it would work. "Kelly, it's daylight. We'll be in a public place. How about it? Something hot to drink has to feel good on such a damp day?" She watched Kelly check the street again.

"Okay, but just for a little while."

"I know you have to meet your dad. Patrick told me."

Kelly smiled for the first time. "I have about an hour before he gets off work."

Claire ordered their drinks while she let Kelly select the table where she might feel most comfortable. Claire reached in her pocket just before the drinks came and turned off her cell phone. She didn't want any interruptions, especially from her brother. She set the steaming drink in front of Kelly. "Do you need sugar?"

"No, I like my cappuccino plain, no sugar, no flavoring."

"So do I," Claire replied. "I'm a purist at heart." Claire let Kelly relax and enjoy her cappuccino for a moment.

"Sarah's backyard was right across the alley from my house," Claire began. "Our houses were identical. That's pretty common in the old neighborhoods. By the time we were twelve, we knew how to climb out of our bedroom windows and down the matching trellises. Sarah's mom smoked like a fiend, so Sarah would steal a couple cigs and matches. In the middle of the night, we would sit in her dad's Mustang convertible in their garage and pretend we were so cool. I have four older sisters, so I really needed to practice. My mom died when I was little. My four sisters were like having four mothers. Sarah was more like a sister than my friend. We shared everything; secrets, make-up, and boyfriends."

Claire let Kelly absorb the information while she drank her coffee.

"I had the same kind of friend," Kelly said. "We were inseparable. Her dad's company transferred him our sophomore year of high school. We were devastated. We lost touch a few years later."

"I bet you could find her," Claire suggested. "The internet does amazing things."

Kelly looked up from her coffee. "Maybe I will. This is my

last day at the Board of Trade. A couple other companies offered me positions, but my heart isn't in it anymore."

Claire calculated how much time she had left before they drained their paper cups and Kelly had to meet her dad. If this was Kelly's last day, then this time became even more precious.

"Sarah and I lost touch for a while, too. She went east for undergraduate school and returned to Chicago for her master's in business before joining her dad. Meanwhile, I finished undergraduate school and went on to medical school. By the time I was a resident, I didn't have time for family or friends. Then I went east to work. I just returned a few months ago. That's why I didn't know about Sarah's gambling problem."

"You're a doctor?" asked Kelly.

"Yes, but not the type you think. I'm a forensic pathologist for Cook County." Claire showed Kelly her work ID and gave her a business card before taking another sip of coffee. "Because of my profession, this is even more important for me to find out the whole truth about what happened to Sarah. The deceased only have us to find the truth about their deaths. This is the last thing I can do for Sarah.

"I know you have no reason to trust me. My brother, Patrick, and his partner will find out the truth, only the person responsible could get away in the meantime. I know that's not what you want to happen. I don't have time to tap dance around the issue. I need your help now."

Kelly squirmed in her chair as she emptied her cup. "Well, I don't know what I can do."

"I think you do. Don't you want to know what happened to Sarah?" Claire didn't wait for a response. "Someone punctured her iliac artery during an egg removal procedure, and she hemorrhaged to death."

Kelly glanced up from her coffee. Her eyes were as wide as saucers.

"This shouldn't have happened during a fairly simple procedure," Claire said. "Besides someone being incredibly careless, no one got help for her. I think this procedure took place at an unlicensed facility. No one could call 9-1-1 because they didn't want to risk discovery. Then they dumped her body in a shallow grave. This could happen to someone else."

"I have to go." Kelly's hands were shaking as she put on her jacket.

"Wait," Claire begged. She pulled the wanted flyer out of her pocket, unfolded it and handed it to Kelly. "Is this what's scaring you? He's the one who buried Sarah in that cemetery."

Kelly went white. It didn't take a trained professional to recognize shock. Claire thought she might faint on her, so Claire moved to the chair next to Kelly. "Give yourself a moment to catch your breath."

They were at the last table so Claire didn't think they had attracted anyone's attention.

"If he finds me, he'll kill me," she whispered.

"How do you know him?" Claire asked.

"I can't tell you, but he knows where I live. The police won't be able to protect me."

"If you don't help me, I'll be doing your autopsy next." Claire knew it wasn't fair play. But she had to use every bit of ammunition in her arsenal. "Call your dad at work and tell him friends are taking you out to celebrate your last day on the job. You're spending the night at my place. Give your dad my name and cell phone number. Don't mention my profession. I'll make sure you are safe. The man in the flyer won't find you. Besides my brother and his partner, I have plenty of help. My building comes with a doorman and security cameras."

"How do I know you don't work for him?"

"Call the number on my business card and ask for me."

Kelly's fingers trembled as she dialed Claire's number.

"Office of the Medical Examiner for Cook County. How may I direct your call?" Claire heard the operator on the other end of the line.

Kelly asked for Dr. O'Shaunessy.

"I'm sorry, but she's off today. May I connect you to her voice mail?"

A few seconds later, she was listening to Claire's voice on her prerecorded message. She hung up. "I'll help you however I can."

***

While Kelly called her dad, Claire called Frankie. Twenty minutes later, Frankie picked them up. Even though Claire lived a short distance away, they arrived an hour and a half later at her apartment. Frankie made sure no one no one had tailed them. "Say Gorgeous, my protection is available for as long as you need me."

Claire gave Frankie a quick kiss on his cheek. "Thank you. I think we're okay, but if I have to go out, Kelly might enjoy some company if you can behave yourself. Oh, by the way, here's the photo you asked for." Claire reached in her purse and handed Frankie an envelope.

Frankie ran the envelope under his nose pretending to inhale a special scent. He kissed it before tucking it in his left jacket breast pocket. He placed his hand over his heart. "If you only knew the passion this stirs in my heart."

"Frankie, you're so full of it," Claire laughed. "Kelly, don't pay any attention to him."

"Miss Kelly, it would give me great pleasure to be your knight in shining armor." Frankie made an exaggerated bow, sweeping his arm across to his heart. "I'll be a perfect gentleman."

Turning towards Claire, Frankie cocked his head. "I'll check in with you in a little while. I still have you on speed dial you know."

"Thanks," Claire said.

Frankie walked them inside before he drove off.

Chapter 25

"Come in. It's safe. I promise, Kelly," Claire said as the frightened young woman stood in the hallway clutching her purse.

"How can you be sure?" she asked, her feet practically glued to the hallway carpet.

"Do you promise not to tell? My brother Patrick would have a field day if he knew I did this. Come here."

Kelly approached the door, clutching her purse tight to her chest.

"Take a look at the base of my door. Okay, now look at the bottom of the door jam. The tape was connecting the two until I opened the door."

Kelly bent down and inspected the areas. "There's a thin piece of clear tape on the door jam. What is it for?" she asked.

"Come in and I'll tell you. First, throw your stuff on the bench and make yourself comfortable while I put a frozen pizza in the oven." Claire disappeared around the corner. She could hear Kelly shut the door and flip the deadbolt. "What would you like to drink? I have pop, beer and the usual drink selection." Kelly followed her into the kitchen like a frightened puppy.

"I think I could use a beer."

"How about grabbing both of us one. We'll make ourselves comfortable in the living room while the pizza is cooking. If you need the bathroom, it's just down the hallway on your right."

Claire took the plates out of the cabinet and set them on the counter. With the timer set, she grabbed the beer and headed into the living room. She found Kelly standing at the sliding glass door to her balcony.

"You have a magnificent view of the city. I never thought of living in the south loop area. How did you ever find this place?" Kelly was mesmerized.

Claire dropped into an overstuffed chair near the view. "When I moved back, my oldest sister, Chevoun, got tired of me sleeping on her couch. Her husband owned several condos in this building for investment purposes. Within a week, they moved my sorry ass over here, called a furniture leasing company, and voilà, instant home. The location turned out to be a godsend. I'm not far from Bridgeport where most of my family lives, and work is a short ride away."

"I still live with my parents on the northwest side of the city. Mom teaches at Gray School, which is south of Irving Park and west of the expressway. Dad owns an apartment management business just off Belmont. I wanted to get a place of my own, but he wouldn't hear of it. Now I can't make up my mind if it's safer for me to stay with my parents, or more dangerous for them." Kelly sat down on the couch across from Claire.

The timer went off. "Be back in a minute." Claire retrieved the pizza and plates. "Dig in. It's not fancy, but it will save us a trip out for dinner."

"You were going to tell me about the tape on the door jam," Kelly reminded Claire as she grabbed a piece of pizza.

"Try not to laugh," Claire said in between bites. "Remember I told you how Sarah and I used to climb out the window?"

Kelly nodded her head as she licked the sauce off her fingers.

"Well, my dad was a beat cop, and he rotated to a different shift every month. Therefore, Patrick became the unofficial head of the house. He is eleven years older than I am, and he had five sisters to keep safe and in line. Even though I knew he was more worried about my four older sisters getting in trouble with their boyfriends, I couldn't chance getting caught. On the nights I climbed out the window to meet Sarah, I would run a piece of tape across the base of the door jam. Then I rolled up a blanket and stuck it under the covers to make it look like me. When I came home, I always checked to see if my door had been opened. If the tape was in place, I knew I was safe. If it was off, then I prayed whoever opened my door hadn't discovered the fake body under the covers."

"Did you ever get caught?" Kelly was on the edge of the couch having another piece of pizza.

"No, and I was damn lucky." Claire reached for another piece.

"Why do you do it now? I saw your doorman, and I doubt anyone could get by him," Kelly said.

"Old habits die hard, as they say. Besides, if maintenance has to do a repair, I can tell if they really showed up."

"Aren't you afraid someone will see you place the tape?"

"No. I either drop my keys or act like I'm picking up something if anyone walks by. Actually, I don't think I have seen anyone but the retired couple down the hall since I've moved in. Their beagle has taken a shining to me. Milo practically licks my face off." She hoped she had Kelly feeling comfortable enough to get her to talk. Claire leaned forward and placed her plate on the coffee table.

"To keep you safe, I have to know the truth. I know you recognized the man in the flyer. And I am pretty sure you know more about where Sarah was and why." Claire prayed she had not scared Kelly off more. "What happened to Sarah could be happening to someone else right now. I know you don't want anyone else to die."

Kelly finished her beer. "No, you're right. I don't want anyone else to get hurt. But if he finds me, I'm dead. He can't risk having me talk."

"This alone is a good reason to help us find him." Claire watched Kelly wrap her arms around herself. She got up and draped the afghan across Kelly's shoulders then sat down beside her. "Why don't you start with how you met him?"

"It's complicated. You'll never understand. You'll think I'm some terrible person for what I did." Worry was taking its toll on Kelly. Claire noticed dark circles emerging under her eyes.

Claire took the last sip of her beer and put the bottle on the table. "In my profession, I see the results of every despicable human behavior. Nothing could shock me or surprise me. I don't think you are capable of such behavior."

"You'll hate me. I hate me. It's my fault Sarah's dead." The tears were back, and Kelly was sobbing.

Claire handed her tissues. "Why don't you let me be the judge? First of all, you are not the one who caused her death. Some idiot did this all by himself." Claire let her regroup for a moment. "Are you ready?"

Kelly took her shoes off and tucked her feet under herself. She pulled the afghan tighter. "A couple of years ago, several of my college friends and I took one of those weekend trips to Vegas. We thought we were so grown up. We agreed if we met someone interesting we could go off with the guy as long as we stayed on the strip, didn't get in any cars, and didn't go to his room or invite him back to ours."

"Those sound like sensible ground rules. What went wrong?" Claire asked.

"This drop dead hunk kept asking me to dance at one of the clubs. After a few dances, he invited me to his booth and ordered champagne. It must have been expensive because I never tasted anything so incredible. We drank champagne and danced. All I remember was the music was beyond loud and the place was dark, except for all the flashing colored lights." Kelly got up and walked to the sliding glass doors. She stared out into the night.

"Were your friends at the club?" Claire inquired.

Kelly watched the Chicago skyline lights play in the dark night. "They were all there having a great time. After a couple of return trips to the dance floor, he suggested we sit out a few numbers. I was feeling all warm inside from the champagne. The next thing I knew he was kissing me on my neck. Then he lowered the strap on my dress with one hand as his other moved up my thigh. I wasn't resisting when he kissed my breast. I told myself I should stop, but my body wanted more." Kelly covered her face with her hands. "I'm so ashamed."

"Why? You and your friends were having a rite of passage. We're entitled to one wild weekend during our youth." Claire could only imagine where Kelly's confession was taking her, but she knew she couldn't rush her to get the answers Patrick and Jack needed so desperately.

She smiled at Claire's support. "I never felt so desired. Before I realized it, he had my panties off. Somehow, he had his pants down, and then he lifted me on his lap. Well you know how it ended."

"I know a lot of women who would love the experience," said Claire.

"I don't think they would have been as stupid as me. He didn't use any protection and I ended up with a severe infection."

"I doubt if it was on your mind. It probably wouldn't have been on mine." Claire thought of several truly stupid things she had done when she was younger.

"I called one of the friends from the Vegas trip for help. She had had a similar experience a few months before. I was on my parents' insurance, so I didn't dare use it for fear they would find out. Also, I wasn't making very much money as a part-time waitress."

"What did your friend suggest?" Claire asked.

"She said she knew of a doctor who would see me for free, but the patient had to agree to donate eggs at his clinic as payment. She said it was no big thing. She had done it several times to pay her bill.

"I was so frantic, I agreed. She took me to the doctor's office. He ran blood work and gave me several prescriptions." Kelly left the window and claimed the overstuffed chair.

Claire steadied her voice, "Do you remember his name, or anything about him?"

"Once I tell you his name, what will you do?" Kelly questioned.

"I don't know." It was the truth, to some extent, Claire thought. "Can you leave out his name for now, and we'll talk about it later?"

Kelly ran her hands through her hair. "I suppose it would work. This doctor owned a private clinic on an estate in LaSalle County where the patients went to donate their eggs."

Claire fought every fiber in her body not to demand Kelly to tell her everything right now, and then call Patrick. "LaSalle County is sort of far out. Did your friend drive you?" Please say yes, she silently begged Kelly.

"No."

"No? How did you get there?" Public transportation didn't seem an option, Claire thought.

"I was picked up in an SUV at Union Station."

"Do you remember what type of car picked you up?" Go slow, Claire counseled herself.

Kelly sighed. "Only that it was a big black SUV."

Claire pushed on. "What about the route you took?"

"It was at night. I recall seeing the Interstate 80 sign before I fell asleep."

Claire tried to remain as casual as possible. "I would be too nervous to fall asleep."

"Me, too, except my friend told me I would be given a Valium to take when I was picked up. Then I would be ready for the procedure when I arrived at the clinic."

Right, thought Claire, they were covering their tracks. Going in the dark of night was a nice touch, and now for the punch line. "Do you remember what the driver looked like?"

"I need to use the bathroom." Kelly ran down the hallway.

Claire went after her the minute she heard Kelly throw up. It wasn't the beer and frozen pizza upsetting her stomach. The sketch of the man on her coffee table had her scared. She was sure of it.

Chapter 26

Claire found Kelly slumped on the bathroom floor as white as a ghost, sobbing between retches. Claire ran cold water over a washcloth and wiped Kelly's face. "You don't have to tell me; I know who the driver was. It's the guy in the sketch, right?"

She looked up. "Yes." The word was barely audible. "If he finds me, he'll kill me. I know too much."

"I'm not going to let that happen." Claire rinsed the cloth with more cold water then bent down to Kelly's level.

"How can you stop him?" Kelly took the cloth and wiped her face again.

"First of all, he doesn't know where you are. And second of all, we have Patrick and Jack to help us, not to mention Frankie." Claire helped Kelly up and sat her on a stool.

"Please, no police," Kelly begged.

"We'll talk about it later. For now, you get in the shower and I'll bring you a set of clean sweats to wear and an extra toothbrush. How does that sound?"

"Okay, I guess."

***

Claire rinsed their dinner plates and waited for the water to boil. She had set out cups and saucers, along with peppermint tea. Claire liked the refreshing flavor. Her sisters had sworn by it to ward of morning sickness. She put out a plate of saltines and shortbread cookies, too.

After the water boiled, she filled her mother's china teapot with the tea leaves, the hot water and covered it with a tea cozy. As much as she enjoyed a steaming cup of cappuccino, there was nothing quite as comforting as a cup of tea brewed in her mom's teapot.

Kelly appeared dressed in the sweats with a towel wrapped around her hair. Her face was rosy from the hot shower, but it wouldn't be long before the color faded. Then her pale skin would make her look like a walking ghost.

"Let's sit here in the kitchen where it's warmer."

Kelly took a seat without saying a word.

"I made peppermint tea. It should help to calm your stomach. I didn't know if you were up to shortbread, but there're saltine crackers."

"Thanks," was all Kelly could get out.

"We both know who the driver was, but who were the other people at the clinic?"

Claire continued to push as she served the tea.

"I barely remember their faces. There was a doctor at the end of the table behind my head. The first time I went, I remember seeing a female nurse, but I never saw her again. After that, the driver assisted the doctor. They never addressed each other, so I don't know their names."

"But you knew the name of the doctor your friend took you to, didn't you?" Claire feared this was a fly by night abortion clinic, but Kelly only mentioned donating eggs.

"Yes. I only saw him once in his Michigan Avenue office. He was never at the clinic. He explained his partners cared for the patients at the clinic. After the office visit, I only had contact with the doctor through the driver." Kelly nibbled on a saltine.

Claire poured them more tea. Since Kelly seemed comfortable talking, she wanted to keep her going. "Did you ever try to contact the doctor again?"

Kelly quickly looked away. She put the teacup down, pulled her knees up and wrapped her arms around them.

Once again, Claire had to push her. "I'm guessing you donated eggs to pay your bill. How many times did you have to donate to clear the bill?"

"I hated having to give myself the hormone injections." Kelly rocked back and forth, hugging her legs. She was lost in her pain. "I used to do it in the bathroom at work. Can you imagine? I had to do it in a bathroom stall because I couldn't risk my parents finding out how deep I was in!"

The tears streamed down her face, her voice trembled with anger, and her body shook. "If I was married and having infertility problems, my husband could have helped me. We could have done it in the privacy of our bedroom, not a public bathroom."

Kelly was falling apart right in front of Claire. They had scratched only the surface of the operation. Claire needed the name of the doctor at the very least. She asked again, "Why didn't you go to the doctor's office if you wanted to talk with him? Why did you have to go through the driver?"

"I was told I couldn't see him at the office."

"You mean he didn't want you seen at his office. Were you threatened?"

"Yes."

"What was the threat?" Claire knew it wouldn't take much to scare Kelly. So whatever she was told she believed to the core.

"The next time I was picked up, there was an envelope addressed to me on the car seat. Inside was a recent picture of my parents out to dinner. A large 'X' was across their bodies. I got the message." Kelly grabbed a tissue and blew her nose. "I never meant to put them in danger."

"Why did you want to see the doctor?"

"I was desperate. I wanted out; only I couldn't risk harming my parents." Kelly's eyes were red and swollen.

"How long had this been going on?"

"Two years."

Claire couldn't believe it. "How many times did you donate a year?"

"At least six or seven."

Claire was frightened what Kelly's answer would be to her next question. She could see Kelly was physically and mentally drained. "Did they ever offer you a way out?"

Kelly sat up and put her feet on the floor. "Yes, if I wanted out, I had to find a replacement."

Blackmail! That was how they kept the operation going. "So, if I have this right, the friend you went to Vegas with got out because she gave them you, and you gave them Sarah."

"It's my fault Sarah's dead."

"It wasn't your fault. You had no idea a doctor was going to pierce the iliac artery. He killed Sarah, not you. Why did she go to the doctor in the first place?"

"She thought she got pregnant on a trip to Vegas a few months ago. I found her throwing up at work. The doctor told her she had a tubular pregnancy and it had to be removed at once or she would die because her fallopian tube would rupture as the pregnancy grew. She had huge credit card debts and didn't know how she would pay for the emergency surgery. She was always a little cavalier when it came to sex, so I didn't think it would upset her to donate eggs for payment, as it did me."

Claire was taken back for a moment. Dr. Sage had emailed her a copy of Sarah's autopsy report this morning and there wasn't any mention of a recent tubular pregnancy. Could Sarah have had food poisoning or the flu and thought she was pregnant? Did the doctor lie about her pregnancy just to get her on board for donations? If Sarah took a home pregnancy test, she may not have been aware that there is a slight chance you could test false positive or negative.

Claire reached for a pen and paper. "I need to go over some of this to make sure I have it straight. Can you hang in there a little bit longer…for Sarah?" This was not the time to tell Kelly that Sarah may have been lied to. She needed information that only Kelly had to prevent anyone else from suffering Sarah's fate. The thought that possibly Sarah was lied to and then died as a result of that lie made Claire sick to her stomach, but she didn't have that luxury right now.

"I owe Sarah that much." Kelly sat up straight and put her shoulders back.

"Good." Claire took in a deep breath pushing what she just learned to the back of her mind. "Okay, here we go." She wanted Kelly to feel they had formed a team and she wasn't alone any longer. "You acquire a bad gynecological infection. A friend, who had the same experience before offers to take you to a doctor to help you in exchange for an unknown number of egg donations. You never ask the obvious question, like how many donations you will have to make, because you're understandably upset. After a while you feel used. You want to know what's left on your tab. They tell you it is never ending unless you find a replacement. You feel used twice because of the person who got you involved. But now you are in her shoes with no other options. Does this sum it up?"

"Yes." Kelly's voice sounded stronger.

"Did you ever see any other girls there when you were at the clinic." Claire had heard Patrick talk about how sometimes when they were interrogating a suspect; they would hit them hard, and hit them fast.

"No. I think I was the only one scheduled when I went, but I remember the driver making a comment to the doctor how last night's donor had given him trouble."

"Did you ever hear the name of the driver?" Claire fired the question fast.

"Once. He thought I was asleep when he answered his cell phone. He said, "Edwards.""

"What was the name of the doctor you saw on Michigan Avenue?"

"Dr. Rothschild. Oh my God," Kelly cried. "Now you know his name!"

Claire took Kelly's hands. "Look at me. We have to stop this operation. We don't want any more 'Sarah's'. We don't want one more person to go through what you went though. Are you with me?"

"Yes, but I'm still afraid he'll kill me."

"I know. Frankie and I will protect you, Kelly."

Chapter 27

"Miller, here's the tire report from Sheriff Wilson." Captain Ramos handed Jack a fax. "We could be looking at a stolen vehicle. Keep me posted," Ramos said as he left the office.

"Thanks, Captain." Jack scanned the sheet of paper.

"Well, partner, are you in a sharing mood?" Patrick threw a wadded piece of paper at Jack.

"Hang on, Patrick." Jack threw the paper ball back. "The tire marks from the cemetery are a high end brand, usually found on expensive SUVs, such as a BMW X5 or a Lincoln Navigator. Both back ends could easily carry a body or two." He passed the report over to his partner.

"Not bad," Patrick remarked, as he looked over the report. "Now all we need is a miracle and we'll have the owner. Did we hear back from the rehab facility in North Carolina yet?"

"The answer is yes, but as I expected they quoted policy. We can cross them off our list of hopefuls. Do you think I would have any luck getting Finch to run his magic fingers over his keyboard to check for stolen vehicles if I asked nicely?"

"Did I hear my name called?" Finch entered the homicide room. "Was someone looking for a favor?"

Jack knew Finch had him cold. "What brings you down to our humble home?"

"I just finished running a background check on a Dr. Arthur Rothschild. I found more twists and turns than the folklore surrounding Chicago's most famous ghost, Resurrection Mary." Finch held papers behind his back. "Let's see what these are worth to you, Patrick. How about tickets for opening day for the White Sox next spring?"

Patrick stretched. "You would have to have the six winning lottery numbers for me to part with those tickets."

Jack knew everyone around the station was aware Patrick's prize possession was his season tickets to the White Sox home games. He often shared them with family and friends. "What do you have, Finch? What makes you think Patrick would part with those tickets?" Jack asked.

Finch dragged his answer out. "Would identity theft count?"

"Whose identity was stolen?" Jack asked. Finch was right; this case had more angles than sightings of Resurrection Mary. Mary's ghost had appeared along Archer Avenue by the Resurrection Cemetery and the old Willow-Brook Ballroom since the 1930's. She always appeared in a white dress along the road or in the ballroom. She would accept rides only to vanish by the cemetery. Men who danced with her remembered how cool her touch was, but the smile on Finch's face told Jack his news was hot.

"I'm still waiting for Patrick's answer. So, what do you say to my offer?" Finch just stood there grinning.

Patrick burrowed his eyebrows. "You would have to tell me you have Dr. Parks' and Sarah's killer locked up in a holding cell for an opening day ticket. But, if you truly have something to barter with, I could come up with tickets for another game."

"Make it a pair for a Yankee game, and it's a deal. My dad would really appreciate it."

"Patrick," Jack jumped in, "he *has* to give us the information. It's his job. You don't have to part with the tickets." Finch could really be a weasel sometimes. Because he was a computer wizard, he had no trouble collecting IOU's from grateful detectives. Jack hated the power Finch held over him.

"Jack, you're right. I could dole the information out to you and Patrick in fragments over the next few hours. I would hate to make you two sweat." Finch must have something big, or he wouldn't be working Patrick over so hard. Jack was ready to tackle the man. Whose alias did Finch come across?

"It's your call. I'll take him down while you go for the papers," Jack suggested, sizing up the computer geek.

"Okay," Patrick said. "The tickets are yours, but this better be worth it, or we'll never deal again. Understood?"

Finch pulled out a chair and straddled it backwards. "Hold on to your seats. This will totally blow you away. I started with the American Fertility Association. I was surprised they had Dr. Arthur Maynard Rothschild's date of birth. So I searched one of my sites for his birth certificate. I found two Arthur Maynard Rothschilds, one for his date of birth and another for six months earlier. I printed up the information for our Rothschild. Then I got to thinking how it was odd for two people to have this particular name, especially with dates of birth so close together. I printed up the other one. To my amazement, I discovered they had the same parents."

"You've got to be kidding me?" Patrick reached over and started thumbing through the papers Finch left on his desk.

"Both mothers had the same birthday, along with the same maiden name. Your Rothschild was a term pregnancy. So I asked myself, how did Meredith Wellington Rothschild deliver a full term child in Savannah six months after her prior delivery in Long Island?"

"It can't be! There must be a mistake somewhere," Jack said.

"It gets better," Finch said. "I dug a little deeper. I researched Meredith and found she had two death certificates. Also, I located a death certificate for the first Arthur Rothschild baby. He died several hours after birth. His mother died in childbirth. She is buried next to the first Arthur Rothschild baby in Long Island. The second Meredith Rothschild died a few years ago in Savannah, Georgia. Both babies had the same father."

There had to be a catch. Between conception and birth, a term pregnancy took nine months. Jack asked, "What do we know about the father?"

Finch continued. "I went on the internet and discovered not only was the father an Ambassador to England prior to his death, but he was a billionaire and a well-known industrialist. After contacting several of his companies, I acquired the name of the law firm which handled his will. Spoke with an older gentleman who had been with the law firm since he finished law school. He hadn't handled the Ambassador's affairs during the early years, but currently he is in charge of the trust."

"This sounds like a soap opera," Jack said. "So, is our Arthur Rothschild really who he says he is, or does he have another name. And who is the second Meredith Rothschild?"

"Mr. Goodwin was definitely surprised to hear about the second Meredith Rothschild and her death. He believes she was Alice Monroe, a maid at the Rothschild estate when Meredith was pregnant. Arthur Sr. was a notorious ladies man. After his wife, Meredith, died, Alice told him she was three months pregnant, expecting to slip into the role of Mrs. Arthur Rothschild. But she didn't know Arthur very well. He believed God was punishing him for his infidelities. Arthur never looked at another woman after his wife's death. He gave Alice a check, told her to terminate the pregnancy and be gone by morning. Several months later, she called Arthur. It seems Alice was too far along to terminate the pregnancy, and she wanted to make a deal."

Patrick stopped taking notes for a moment. "I bet Arthur Sr. wasn't too thrilled with Alice. She's lucky he didn't hire a hit man."

"Keeping this private had to be foremost on his mind if he was an ambassador." Jack couldn't believe the information Finch had dug up. He really did deserve the opening day tickets. "What else did he have on this Alice Monroe?"

"Mr. Goodwin said the Rothschild estate is still sending Alice a check every month, and someone is cashing them," Finch stated. "I gave Goodwin all the information. He will have the law firm's investigator look into the matter immediately and see if fraud charges can be brought against whoever cashed the checks."

"If our Dr. Rothschild is involved in Sarah's and Dr. Parks' murders, I would hate to see him get arrested for fraud and skip out on the murders. Jack, it's time we made an unannounced visit to upper Michigan Avenue," Patrick said. "Finch, the tickets are yours. Thanks for your help."

Patrick shook his head. "It's amazing where one dead body behind some unwanted buckthorn can lead you. This certainly is some can of worms."

Chapter 28

"Good morning, Gorgeous," Frankie announced as Claire opened the door. He juggled two large shopping bags. "I assume your cupboards are empty as usual."

"You know me, I'm not a cook," Claire responded as she took one of the bags from Frankie. "How much do I owe you?"

"The pleasure of your smile is payment enough for me." Frankie blew Claire a kiss.

"Frankie, you haven't changed one bit. Kelly, whatever you do, don't encourage him." She glanced at Kelly as Claire began her morning ritual of searching for her keys.

"You lose something?" Frankie held Claire's key ring on his finger.

Claire grabbed them. Some people never grow up, and right now, she was glad Frankie hadn't lost his spunk. "I'm leaving you in good hands. Besides being safe, Frankie will put ten pounds on you with his cooking." Claire watched Kelly's eyes dart around the room, still uncertain of her safety.

"What, you're not staying for one of Frankie's special breakfasts?" Frankie put his hand over his heart and looked toward the heavens.

"Remember, I have to go to work, just in case my smile won't pay for groceries."

"Is he always like this?" Kelly had barely said a word since she got up.

"Miss Kelly, what you see is what you get, *kapish*?" Frankie strutted around Claire's bare kitchen. It was obvious he was in search of something.

"If you're looking for the frying pan, it's in the lower cabinet next to the fridge," Claire offered.

"What, no omelet pan? How do you expect me to make Kelly one of my famous Italian omelets?" Frankie placed thick slices of bacon in the pan.

"I imagine you'll think of something, Frankie. I've got to go. The thought of bacon is already killing me. Kelly, you have my work and cell phone numbers. If I don't answer right away, I'm probably in the autopsy room. Don't call anyone except your folks. And, remember, you are having a great time and make them believe it."

"What if Edwards tries to contact them? He could hurt them." Kelly squeezed her clasped fingers tighter together.

"His picture has been on the news. The last thing he is going to do is show his face. I have to go. I'm already late. We'll figure out the next step when I come home. The only thing you have to worry about is Frankie's charm." Claire shifted her eyes to Frankie. "Take good care of her. I'll call you later. And, thanks." Claire favored him with one of her smiles.

Frankie walked her to the door. "You be careful out there." He handed her a folded envelope.

Claire took the envelope and stuffed it in her purse. "How many do you have outside?" She whispered under the cover of a light kiss on his cheek. She knew Frankie wouldn't be here alone.

"Plenty. Frankie's got your sweet ass covered and Kelly's, too." He gave Claire a pat on her butt as she left.

***

"You can take me this afternoon at four? That would be wonderful. Yes, my name is Claire O'Reilly." Claire gave Dr. Rothschild's receptionist the fake name and the address for an empty condo Chevoun's husband owned. She had her name blocked on her cell phone so they couldn't trace her. Her pulse raced a little bit knowing she would be one-step closer to finding Sarah's killer.

Sarah had lost her life through someone's carelessness. More young women would die, if they hadn't already, at the hands of this monster. Claire was sad her old childhood friend had made horrible choices, but Sarah didn't deserve to die because of them.

She could drive herself crazy with all the whys, like why hadn't she kept in closer contact with Sarah in recent years. But as a doctor, Claire knew the path of most addictions only went one way. She still had time to back out from her appointment with Dr. Rothschild, but she wouldn't be her father's daughter if she did. He never took the easy way out, and Claire wasn't about to either.

Since the day her father, Shawn O'Shaunessy, died she had measured everything she did by his standards. Her father was a good, kind man. As a patrolman for the Eighteenth District during the days of the homeless men sleeping in doorways on LaSalle

Street, he often passed out day old donuts from the local bakeries and fruit from the wholesale district. Now there were high-rise buildings fighting for the skyline along LaSalle Street.

Her dad made sure the sick ones got a ride up to Henrotin Hospital, which was on Oak Street, between Clark and LaSalle. The land where the hospital once stood was home to expensive townhouses today. Claire's father never judged the less fortunate.

He was the best father a girl could have. He had raised his six children after his wife died of pneumonia when Claire was little. Yes, her grandparents and other relatives helped, but it was her father sitting in the stands rooting for Claire at her hockey games along with her brother. And her dad never turned on a friend.

Once he heard a fellow cop was shaking down a couple liquor stores. He went to the cop and asked him why he was taking such risks. The cop was trying to support both his family and his sister's. Shawn went to each store and found out how much the cop owed them. He guaranteed repayment for the cop and helped the guy get assistance for his sister's family. Later the cop went back and paid the storeowners back. Claire's father never turned the cop in to his district commander.

Claire turned her attention to the caseload in front of her. She opened the top file and began reading the lab, radiology, and the autopsy reports on an elderly female. The woman had been found by her son in her backyard. She had died from the head trauma she sustained after passing out from a low blood glucose level. Since the woman had not seen a doctor in over ten years, the medical examiner's office was required to rule on the cause of death. Claire signed off on the death certificate and moved on to the next file when she heard Patrick's voice.

"Hi Sis," Patrick called as he and Jack entered her office.

"What brings you over to my neck of the woods?" Claire set the unopened file down.

"I came with a peace offering." Jack produced Claire's favorite cappuccino from behind his back.

Claire reached for the welcomed hot drink, but Jack pulled it back.

"Not so fast," Jack said. "I need to know if my apology for my abrupt tone of voice the other day is accepted."

Claire could almost taste the rich flavor of the cappuccino. She hadn't taken time to stop for a cup on her way to work. She rationalized accepting one cup of coffee did not mean she would let men dictate her life. "It never hurts to be polite," her sister Chevoun would say. Claire was usually short in the manners department.

"I wouldn't want to hurt your feelings, Detective Miller, since you went to all this trouble just for me. Apology accepted. I may have reacted a little too hastily myself." Claire waited patiently for the cup to pass into her hands.

"The name's Jack, not Detective Miller," he said, "and this is partially for Patrick's welfare." Jack handed over the coffee.

Claire noticed a small smile on the edge of Jack's mouth. "Thank you, Jack." She savored the cappuccino as she rolled it over her tongue.

"Are you two done with this duet?" Patrick pulled over the other office chair while Jack leaned against the side of her colleague's desk. "Claire, I promised to keep you in the loop, so here goes."

Patrick summarized his phone conversation with Mr. Barron, Dr. Park's friend and attorney, from Parks' fall from grace to the last time Mr. Barron tried to reach him. "And get this," Patrick went on, "Parks took up running while in rehab. Mr. Barron is having Parks' dentist forward dental records to you."

Jack picked up where Patrick left off. "I called the rehab center to find out who Parks hung out with. The director said Parks kept to himself, but I have a feeling this is where he picked up the link for his current position. I don't think the medical director will give up the name."

"This morning Jack and I swung by the Board of Trade to have another chat with Kelly. Imagine our surprise to find out she quit. I talked with her mother and guess where she's staying? Is there anything you would like to share with us?" Patrick sat perfectly still with his fingers interlocked across his round abdomen.

Claire held on to the cappuccino like it was the last one she would ever have until she was released from jail. "Well, I've been meaning to call you, but I was busy."

"Define, 'busy'," her brother commanded, not moving an inch.

Claire caught Jack's face out of the corner of her eye. He was relaxed and smiling. Damn, he knew Patrick was going to skin her alive. He didn't have to enjoy it so much, she thought. "I can explain."

"Please do," said Patrick.

"I remembered you told me Kelly appeared scared during your interview. I couldn't help but think perhaps if Kelly had a woman to talk with, she might open up. I stopped by the Board of Trade when she got off work and offered to buy her a cup of coffee."

Jack laughed. "We bought her a cup of hot cocoa the day before. Kelly's doing all right for herself."

Claire glanced Jack's way. "No, she's not. She's scared to death Edwards will find her and kill her." Claire hadn't meant to snap at Jack. She was just feeling very protective of Kelly.

"Who's Edwards?" Patrick and Jack asked at the same time.

"Let me start over." The relaxed atmosphere was charged. Claire could feel her muscles tighten. She was going to have to spell out the information she'd obtained without her brother and his side kick going ape on her.

"At first, I couldn't get Kelly to talk much, but I noticed on our walk over to the coffee shop, she kept looking around as if someone was following her. When she told me it was her last day and she had to catch the 'L' to meet her dad, I knew the window of opportunity was about to slam shut. I know this was a cheap shot, but I pulled out the sketch we have from Zenna. When she saw it, Kelly turned white. I knew I had hit a nerve. She needed protection."

"You risked her safety by taking her over to your place?"

"Not exactly, Patrick," Claire said.

"What do you mean, 'not exactly'? From where I'm sitting, this guy could have grabbed both of you at any time!" Patrick's face flushed.

Claire cringed. Patrick sounded just like he had when their sister Colleen would come home late from a date, especially the time her summer shorts where inside out. Claire took in a deep breath and just went for it. "Frankie would never let that happen."

"*Frankie! Frankie Biaggi?* You've got to be kidding me! Jack, she's killing me!" Patrick yelled. He jumped out of his chair and slammed the palm of his hand against the door jam.

"Who's this Frankie Biaggi?" Jack asked.

"Patrick, now calm down," said Claire. "You're going to

stroke out. Think about your blood pressure. Now you see why I didn't call you."

Patrick sat back down.

"Wait a minute, is this the same guy who stuffed Claire into the gym locker?" Jack questioned as he rubbed his forehead.

Patrick ignored his partner. "How did you find Frankie so fast?"

"You told your partner about the gym incident? I was a kid. Isn't anything sacred anymore?" Claire wanted to box Patrick's ears, remembering her embarrassment.

"How did you find Frankie so fast?" Patrick repeated his question resting his elbows on his knees.

"I have him on speed dial." The worst was out Claire thought. If she could get Patrick past Frankie, all would be okay. "We've talked since I got back in town." This was almost accurate, she thought.

"Why do I get the feeling Frankie is Italian and from the old neighborhood." Jack just widened his stance and stared at Claire with his hands on his hips, his unbuttoned jacket pushed back.

"You're right. Frankie is one of the good guys from the old neighborhood," said Claire. "I trust him with my life; that's why I called him. I knew he could get Kelly and me back to my place unnoticed. You and Patrick couldn't have done that. Half of Chicago can recognize unmarked police cars. And with you two, there would be a scene. You might as well have called out the Channel Five news team and sent up flares."

"She's right, Jack. Only Frankie could pull it off, especially if someone was following Kelly."

"But Claire, you only had one guy watching Kelly. We could have set up surveillance, provided back up." Jack raised his hands in disbelief.

"I hate to say it, but Frankie has more manpower than we do for protection, Jack. Actually, Claire picked the perfect person. Frankie can cook, so I know Kelly will eat well. Claire can't even boil water without causing a three-alarm fire."

Claire laughed. "Thanks Patrick." She felt relieved the air was cleared between her and her brother, even though Jack still looked skeptical. "Okay, you two," Claire continued, "this is the part you would never guess, so take notes."

Patrick took out his note pad while Jack leaned back against the desk with his arms folded.

"A couple of years ago, Kelly acquired a gynecological infection after a fling. At the time, she was broke and covered by her parents' insurance. A friend who had had the same problem offered Kelly an out. She knew a doctor who would treat her for no money, but he asked his clients to donate eggs for infertile couples. Kelly bought into the plan because of her finances, and she didn't want her parents to know. The part her friend failed to tell her was her tab for his help was never-ending. When Kelly asked how many more times she had to donate before her bill was considered paid, she was told the only way out was to find a replacement."

"Who was this doctor, and who is this Edwards you mentioned?" asked Jack.

"I'm getting to that part, Jack. Kelly worked with Sarah. Sarah thought she was pregnant, but there is a chance she was lied to, just so the bad guys could harvest her eggs. Sarah was broke, badly in debt and Kelly wanted out. Kelly set up an appointment with Dr. Rothschild for Sarah."

"Shit, this case just took on a whole new dimension," exclaimed Patrick. "This *has* to be the same Dr. Rothschild's office that sent Sarah the yearly appointment reminder."

Jack let out a low whistle. "This is a far cry from one dead body behind some buckthorn in Jackson Park. Claire, what about this Edwards character?"

"Hang on, and I'll answer your questions. Kelly said the way the operation works is the girls are picked up at the Union Train Station downtown. This always happens at night. The donor gets in the vehicle and immediately takes a Valium, supposedly so she will be relaxed for the procedure when she arrives at the clinic. The best Kelly could remember was the trip took at least ninety minutes to get to the clinic. She remembers seeing the sign for Interstate 80. Also, wherever this clinic is, it is dark. No lights.

"Because of the medication, she only has scant memories and often does not remember getting in or out of the vehicle, but once the driver answered his cell phone by saying, 'Edwards'. Kelly identified Edwards as the man in the sketch. She only saw Dr. Rothschild for the initial visit. When she requested to speak to him personally regarding her bill, she received a photo of her parents with an 'X' across their faces. She never saw any other patients at the clinic either."

"This doesn't make sense," Patrick stated. "Why this clandestine approach to infertility? There are clinics and specialists all over the Chicago land area. What's in it for him?"

"Money," replied Jack. "I'm willing to bet he's selling the eggs. It would be clear profit. And, if Kelly said the area was dark and she saw an Interstate 80 sign, then that accounts for Sarah's burial in LaSalle County. But why he finds it necessary to do it out there is beyond me. I think it's time we gave Sheriff Wilson an update."

Patrick and Jack got up to leave as Ian charged in from around the corner. "Dr. O'Shaunessy...I'm sorry I didn't know you had visitors. We're ready for you."

"No problem Ian, I'll be right there. Well guys, duty calls."

"Not so fast." Patrick blocked the doorway. "I'm going to pretend I didn't hear Kelly is your house guest only because of Frankie. But if you do anything stupid, remember Sylvia and your nieces won't be too happy about sharing your apartment with you if I lose my job. I promised I would keep you in the loop with the information, but you have to do the same. I might add, in a more timely manner. Do we understand each other?"

"Not a problem," she said. "Now I have to go cut up dead people, as Frankie would say, okay?"

"Did he really say that?" her brother asked.

"Yup, he sure did."

"Oh Claire, you make it sound like you enjoy it, how disgusting. Come on, Jack, let's see if Finch dug up anything on Sarah's credit card information. Claire, I'll check in with you later."

"Okay," Claire replied. "Now get going, I have work to do. And Jack, thank you for the cappuccino."

"My pleasure," he nodded.

As they left, Claire could hear Jack ask Patrick if she and Frankie were an item. Patrick insisted no, they were not. If only they knew who she had lost her virginity to in college after Frankie and Sarah broke up.

Chapter 29

Jack wasn't sure he agreed with Patrick. This Frankie character may be from the old neighborhood, but he was hardly a trained professional. He was probably a thug, not a skilled officer. Another thing Jack wrestled with was Claire's relationship with Frankie. He didn't like Claire depending on him. If she needed support, he and Patrick could take care of her.

He was half way up the stairs to see Finch when he realized he was having this one-man argument with himself. Patrick was right. Claire definitely was a handful.

"Well, if it isn't Detective Miller invading my domain," Finch said without taking his eyes off the computer screen. "I imagine you are looking for the credit report on Sarah. Hate to tell you, but you are going to be disappointed with what I found."

"What do you mean?" Jack stood next to Finch's computer. This day had too many roadblocks and it wasn't even lunchtime. "Okay, give it to me straight."

"Her credit rating was low, which wasn't too surprising after what we learned about Sarah's financial problems. But here's the kicker, she doesn't owe anyone a dime. Go figure. Personally, I don't think this adds up."

"You're right, something doesn't add up. Why would Kelly tell us Sarah's gambling had pushed her into abusing credit cards and causing major debt? Because if Sarah wasn't in debt, why didn't she just pay for treatment instead of agreeing to multiple egg donations?"

"I can't answer that question for you, but I can tell you which credit cards she was behind on before she caught up." Finch hit a few keys and his printer spit out a list. "There you are."

Jack took the list from him. "Finch you truly are the wizard! I'll call them as soon as Patrick and I get back from seeing Dr. Rothschild. Thanks a lot."

"Don't mention it. If you happen to pass the Golden Arches, I would like a number three on the menu with a large Coke."

"A number three with a large Coke, not a problem," Jack answered. Kelly had managed to score a hot cocoa and a

Starbucks cappuccino. Finch would get his Sox tickets plus a number three special from McDonalds. This case was getting expensive. Jack wondered if these were considered tax-deductible business expenses.

Jack met Patrick downstairs and relayed Finch's findings. They decided Dr. Rothschild's visit was long overdue. Jack would call Sheriff Wilson after the visit, hopefully with more information.

***

"Nice digs," Jack commented as he and Patrick entered the elevator for the twentieth floor. "I can imagine what the office will look like."

"I don't think these are called offices on North Michigan Avenue. I believe the word is 'suite'." Patrick straightened his tie in the mirrored elevator.

When the elevator door opened, Jack stepped out into a hallway glistening with glass, marble and rich mahogany wood. "I think the 'suite' is down this corridor," he directed Patrick.

"Trust me, if it's a suite, then there will be a lake view," Patrick said. "Nothing, but the best for our Premier OB, GYN and Infertility Specialists." Patrick rolled his eyes as he elbowed Jack.

Jack caught his drift. He let out a low whistle as they approached the expansive glass doors. "Our front desk doesn't look like this." He took in the expensive furnishings and the slender blonde receptionist manicured to perfection. Jack wondered what type of salary she made to afford full carat diamond stud earrings.

"Welcome to Premier. How may I help you gentlemen?"

Jack couldn't help but notice the receptionist's voice was as smooth as rich chocolate. He wondered if yearly pap smear tests really paid this well. "I'm Detective Miller, and this is my partner, Detective O'Shaunessy. We would like to see Dr. Rothschild." Jack flashed his badge for the receptionist to see. If she was concerned about their visit, she didn't flinch even an eyelash.

"Would you take a seat please," she indicated the chairs and couches strategically placed to offer the clients views of the city and the lakefront. "The refreshment center is to your right. I will have someone see you immediately." A few other women seated in plush velvet chairs seemed to be enjoying the refreshments.

"Thank you." Jack felt just like his fifth grade teacher had told him to sit down.

Patrick sat on the soft beige leather sofa. "This place is a little too rich for my taste," he whispered under his breathe to Jack.

"This should prove interesting. I'll bet you lunch at Rock N' Roll McDonald's, she'll have someone here in five minutes to see us."

"Nah, she's already here. You're buying." Patrick nodded towards the approaching tall blonde.

"Officers, I'm Renata, the office manager. How may I help you?"

Jack stood first and introduced himself and Patrick. "We need to speak with Dr. Rothschild in person regarding a patient."

"As you already know, we can't discuss our patients with you without a subpoena." Renata lifted her chin slightly to stress her level of importance.

"As I mentioned before," Jack pushed, "we need to speak with Dr. Rothschild personally."

"Who is the patient you want to know about?" Renata crossed her arms and stood with her feet slightly apart.

"I'm sorry, we can only release the name to Dr. Rothschild. Can you tell us where we can reach him?" Jack purposely raised his voice to capture the attention of the other women in the waiting area. He figured the office manager would take him and Patrick to an inner office if they drew attention to their visit. And his ploy worked.

"Follow me." Renata turned and walked down the inner hallway to an office. "You can wait here for Dr. Rothschild."

The minute Jack and Patrick entered the impersonal, high styled office with more mahogany furniture and windows to the east, Renata pulled the door shut.

"Smile for the cameras." Jack dropped the line as he bent close to Patrick before they sat down in the only two chairs present facing a desk.

Patrick pulled on his left ear. A sign to Jack, he believed they were being recorded. "You can catch a nice view of the lake front from here."

Jack knew as well as Patrick there were several cameras recording them since entering the office. He pulled on his right ear to let Patrick know he got his message. They would need to talk about the weather, sports or family. He knew the woman, Renata, was waiting for him or Patrick to discuss the reason for their visit.

"Say, Patrick, how are your sons' soccer teams doing this year?" Jack knew Patrick's daughters were into cheerleading, but offered the ploy to let Renata think they were divulging personal information because they had privacy. In addition, Renata should tire soon of the family trivia and appear, or send in Dr. Rothschild.

Patrick went right for the bait. "Ron's traveling team is on a winning streak. He even made a goal last weekend. Dan is benched for two more weeks because he wiped out his left knee in practice. My wife sees more of the orthopedic doc than she sees me at this time of the year. Next year I'm signing Dan up for something safe, like chess. If you have nothing to do next weekend, you ought to join us on Saturday morning. Ron's team will be playing out in Oswego."

"Thanks. It sounds great, but it's my nephew, Timmy's fifth birthday. And you know how my sister gets out of whack when I miss any of these important milestones in Timmy's life. She needs to have another child so Timmy can get some breathing room." Jack crossed his right leg. He glanced down at his watch. Someone should be coming in just about now.

The door opened almost on cue. In walked Dr. Rothschild.

"Good morning officers. I'm Dr. Rothschild. What can I do to help you?"

Jack and Patrick stood. Jack offered introductions for himself and Patrick.

"Please sit down." Dr. Rothschild walked around his desk and took his place. "I understand you have questions regarding a patient of mine? Unless you have a signed subpoena from a judge, you already know the answer to your question."

"Dr. Rothschild," Patrick said, "this is your lucky day. I just happen to have one for you." Patrick took an envelope out of his breast jacket pocket and slid it across Dr. Rothschild's desk.

Dr. Rothschild's fingers slowly reached for the subpoena and opened the envelope. Acting as casual as possible, he opened the envelope and read the contents. "I don't see how this concerns me. I saw Sarah Morgan once for a routine gynecological exam."

Jack leaned forward and rested his elbows on his knees. From Kelly's story, this part was true. Dr. Rothschild only saw the girls on their first office visit. Afterwards all business was conducted through Edwards. "We're following up on a missing person's report. My partner and I were at Sarah's apartment when she received a reminder from your office for her yearly exam."

Dr. Rothschild remained in character, the innocent physician. "That may be, Detective Miller, but to the best of my knowledge she hasn't scheduled the appointment."

"She's been missing about seven days. You are one of our few leads." Patrick shifted his body in the uncomfortable, high styled chair.

"I'm so sorry to hear she's missing," Dr. Rothschild responded without moving a muscle. "Perhaps she is out-of-town and forgot to tell anyone her plans. Have you checked her place of employment?"

Jack couldn't believe what a good actor Dr. Rothschild was. He reacted just as if he had read a script.

"We're not at liberty to discuss the case. We'll be on our way. Thank you for your time," Jack said. As the three men stood, Jack removed a copy of the sketch from his coat pocket and handed it to the doctor. "Do you recognize this man?"

Dr. Rothschild, shaken, recovered quickly, but not before stuttering over his first "No."

"Thank you again. We'll let ourselves out." Jack and Patrick walked out of the office before Dr. Rothschild could call for an escort.

Back in the elevator, they 'high fived' each other after the door shut. "Jack, I think you're buying lunch."

"Stop gloating. I owe Finch lunch, too. He wants a number three from the Golden Arches. Would the Rock and Roll McDonalds be okay?" Jack hardly minded picking up the tab after all the dinners he had shared with Patrick's family. Patrick's family put the warmth back into his life after Tad's death and losing his cousin, Irene.

Irene had been good to him and his mother. While his mother worked and finished college so she could make something of herself, Irene had raised Jack. Irene may have died in her early eighties but she had had more spunk than most sixty-year-olds had when he was growing up. If there is a Heaven, Jack was sure Irene was in charge of the sunshine.

"Sounds good to me, then we'll drop off Finch's lunch. Gotta keep our computer wizard happy," Patrick said.

Chapter 30

"Hi, Gladys. Is Sheriff Wilson in?" Jack dunked another French fry in catsup, savoring every bite. He promised himself he would drag Patrick to the gym as soon as this case was over. His and Patrick's days of burgers and fries were about to come to an end.

"Yes, he is, Detective Miller. I'll put you right through. Now don't you be a stranger, you hear? Just give me a day's notice, and I'll whip up one of my sticky bun cakes for you and your partner."

"I'll hold you to it, Gladys. Thanks."

Gladys connected Jack to Sheriff Dave Wilson.

"Sheriff Wilson, here."

"Dave, this is Detective Jack Miller calling."

"How's the investigation going from your end?" Dave asked.

Jack proceeded to fill Dave in on the information he and Patrick had gathered, along with what Claire had come across.

"I haven't gotten very far," reported Dave. "From what you're telling me, I'm going to guess this clinic is operating out of an old estate somewhere in my neighborhood. I'll put Gladys on it. She can check the property records and start a Google Earth search on the internet. Her family has been in LaSalle County for four generations. If the estate is out here, she'll find it."

"Much appreciated," answered Jack. "I'm going to check to see who paid off Sarah Morgan's credit cards. For someone who is supposed to have a gambling debt, her credit card balance is zero. That doesn't seem realistic."

"Did she play at the river boat casinos?"

"No," Jack said, "she liked Vegas and the dice. Did you get a confirmation on the tire design?"

"We just got a call from the state lab. We're looking for a recent model of the Lincoln Navigator. We don't usually see this style of car out this way, except for the tourists over at Starved Rock State Park or the Grand Bear Hotel in Utica. I'll tell my men to be on the lookout. We're still maintaining silence as you requested on the sketch of Edwards. Only police agencies have the information. I don't want to put the two girls at Bali Imports, or my daughter and her friends, at risk."

"From what we have learned about Edwards, he sees people as disposable. Between the two county agencies, we'll find him Dave. If you hear anything, this is my cell phone number." Jack recited the number.

"After this case is over, you and Patrick, and your families should come spend a long weekend in Ottawa. Life is slower. We have great golf courses and incredible trails at several locations. And my wife puts on a super barbeque."

"Sounds like my kind of weekend," Jack said. As much as he loved Chicago, a quiet weekend away would be nice. Sylvia, Patrick's wife, would agree. Some fresh air and easy trails would be healthy for Patrick, no matter how much he complained. Maybe Claire would put down her scalpel and join them.

Jack also liked the idea of building friendships with agencies from other counties. Criminals don't stop at county lines. A department never knew when it would need help from another county. "I'll check in with you in a few days, unless Patrick and I come up with something sooner."

"Same here," Dave answered. "And I'll get Gladys looking for the estate."

After hanging up the phone, Jack took another bite of his burger and looked up at Patrick. "Okay partner, which credit card should we go after first?"

Patrick ran his finger down the list Finch had given Jack. "How about we start with the one with the largest prior debt, Monroe Trust and Savings? Their main office is in the loop."

Jack indulged in another fry. "We don't have a subpoena."

"You're right, we don't, but I'm willing to give it a try since it is already Friday afternoon. If we go for the subpoena first, we'll spend half the time trying to catch a judge to sign it. By then the office will be closed for the weekend."

Jack finished the last of his burger and fries. "Do you want to call in advance?"

"Nope. Let's go for the element of surprise. I love living dangerously at the end of the week. If it doesn't work, then we'll get a subpoena on Monday." Patrick stood up and brushed the crumbs off his tie. "Ready to check out the bank?"

"Let's do it." Jack wanted to get this last stop out of their way. The weather was incredible, clear blue sky, gentle southwesterly breeze and sixty degrees. He had his running gear in the car, and he was headed for the lakefront to stretch his legs after work. He was still curious about the Frankie situation though.

On the way to their car Jack proposed the question, "Shouldn't we stop and see how Claire and Kelly are doing?"

"Nah," replied Patrick, finishing his ice tea. "If there's a problem, Frankie will call me."

"You're kidding? Why Frankie and not Claire?" Jack couldn't believe Patrick's response.

"Because Frankie isn't stupid, and he doesn't take risks he can't handle, but Claire would without question. Do you want me to drive?"

"Sure." Jack tossed him the keys and slid into the front passenger seat.

"For example, when Claire was about thirteen, the whole neighborhood knew the Jackson brothers robbed the local grocery store and beat up the owner. Mr. Pong was too scared to talk to the police, which was exactly what the Jackson brothers were betting on. For several days, all anyone talked about was the robbery. The Jackson brothers didn't even try to hide.

"Claire got it in her head she was going after the Jackson brothers. She must have mentioned it to Frankie because all of a sudden he stuck to her like glue, even though she didn't realize it. Apparently, Claire had watched where the Jackson brothers hung out. And on her way home from baseball practice, she walked by them swinging her bat. Just as she was about to take out the older brother's knee cap, Frankie jumped out of his cousin's car, grabbed Claire and the bat, and threw them into the back seat. He promptly turned her and the bat over to my dad. She was so pissed at Frankie. I don't think she talked to him for six months."

"What happened to the Jackson brothers?"

"Let's say my dad convinced them to leave the neighborhood, or he promised to turn Claire on them. After Mr. Pong recovered, he was so grateful to Claire he went down and filed a report with the police. The Jackson brothers each did eighteen months." Patrick pulled into a 'No Parking' spot on Monroe just around the corner from LaSalle Street.

"Don't worry, Jack. Frankie will keep a good eye on her."

That was precisely what concerned Jack. He intended to keep a good eye on Frankie.

After a few inquiries, Patrick and Jack headed up to the seventh floor where the credit card department was located. The receptionist directed them into a Mr. John Gimble's office.

"Mr. Gimble, I'm Detective Patrick O'Shaunessy, and this is my partner, Detective Jack Miller. Sorry to catch you so late on a Friday, but we have a problem we are hoping you can help us with."

"Detective I'll do what I can, but I know you understand the privacy laws."

"We are investigating a missing person's report on a Sarah Morgan. We've learned she has a gambling problem and took multiple cash advances on her credit card. Other people who know her said she told them she was having a hard time paying her bills. We've learned her bills were paid off all of a sudden. We wondered if it is possible to see who paid off her bill. This might have something to do with her disappearance."

"I'm afraid I can't help you. Our records will only show if a bill is paid, not who paid the bill."

Jack didn't buy Mr. Gimble's answer. His mother had worked in the trust department at another Chicago bank. She said something about how the bank routing numbers were recorded electronically. He couldn't recall how this actually was accomplished. "In other words, if we had a subpoena it wouldn't make a difference."

"You're correct, Detective. Now if you could excuse me, I have a meeting I must get to."

"What a lousy time for a meeting. Hope it doesn't keep you late," Jack said. "Thank you for your time."

Patrick placed his business card on Gimble's desk without lowering his eyes. "Here's my number, just in case you remember something."

"No problem. Have a nice weekend." Mr. Gimble dismissed them as he stuffed papers into his briefcase.

Half way to the elevator Jack said, "I'm sure he's lying. Let's see where he goes."

Patrick and Jack didn't have to wait long before Mr. Gimble left the bank and grabbed a cab.

Chapter 31

"Edwards, you're an incompetent idiot! I just had two Chicago detectives here asking about Sarah Morgan." Dr. Rothschild screamed into the phone. "They had a missing person's report and a subpoena. I thought you said you cleared out her apartment and picked up her mail? They found one of our reminder cards in her mail."

"I did," Edwards said. "Go talk to your precious Renata. She should've made sure the card didn't go out and Sarah's file was deleted from the system."

Dr. Rothschild opened his private bar and reached for his personalized crystal decanter of Maker's Mark Bourbon Wisky. He poured two fingers into an accompanying glass. "They also had a sketch of you with them. I don't like this. They must have discovered some connection between Dr. Parks and Sarah, otherwise why would they ask me if I recognized you?" He watched the sailboats out on Lake Michigan through his large office window as the first sip of bourbon anesthetized his throat. He didn't like anything threatening his position.

"They don't have any connection. They're probably fishing," Edwards said.

"What about Sarah's landlady?" Dr. Rothschild searched for the break in their plan.

"Her memory isn't too swift. I doubt if she even remembers I said I was Sarah's brother. She never even checked on the apartment application."

"Where are you now?" Dr. Rothschild questioned.

"I'm almost at O'Hare Airport. Your clients should land shortly. Wait a minute; you said they had a missing person's report. Maybe they don't know Sarah's dead. The landlady must have forgotten to tell them."

"You better hope so. Take the client back to the estate cottage and stay put. Renata should be there before you arrive. Have you found Kelly Davis?"

"No," answered Edwards. "I checked with the Board of Trade, but she quit yesterday. I called her home, but her parents said she flew to New York for a job interview."

"I don't like loose ends. For now we'll let her be. She most likely ran because she is scared. A little fear is good for people, keeps them from making stupid choices. I'll check in with you later." A knock at the door interrupted his conversation.

"Dr. Rothschild, your new patient Claire O'Reilly is in exam room five," a slender blonde announced.

Dr. Rothschild disconnected with Edwards without a goodbye; it wasn't warranted with staff.

He walked down the hallway, stopped at exam room five and unlocked the file box outside the room. He took Claire O'Reilly's chart out and read it. Ms. O'Reilly sounded like a good prospect, a business woman, not a wimp like Kelly. Besides, right now he was down one donor after the accident with Sarah.

Dr. Rothschild knocked on the door and entered. "Good afternoon, Ms. O'Reilly. I'm Dr. Rothschild. May I call you Claire?" He extended his hand.

"Please do." She shook his hand.

"What can I do for you?" Opening the patient folder in front of him on the small exam room desk, he pretended to review it. He already knew everything he needed to know. Ms. O'Reilly had participated in egg donations before.

"Recently I moved to Chicago. I ran up a substantial amount on my credit card during a European vacation. Just before I moved, I was preparing for a private egg donation. At the last minute, the couple had money problems. Besides moving expenses, I have tuition due in January at Circle Campus."

"I understand. Why did you select to see me?"

"You advertise you're an infertility specialist. With an upper Michigan Avenue address, I thought you might have clients who are in a position to afford such services."

Dr. Rothschild looked directly at Claire. She definitely was resourceful. "I do have such clients from time to time with checkbooks which can accommodate my fees." He looked her up and down. "I need to be sure all my donors are healthy. I insist all donors be drug and alcohol free, and not carriers of various diseases."

Claire spoke, "I know you'll find I fit into that category."

"Good. Would you be opposed to a pap smear test and blood draw?"

Claire squirmed in her chair. "I noticed you advertised as having a nurse practitioner on your staff. I would be more comfortable if she could do the Pap smear."

"No problem at all." Dr. Rothschild loathed performing the test. Nothing is more pathetic than a woman with her legs up in stirrups wishing she was any other place. The sight of a woman's buttock hanging over the edge of the exam table left a lot to be desired. It was the most undesirable view of a woman.

"I'll send in Sophia. You'll like her. After she completes the test and draws your blood, you will redress and meet me in my office. Then we can discuss some options."

"That would be fine," Claire responded.

"Good. Now change into the exam gown, and Sophia will be right in."

***

After Sophia was finished with the testing, she directed Claire to Dr. Rothschild's office.

"Claire, please come in and sit down." Dr. Rothschild made sure the tone of his voice was gracious. He liked Claire's straightforwardness. She wasn't crying about an unwanted pregnancy or an infection like most of his donor patients. She apparently had a goal to accomplish, and she was working on a plan. This had potential for a happy business arrangement. "I hope you found Sophia acceptable?"

"Yes I did. Thank you very much for honoring my request." Claire sat back in the chair with her legs crossed. "You have a lovely view."

"It is quite stunning, isn't it?" At least the afternoon was going much better than this morning. Usually nothing could rattle him, but the two detectives had unnerved him. He wished he knew how much information they truly had on Sarah.

"Claire, I don't want to keep you too long. The weather is spectacular, and I'm sure you want to get out and enjoy it. Before I can ask you to work for me, I must have your test results. I'm sure you understand." Dr. Rothschild relaxed back into his leather chair. Claire definitely was a possibility, and he was short a donor.

"Not a problem. I appreciate your concern for healthy donors," she said.

"What day are you in the cycle for your medication?"

"This is my seventh day," Claire answered.

"I'll keep this in mind. All right then, let's discuss our business arrangement. We should have your lab results back by Monday. If everything is fine, I'll have my assistant call you with the details as soon as we have something for you. If we don't have something for you in the near future, Renata will schedule your next round of medications."

"That sounds reasonable," answered Claire. "Do you perform the procedure here?"

"No. My clinic is a short drive from Chicago. Generally, we have our driver pick up our donors at the Union Train Station since some come in from the suburbs. Because you live locally, you can have our driver drop you off afterwards at either your home address or the train station. I may not be on call when you are scheduled. I work with a team of highly skilled physicians. We will let you know who will perform your procedure. Do you have any problem with this?"

"No, I find it quite acceptable."

"I usually send the driver with a low dose of Valium to help you relax. I'm going to ask you to take it right away. I find my patients are so much more comfortable for the procedure. Here is an explanation of the procedure." He gave her a folder filled with different instructions. "Afterwards, you will rest for an hour. Then, you will be brought back."

"This sounds simple enough. Is there anything else I should do?"

"All the pre-op instructions are included in this packet for you. If you have any questions, Renata will help you. As for your payment, may I ask how far in debt you are?"

"This will seem small to you, but ten grand sort of set me back."

"Oh, no, ten grand does seem sizeable to me. Well, I don't think we can wipe out your bill in one donation, but I have enough business to foresee no problem in taking care of it. My dear, I want you to go home and relax, knowing your problems are solved. If you could bring a copy of your last credit card statement in a sealed envelope with you the first night and give it to my driver, I will see to it everything is taken care of."

Claire sat on the edge of her chair. "You mentioned first night?"

"Oh, I'm sorry. I forgot to mention we do our procedures at

night because so many of our donors work during the day. The less amount of time they have to take off from work, the fewer the questions they're asked by nosey co-workers and friends."

"How thoughtful," Claire said. "Do you write me a check for the donation?"

"No. When the recipient pays, it is applied directly to your account. This way you won't be tempted to use the funds. We have found this to be most helpful for getting our young ladies back on track." Dr. Rothschild leaned back into his chair again. He had just snared another one. It's her own fault for being so stupid with her money.

"We have just one more piece of unfinished business. We ask all our donors to sign a confidentiality agreement. Competition is stiff in the infertility field. We wouldn't want to give our competition an edge, would we?" asked Dr. Rothschild.

"No. I have no problem with that."

"Good." Dr. Rothschild pulled a form out of his desk drawer, filled in a few blanks and slid it across his desk to Claire. "Just sign and date by the 'X'," he instructed.

Claire did as he asked.

"Do you have any questions?"

"I think you have covered everything. Thank you for your help." Claire stood and shook his hand goodbye.

"You're welcome," Dr. Rothschild answered. "Would you like me to have someone show you the way out?"

"No, I remember the way. I'll look forward to hearing from your staff."

Chapter 32

Oh, shit! How could she be so stupid? Claire's elevator reached the lobby as the realization of what she had just forgotten hit her. A quick look out into the lobby told her no one was waiting for the next elevator. She stepped back in and pushed the button for one floor below Dr. Rothschild's office.

Claire could hear her heart pounding above the sound of the ascending elevator. She rifled in her purse for the set of lock picks Santa left in her stocking the year before her dad died. She carried them with her all the time, not because she was planning a career of breaking and entering, but because they had been the last things her dad had given her. They were a memento for all the nights they sat at the kitchen table and discussed his day.

The elevator door opened, jerking her back to the present. Claire stepped out into a hallway for a surgeon's office. The entrance to the surgeon's office was in the same place as Dr. Rothschild's office. A quick sweep of the area told her the exit sign was to her left. As she approached the exit she noticed an unmarked door around the corner with a white lab specimen box sitting on the floor. This was undoubtedly the back entrance to the office. Now, if Dr. Rothschild's box would only be in the same place on the floor above, she thought.

After checking the exit door to the stairs to make sure she could get back in, Claire slipped up the flight of stairs. Through the stairwell door's glass window she peered into the side hallway. The white lab box was in the same position as the floor below. Her pounding heart was now in her throat. If she was going to find Sarah's killer, she had to remove the tube of blood with her name on it and leave before being discovered. Just as her hand touched the door handle, Claire heard the side door open and saw Sophia step out of the office. She opened the white lab box with a key, placed several plastic specimen bags in it, locked it and disappeared back into the office.

Quickly Claire stepped into the back hallway and bent down to the box. The last time she used the picks, she and Sarah were breaking into Sarah's garage to smoke cigarettes. Claire inserted the first pick and rotated it with no luck. The second pick wasn't any better. As she inserted the third pick Claire could hear voices by the elevator. *Please get on the elevator,* she prayed.

Then she heard Sophia's voice.

"I think I forgot to lock the lab box when I put the last specimens in it. It will only take a second to check."

Claire pulled out the pick and stepped back into the stairwell. She ducked behind the door.

"Hold the elevator," Sophia called out. "I locked it."

Claire wanted to slide to the floor and sit. If she didn't do it now, she wouldn't be able to get justice for Sarah. And how many other young women like Sarah were risking their lives? She opened the door and stepped over to the looming white box and inserted the pick. On the final rotation the lock clicked open. Claire could have kissed the floor, but there wasn't time to celebrate.

She grabbed her specimen bag and then a second one to divert attention away from her. Tomorrow, the office and the lab could argue who was responsible for the lost specimens. She stuffed the plastic bags in her jacket and disappeared down the stairwell.

Chapter 33

John Gimble tightened his grip on his briefcase. His head felt as if it were ready to explode. His heart pounded so hard he was amazed it remained inside his chest. He could taste the acid reflux in the back of his throat. He had been expecting the police to knock at his door for years, yet today it still caught him off guard. Life as he knew it was almost over. Even his marriage had been shaky the last few months.

Nothing pleased his wife any more. She was bored with shopping, her charity work and her private tennis lessons. The twins were pretty self-sufficient as high school sophomores. Their studies, friends and school activities were their lives. They were good kids, growing more independent every day. Perhaps his wife's problem was she didn't feel needed any more, but she had no idea how much he still needed her. He had loved her since he first spotted her studying in the college library.

John tapped on the glass divider to get the cab driver's attention. "Could you pull over at the cash station on the next corner please?"

"I'm keeping the meter running, understood?"

"Understood." John leaned back for a moment and closed his eyes. He couldn't live like this anymore. He had made up his mind. The next time Rothschild called and demanded he change someone's account, his answer would be no. He already felt the weight of his decision. Rothschild would be furious. No one said no to the man.

John was exhausted. He would tell his wife the truth soon. He was waiting for the right moment, if there ever would be one.

Consumed by his thoughts, John didn't realize the cab had stopped.

The driver banged on the glass divider. "Well, are you getting out?"

John opened his eyes and looked around for a moment. "Yes, thank you. I'll be right back."

He stepped out of the cab and made his way to the cash station with his briefcase in hand. He pulled out the plastic card from his jacket pocket and fed it into the machine. His fingers slid over the selection on the key pad and made the first of several money transactions. After each transaction, he put the card in his pants pocket and pulled another one out of his jacket pocket. On the last transaction, he took out a couple hundred in cash and stuffed it into his pocket.

***

"Jack, can you see what he's doing?" Patrick slumped down in the driver's seat.

Jack watched Gimble through his binoculars. "It looks like he is using several ATM cards. I think he only took cash on the last card."

"I wonder if he's trying to steal money from customer accounts, using a machine away from the bank so he can escape before being caught," Patrick said.

"Okay, Patrick, he's in the cab, and they are leaving. Gimble seemed pretty engrossed in what he was doing. I doubt if he saw us."

Patrick followed the cab at a safe distance. "Let's see where he's going." The cab stopped at Union Station. "I don't think he's making a break from the country. My guess is he's headed home to suburbia."

"Let's go back to the police station. If he's going anywhere, it's not from here."

***

Back in the cab, John had requested the driver take him to Union Train Station. As he exited the cab, he handed the driver a sizeable tip. The driver nodded his head in appreciation and drove over to the pick-up line to catch another fare.

John headed for the train track which would take him home. He could relax a little now knowing he had moved funds into accounts for his wife and kids, and no one could touch them should anything happen to him. This wasn't bank money. It was his money. If arrested for fixing credit card debts for Rothschild's patients, he knew all his assets would be frozen. The accounts for his family were in his wife's maiden name. The money transfer would take care of them long after he was in prison.

His deepest regret was the pain his family would go through because of his actions. All of this had happened because he wanted to give his wife what she so badly wanted, babies. His low sperm count had prevented him from impregnating her, so he enlisted the help of a fraternity brother starting out in the infertility field.

Dr. Rothschild had told John's wife her eggs wouldn't fertilize inside her body. With John's help, Dr. Rothschild informed her, he could fertilize her eggs outside her body with her husband's sperm and plant the embryos in her womb. All she needed to be pregnant was a little help from him.

And so the deception began. John made his wife happy, and Dr. Rothschild had his first successful case. One hand washed the other, and John's wife never knew. On the first round, the pregnancy took. Nine months later Dr. Rothschild delivered healthy twins for the ecstatic couple. Life was incredible for John and his wife, in spite of all the long sleepless nights, piles of diapers and nothing in the refrigerator but baby bottles.

Then one day Dr. Rothschild called.

At first he thought Dr. Rothschild wanted John to tell his happy story to another couple. He hadn't had the money to pay for the procedure without his wife knowing, so Dr. Rothschild did it free.

"Someday perhaps you can return the favor," Dr. Rothschild had said.

John had no idea how dearly he would pay for the pregnancy. Rothschild didn't want John to talk to a perspective couple; Rothschild wanted John to erase a sizeable credit card bill for a young woman. At first John balked at the idea, but Rothschild made it clear he would hate to have to tell John's wife the truth.

John had no power to eliminate the bill, but he could send it to a collection agency and set up minimal payments, which he himself covered. This was only the beginning.

Rothschild called on him many times over the years for the same service. Since he was the banker in the family, his wife was happy to leave all the money handling to him as long as she had what she wanted. His father-in-law's death eased John's burden considerably.

As the years passed, he moved right up the corporate ladder because he had married into the right family even though his own pedigree was tacky. Finally, he had the power to eliminate a debt.

He lived in constant fear someone would realize how often he had done it and would blow the whistle. Rothschild demanded more, so John went back to his old system of turning the bills over to collection and then anonymously paying them.

***

The house was empty when John arrived home. A note on the kitchen counter told him the twins were at a school event and his wife was having dinner with her sister. He immediately went to his private study. The walls had floor to ceiling shelves stuffed with books and family photos. His desk faced sliding glass doors which opened to an outdoor patio. In the corner of the room was an overstuffed couch with too many pillows. The twins loved to curl up on it when they played games in front of the wood burning fireplace.

He set his briefcase on his desk and opened a hidden wall safe. From it, he removed a large brown envelope and dumped the contents on his desk. Over two dozen labeled cassettes fell out. He reached inside his brief case for an additional six. From a closet, he removed a brown box and placed the tapes inside in order of date and time.

Then he sat down at his computer and put in a code no one would guess, the date he first kissed his wife. He pulled up the complete history of his transactions with Rothschild and placed a copy in the box.

Next, he emailed his brother, Paul. John told him if anything ever happened to him, he was to take this box to the police and tell him about the bank accounts. John gave him a hint where to find the box. After sending the letter, John took the box out to the garage and shoved it under the tool bench. This was the first time he had technically used the tool bench. The bench had come with their custom designed home. It really belonged in his brother's home. John much preferred his hands on a computer keyboard to a workbench. After John threw some rope on top of the box, he placed the circular saw box in front of it.

He felt relieved. The deed was done. He was ready to say no to any further requests from Rothschild, and face the consequences.

Chapter 34

Claire tried to remain calm as she hailed a cab outside Dr. Rothschild's office just in case he had someone watching her. Once she was safe in the backseat of the yellow cab, she said mentally, *"Yes, we've got him. What a dirtball!"* Her heart raced as fast as the cab did through mid-afternoon traffic down Michigan Avenue to the south loop neighborhood where she lived.

She stopped outside her apartment door to listen for any sound. Claire heard Kelly laugh as Frankie yelled, "I won."

Good, she thought, all was well. She knocked so Frankie could answer the door.

"Gorgeous, you're home!" Frankie grabbed Claire in his arms and pretended to dance her across the room.

"Do I smell my favorite spinach lasagna cooking?" Claire dropped her purse and jacket on the living room chair.

"I slaved all day for you. I have garlic bread, too." Frankie beamed as Claire and Kelly laughed.

"It certainly sounds like the two of you have been having a good time. Kelly, how are you doing?" Claire had been worried about her all day.

"Actually, much better than I thought," Kelly said.

"Might I throw in a little footnote to Miss Kelly's status?" Frankie poured three glasses of red wine.

"What am I missing Frankie?" Claire knew she could always trust Frankie to give her the truth.

"It's okay, Frankie, I'll tell Claire."

Kelly took the glass of wine from Frankie. After a sip, she began. "I called my mom right after you left this morning. I let her think someone has been bothering me at work, and if he calls she is to say I flew to New York for a job interview and to visit friends. She was worried at first, so I told her your brother is a cop and he was watching out for me. I know that isn't exactly the truth, but I didn't think she would believe I was safer here with a wild Italian."

Claire gave her a hug. "You did great. Good thinking. The

only part you have turned around is the fact you *are* safer with Frankie. He can do a better job than my brother does. Patrick can be too obvious."

"Frankie's your man," said Frankie. "How about you two lovely ladies set the table while I check on our feast? Then we'll eat." Frankie pulled a tossed green salad out of the refrigerator and passed it over to Kelly.

"I'm going to change. While we are enjoying Frankie's dinner, I have news to share." Claire disappeared down the hallway in search of her jeans and sweatshirt. Minutes later, she appeared dressed more comfortably with a big pair of moose head slippers on her feet.

Frankie took one look at her slippers and asked, "Did you just kill those and have them mounted?"

"He has no sense of style," Claire said to Kelly.

"Frankie has lots of style, but those slippers belong north of the Wisconsin border."

Kelly laughed.

After everyone finished their first serving of Frankie's lasagna, Claire began sharing her news. She let Frankie know Patrick had personally endorsed him as their knight in shining armor. Claire had a funny feeling Jack wasn't as pleased, but kept it to herself.

The best part was her visit to Dr. Rothschild's office. "That guy is so full of himself, I wanted to puke. He basically told me everything you said about the set up. He said he might be able to use me the first part of next week."

"*What! Are you nuts, Claire?*" Frankie was out of his chair walking circles around the table. "He is not going to touch you again."

"Frankie, calm down. He didn't touch me today. I requested a nurse practitioner. She was very good, and I wouldn't be surprised to find out she has no idea about this side of his operation. His assistant, Renata, will call me with the particulars. I put my money on her.

"I loved the way he had me sign a confidentiality agreement. I wanted to tell the guy it wasn't worth the price of the paper it was written on. I can see how he easily obtains everyone's silence."

Kelly took a second serving of the lasagna. "Claire, how can he harvest your eggs when you haven't been on any meds?"

"I told him I just moved here and was taking the shots because I was going to donate eggs for a couple this week but they ran out of money."

"Nobody's touching your eggs. Does Patrick know about your office visit?" Frankie asked, still showing his anger.

"No, and he's not going to either." Claire finished her wine. Between the food and the wine, she was going to sleep well tonight.

"Your blood level won't come back high enough for him to send for you," Kelly voiced her concern.

"You're right, it won't, but not for the reason you think." Claire explained how she retrieved her specimen, with hopes that Rothschild would need her and have to forgo the lab results.

"You're not going out to the clinic," Frankie said as he cleared the table of dishes.

"I don't have a choice. How else are we going to find out where he takes the girls? Besides, I thought you could follow. Right after I get there I'll make an excuse to go to the bathroom and slip out the door. You'll be waiting down the driveway to take me home. Then we'll call Patrick."

"But Claire, Edwards gives you the Valium and watches to make sure you take it," Kelly warned her.

"Well, I guess I better make it look good so Edwards is convinced. I'm going to need a credit card bill in Claire O'Reilly's name showing ten thousand dollars in cash withdrawals. Do you think you can fix it for me?"

"Consider it done," Frankie said. "I still don't like this, though."

"It's okay," Claire smiled up at Frankie. "Enough of this for now. What's for dessert?"

"Tiramisu, what else?" he said. "The coffee should be about ready."

"Both of you sit and I'll serve," Kelly said. "I want you to be ready for me to beat you at War."

Claire laughed. "I wonder how many decks of cards we wore out as kids playing that card game. You have to watch Frankie, he's fast."

"Gorgeous, you haven't even seen fast!"

Chapter 35

"Why do I feel like we are ending the week empty-handed?" Patrick flipped through his notebook to see if he had missed anything.

"If Gimble had done something besides get on a north bound commuter train for suburbia you would be happier," Jack said. "Admit it, you were hoping he would head for the airport so we could go into high gear and call in SWAT." Jack leaned back in his chair and smiled. Patrick never got tired of the high drama or the boring routine part of the job. It was in his blood. And Jack was sure a Claire had the same DNA.

"What were all the bank cards about? Were they his cards, or did they belong to bank clients?" Patrick questioned. "I hate waiting for Monday. Even if we had a subpoena, the bank is closed until Monday."

"Just maybe for once we could act like regular people and enjoy the weekend instead of playing cops and robbers. I, for one, am ready for a run on the lake front and a session watching the entire Bears game on Sunday without interruption." Jack sorted through the files on his desk and locked them in his drawer.

"Do you think Gimble knows Sarah is actually dead or believes what we told him, that she is missing? I'm sure he lied about not being able to track the payee for the credit card bill. Who do you think would benefit besides Sarah with the bill paid?" Patrick didn't let the subject go.

Jack chewed on this question for a moment. "I'm back at square one."

"What do you mean?" asked Patrick.

"Do we even have enough for a subpoena? From where I'm sitting, all we have is a list from Finch showing which credit card carried the highest balance and the payment dates."

"Bingo! I'm calling Claire," Patrick said and dialed her cell phone.

Jack sat forward. He knew Patrick was just like a dog with a bone. He wasn't going to give it up. Not even for one Friday evening, not for one fall weekend.

"Hello Patrick. What's up?" Claire said on the other end of the line.

"I have a quick question or two for Kelly? Do you think she would talk to me?"

"Are you going to be the nice, polite detective we all know and love, or are you here to instill fear and scare Kelly half to death?"

"Okay, I promise to play nice. I'll give you an update afterwards."

He could hear Claire pass her phone to Kelly. "Patrick wants to ask you a question. Is that okay?"

"This is Kelly," she answered.

"Hi Kelly. This is Detective O'Shaunessy. I have a couple quick questions. Do you remember when Sarah started donating eggs?"

"Yes, it was just after Labor Day last year," Kelly answered.

"Since that time did she ever seem at ease, like her money problems were getting better?"

"She did for a few months, but then she started gambling again. Over Thanksgiving, she flew out to Vegas, and then again at Christmas. Now that I think about it, she went every time there was a holiday."

Kelly started to cry.

"What did you say to Kelly?" Claire asked, coming on the line.

"I don't think it was what I said, but what Kelly realized," Patrick confirmed.

"What are you talking about?"

Patrick rubbed his forehead. "Kelly just put two and two together. Sarah flew to Vegas during all the holidays, probably looking for excitement to cover up her pain. She was searching for a way to handle the loss of her parents."

"Oh," Claire replied.

"Finch pulled up Sarah's credit report. Her score was low, as to be expected, but her bills which she was past due on were suddenly paid off or up-to-date. We're looking to see if we can find a tie to Dr. Rothschild. Jack and I stopped at his office this morning. We used the excuse of the appointment reminder card to investigate a missing person's report. Rothschild was perfectly calm until Jack showed him the sketch of Edwards, then he tripped over his own response. He said he didn't know the man but I have my suspicions. How are things at your end?"

"We're doing fine. Actually, Kelly and I are doing great. Frankie's not. He's losing at War," Claire answered, realizing how close she came to running into Patrick at Rothschild's office caught her short.

"What do you have planned for the weekend?" Patrick asked.

"We haven't gotten that far yet. I'm on call Sunday."

"I'll have Jack pick you and Kelly up at five for dinner on Saturday. Frankie is also invited, or he might want the night off from you ladies. You and Kelly will be safe. I'll have an extra unmarked car follow you and keep an eye on my neighborhood."

"Wait a minute," Claire replied, "don't you think you should ask Sylvia first? She may not want to feed a crowd."

Patrick caught the crunched up paper ball Jack threw at him. "Ask Kelly if she can make potato salad."

Claire asked Kelly and gave Patrick her answer. "She said yes. She wants to know if she can put sliced green olives with pimento in the salad."

"Sylvia will love it. I'll have the girls soak sweet corn, and I'll make sure there are plenty of ribs. Tell Kelly thanks for the information. See you tomorrow. And Sis, please stay out of trouble."

Patrick hung up.

Jack sat back in his chair again and rolled his eyes. "Patrick."

Patrick looked up at Jack. "What?"

"You never asked if I had plans for Saturday night. I might have a hot date, not to mention Sylvia and the girls might have plans."

"When was the last time you had a hot date any night of the week? Besides, if I recall, you were asking if we should check up on Claire and Kelly. So which is it?"

"Which is what?" Jack looked confused.

"Did you want to see Claire, or was it Kelly?"

Jack almost choked on the bottle of water he was drinking. "Where did that come from?"

Patrick shrugged and grabbed his jacket off the back of his chair. "Come on. It's time to go home."

Chapter 36

Gladys had whittled her list of possible sites down to seven. She and her husband, Hank, had spent Friday evening making their final selection. Armed with the information, they mapped out their route. It was just like old times. It had been a while since they worked a case together and she was looking forward to the adventure.

Since the weather was beautiful, they decided to take out their antique, red, 1963 Ford Mustang convertible for a spin. They threw a cooler in the back seat with an assortment of drinks and snacks. The stack of well-used bird books with many pages marked with scraps of paper sat beside the cooler. They each had a pair of high-powered binoculars and a camera with a telephoto lens. To top it off, they had flyers on Starved Rock and Matthiessen State Parks and the Sandy Ford Nature Preserve just south of the state parks on the Vermillion River.

Hank was in charge of the finer details of their cover. From the hidden floor safe in their basement, Hank had selected Illinois drivers' licenses for Ralph and Shirley Pfiefer. He included their membership cards to the National Audubon Society. He also had LaSalle County road maps. They were all set just in case they ran into the very person they were looking for.

The first two properties on their list were south of Ottawa. The driveways were short, and they could easily see the houses from the road. They decided to try for the third address on the list. This property was located on the northeast side of the Vermillion River just south of the Matthiessen State Park. Open fields of cut corn left a thin dirt road visible.

On their first pass, Gladys and Hank had missed it. Nothing marked the entrance, not even a mailbox. Just beyond the fields was an area of dense trees. The location was perfect for their cover as bird watchers.

Gladys got out of the car. "This has to be it. Someone doesn't want this place discovered. I'm going to call Sheriff Wilson and give him our location."

After Gladys completed the call, she placed the phone in her fanny pack next to her 9mm Beretta. The weight of her piece felt good. She knew Hank had his piece in the back of his waistband under his sweatshirt. With the field guide in hand, they walked down the road giving the false impression their eyes were sky bound.

"Shirley, is that a White-Breasted Nuthatch up to your left? I think he is on the move." Hank spanned the trees in search of cameras.

"Keep quiet Ralph, or you will scare him away. I'm going to try and get his picture." About twenty feet ahead, Gladys could make out an iron fence topped with barbed wire. "I think this is a female. Do you see the gray cap? The male has to be around here somewhere." Gladys referred to the field guide. She walked over to Hank. "Look Ralph, here's a picture of the Blue Heron we saw at the nature preserve earlier this morning."

Hank gave the illusion of reading the field guide as he whispered, "Gate to your right. Visual on two cameras." To complete the picture of the two happy birdwatchers, he kissed Gladys.

"Now Ralph, there will be plenty of time for that later tonight at the hotel. Look, there's the male." Gladys pointed to the fictitious bird off to her right just as she heard the loud bang of the metal gate opening. Within seconds, a black Lincoln Navigator pulled to an abrupt stop next to them. A large man with short hair got out.

"This is private property. What are you doing here?" the man asked.

"Oh Ralph, I didn't see any sign, did you?" Gladys said.

"We must have overlooked it in our excitement. Hi, we are Ralph and Shirley Pfieffer." Hank extended his hand, but the man didn't take it.

Gladys spoke. "We are so sorry we disturbed you. We're out bird watching. I can't believe we just saw a female White-Breasted Nuthatch!"

"You need to leave." The man stood there with his arms crossed.

"Come on Shirley, we'll head over to the Matthiessen State Park." Hank took Gladys' arm and walked her to the Mustang. They were gone in seconds.

Gladys phoned Dave Wilson, the sheriff, as soon as they

drove around the bend in the road. She told him about the fence and cameras, and how difficult it was to even see the entrance from the road. "Also, the driver of the SUV looks just like the man in our sketch. This time the vehicle has Missouri plates. I think we found the place."

"Come on in. Good work you two," Dave congratulated Gladys and Hank.

***

Thirty minutes later, Gladys and her husband walked into the Sheriff's Office. "Hank, good to see you," Dave shook his hand. He gave Gladys a hug. "And how's my favorite ex-FBI Field Agent?"

"Actually, it was fun pulling the scam. Edwards was annoyed to find us looking for birds." Gladys took her gun from the fanny pack and removed the ammunition clip.

Hank had his weapon out also.

"I didn't expect the two of you to be packing weapons?" Dave smiled.

"Don't laugh," Hank remarked. "We both qualified at the range last week. We may have gray hair, but we can both hit the target dead center."

"Come on into my office and let's see if we can figure out any other entrances to the property. Stacy just dropped off lunch. How about we eat as we work?"

"That would be great," Hank said. "Come on Gladys, let's circle the wagon." Hank made a beeline for the picnic basket Dave's daughter had brought.

"God bless that daughter of yours, Dave. She even marked the sandwiches. Gladys, I'm having a chicken salad sandwich. What would you like?" Hank said.

"Is there a ham salad in the basket?" Gladys asked.

Hank handed her one as Dave grabbed a chicken salad and opened the bag of chips.

"Looks like my wife made potato salad and brownies, too. Dig in while I pull up Google Earth." Dave ran his fingers over the key board until he had the exact location of the property dead center. He turned his computer screen so Hank and Gladys could see. Using the pencil eraser tip, he pointed out a narrow dirt road which seemed to skirt around the edge of a corn field to the north of the main house.

"Dave, from Rt. 178, we couldn't see where that road went," Gladys said. "It almost looks like it runs along the Vermillion River over to the quarry."

"Well, we do now," Dave said, "only whoever is there doesn't know we're watching."

Chapter 37

John Gimble read the number on the caller ID of his office private number. It was Dr. Arthur Rothschild. What a horrible way to finish Monday afternoon.

"Hello," he answered.

"John, I thought I would give you a heads up, I have a new donor who will be in need of assistance. She starts Wednesday evening and was told to bring a copy of her last statement with her. I'll send it over Thursday morning," Dr. Rothschild stated.

"Arthur, I'm done. I'm not doing this again for you. You have bled me dry." John sighed.

"I don't believe you are thinking clearly. You will handle this for me. I'm sure your wife…"

"You can stop threatening me. I told my wife over the weekend. It's over. I'm done," John insisted.

"You're still not listening to me. You will handle this matter for me, and anything else I tell you to do." Rothschild raised his voice.

"No, Arthur, you're the one not listening." John was aware he was speaking louder. He dropped his voice so as not to attract his secretary from the outer office.

"Well," Rothschild went on, "I hope you also told your wife I used my sperm to impregnate her eggs."

"You did *what?* What happened to the sperm donor I selected from the donor bank?" How could his sweet, wonderful twins have this despicable man's genes in their veins? John wanted to vomit. Searing pain stabbed his temples. How would he tell his wife this?

"And here I thought you would be grateful I had saved you the additional charges."

"Rothschild, you're a bastard. The answer is still no!" John hung up. He would have to tell his wife about this tonight. Surprisingly, she had handled the news that because of his low sperm count, a donor sperm had been used. Perhaps it was because she couldn't bear the thought of not having the twins.

She wouldn't be happy to find out who the sperm donor was,

but John would find a way to put a positive spin on it.

He felt a horrible weight lift from his shoulders. The relief was incredible, but somewhat short lived. He still wanted to resolve the accounts he had canceled. He had contacted his stockbroker to sell some stock and planned to have the accounts cleared. Soon he would be whole again. If Rothschild pushed the issue, John would report him to the medical board. John wasn't sure if Rothschild even deserved a warning first.

In the meantime, it wouldn't hurt to leave a message for his brother. While the tapes and papers were safe, there was a part of John telling him to watch his back. If Rothschild reported him to the CEO, John would need all the blackmail proof. The tapes and payments should prove he wasn't out to steal from the bank, and he was making restitution for the accounts.

He didn't really believe Rothschild would do anything physical to him. Rothschild never dirtied his hands. John immediately unlocked his desk drawer. He removed a list of credit card transactions going back several years. His finger ran down the names until it stopped at Sarah Morgan. Now he remembered her. Her total initial bill for all her credit cards had been high. John had dissolved it. Rothschild reported Sarah had a gambling problem. There were several later entries for amounts he had removed.

Then the reality hit John. The police had access to credit information. That's why they had shown up at his office. Somehow, the police thought he was involved in her disappearance. Had Rothschild done something to her? Had Sarah become too much a liability? John may be guilty of embezzling under the threat of blackmail, but nothing more. And the concept of being innocent until proven guilty never worked in the newspapers when money and a missing body intertwined. He needed a plan, and he needed it *fast* now that he had confronted Rothschild.

John replaced the list in its file and locked the drawer. First, he would leave his brother a message on his voice mail. Anyone could destroy an answering machine, but they couldn't get into Paul's voice mail messages. His brother would be back in town tomorrow. Next, he had to lay this all out for his wife. Hopefully, she wouldn't kick him out of the house. Then, tomorrow he would go directly to the police before he even went to work. Finally, he would tell the CEO and offer to resign rather than embarrass the bank. It was the only right thing to do.

John checked his watch. It was after five o'clock. He was mentally exhausted. He might as well head home now. He had a lot to do before tomorrow, and tomorrow was going to take a toll on him. John called his wife. She wasn't home, and her cell phone went into voice mail mode. He left a quick message telling her he was on his way home and he loved her and the twins.

Next, he left the message for his brother. It might take Paul a few minutes to figure out the message, but John knew he would. He stuffed the last tape deep in his front pants pocket so it wouldn't fall out.

A few minutes later John stepped out into the brisk fall air. The breeze off Lake Michigan dropped the temperature below sixty degrees. He found it refreshing. It helped to clear his head as he walked toward the train.

As he crossed under the 'L' tracks, he felt the pressure of a hard object against his back. His heart pounded. He tried to turn to see who was responsible, but the object was shoved harder into him.

"Keep walking if you want your family to live. Turn into the self-parking garage and go up the stairs to your right," a deep voice spoke softly in his ear.

John froze with fear. Only the thought of his family's' safety kept him from collapsing right there. He entered the stairwell and was almost to the second level when he felt the cold metal muzzle press into his neck. John's last thought was how sorry he was for the pain this would bring to his family. In the next second a bullet entered the base of his skull and blew out his trachea.

Chapter 38

"O'Shaunessy, Miller, in my office now," Captain Ramos yelled as he passed through the squad room.

"What do you think he wants?" Jack asked, staring directly at Patrick.

"I don't know, but we best get in there now," said Patrick as he swallowed a gulp of coffee and stood. "Let's go, Jack."

With a few quick strides, Patrick entered the captain's office first. "Is there something we can do for you, Captain?"

Captain Ramos pulled some photos from an envelope and handed them to Patrick. "A John Gimble was shot to death in a parking stairwell last night. O'Shaunessy, your business card was found in his jacket pocket. Is there anything I should know about this?"

Patrick looked at the photos and passed them to Jack. Was their inquiry responsible for Gimble's death? He didn't want to think so. "Captain, we spoke with Mr. Gimble in his office late Friday afternoon. This was in regards to some high credit card bill of Sarah Morgan's which seemed to be mysteriously paid off. Mr. Gimble told us there was no way to trace the payments. The credit card bill from his bank was her highest debt."

"And you believed him?" Captain Ramos took a seat at his desk.

"No, but we didn't have a subpoena," Jack answered. "We've spent the day collecting information regarding the matter."

"O'Shaunessy, what's your take on this?" Captain Ramos asked.

"He's hiding something. I'm not sure what, but it's connected to Sarah Morgan."

"Perhaps that something got him killed. Head over to the morgue and see if Claire has any answers for you and keep me posted."

"Yes, Captain," Patrick said as he and Jack returned to their desks.

"What made him say Claire's name?" Jack asked.

Patrick looked at his partner and shook his head. "He

probably asked for Claire to do the autopsy."

"But, why?" Jack remarked.

"Because the Captain knows Claire is like a starving dog with a bone; she won't give up until she has the answer."

***

Armed with a large cappuccino and a cranberry scone, Claire checked the schedule for the day. Her first case was a male gunshot victim found in a self-parking structure stairwell at six last night. Claire was paging Ian, her favorite tech, when Patrick and Jack walked in.

"From the look on your face I'm guessing this is not a social call. Hi Jack." Claire worked on her cappuccino.

Jack nodded in return.

"Hi, Sis. We're here to discuss the gunshot victim found last night in a stairwell." Patrick grabbed his usual chair. "I think this case is connected to Sarah."

"You're kidding me? I thought this was a suspected robbery gone bad?"

Jack leaned against the doorframe with his arms crossed. "Normally, you'd be right. The problem is Patrick and I stopped by Monroe Trust and Savings late Friday afternoon. Your gunshot victim, John Gimble, is head of the credit card division. We approached him regarding the missing person's report on Sarah. Finch was able to provide us with her credit card transactions, and the report led us to him. I just don't buy the robbery gone bad theory."

Claire opened the John Gimble file. "What did Gimble say about Sarah?"

"Nothing. We didn't mention Sarah was dead. We inquired about tracing the payee on her accounts. Gimble said it wasn't possible. It was already late Friday afternoon so we didn't take time to get a subpoena before we left. The plan was to return Monday or Tuesday with the subpoena. Jack and I are hoping you'll find a connection between Gimble and Sarah."

Claire took another swallow. She had the connection they were looking for. Dr. Rothschild told her to bring the latest copy of her credit card bill with her on her first scheduled donation date. Claire couldn't risk telling Patrick and Jack anything until she had the proof against Dr. Rothschild for what he had done to Sarah and Kelly. All she needed was one to two days and she would have the evidence for them to arrest Dr. Rothschild.

Patrick hung his head. "I feel in some way responsible for Gimble's death. If I hadn't gone to Gimble with the list of transactions, he'd probably be alive. He left behind a wife and twins."

"There is no way you could have prevented Gimble's death, Patrick. Jack, you tell him." Claire hated to see Patrick in such distress.

Jack uncrossed his arms and shoved his hands in his pants pockets as he stood up straight. "There isn't anything you could say to Patrick I haven't already said to him. We have no proof our visit to Gimble's office last Friday caused this. What we know about Sarah's credit card debts makes us automatically connect the dots in that direction."

"So this could be a random act of violence, a robbery," Claire said. "How did the police identify our victim as John Gimble?"

Patrick stretched the kinks out of his neck. "He didn't have a briefcase or a wallet in his pants pocket. However, in the inside breast pocket the responding patrolmen found his business card with mine. Sgt. Perchowski was at the scene, and he called the bank. Gimble's secretary gave a description of him, and it matched. Perchowski took a photo over to the bank, and she made the official identification."

"As I told Patrick before, this could have absolutely nothing to do with our case. Maybe Gimble was into something else, or this simply was a robbery gone bad."

"I guess we'll have to see what John Gimble's body can tell us. I have to change into scrubs." Claire tossed her empty paper cup away. "You two know the way. We're in the same autopsy room as before."

Claire's phone rang. "Hi, Ian. Detectives O'Shaunessy and Miller are joining us again. I'll be in shortly. Thanks."

***

Claire was already in scrubs and protective gear when Patrick and Jack entered dressed in the disposable gowns. A whiff of Vicks followed Jack to the other side of the exam table.

Claire noticed Patrick grabbed a stool by the work counter instead of hugging the back wall of the room. She was glad to see her brother was a little more comfortable attending this autopsy. He didn't have to enjoy them, but it would be better if they wouldn't take such a toll on him.

Since her first day in medical school, Claire had been fascinated with the concept of having an inside view of the body. Several of her friends were ready to give up medical school because they had to dissect a human body. Eventually they came around. In the meantime, Claire had more time to investigate what lay beneath the skin, the body's largest organ, in spite of what her male lab partner claimed.

Claire may have joked that she liked to cut up dead people, but she really thought of the classic 'Y' incision as the door to the thoracic and abdominal cavities. Most of her gunshot victims had a bullet or two take a ride through the chest wall, ricochet off a rib and high tail it down into the abdominal cavity. There the bullets would nick a section of bowel before escaping out of the body. Sometimes the bullet would lodge in the hipbone.

Stabbings were different. The objects used were thrust into the body before being yanked out. The variety of objects used for stabbing was endless.

But these weren't the only causes of death behind the 'Y' incision. Not every death was a murder. However, every death required explanation. Behind the incision was the private world of each human being. A soul may have left, but the body had been its home until life ended.

Claire realized that just because someone's body lay on her steel table did not mean they gave permission for her to invade their privacy. There were laws written to find the answers that must be sought. Claire had agreed to uphold these laws and find the truth for each one of her patients. She would do this with dignity and respect.

After adjusting her headset, she began dictating the routine information for the case. "John Gimble, a forty-eight- year old male Caucasian, is 69 inches tall. He suffered a gunshot wound to the right side of the back of his neck. Exit wound is visible to the front left side of the neck. Victim appears well nourished and dressed in a suit."

Claire began examining the head and neck area. "Ian, please take photos from several angles on the exit wound. When you're done, we'll roll him over for the entrance wound."

"It will take just a minute," Ian said. "I pulled up the cervical spine x-rays on the screen."

Both Patrick and Jack followed her to the computer. Claire pointed out the findings. "You can see the bullet damage. The bullet appears to have entered from just right of the center of the spine at C6 and traveled slightly upwards through the trachea and exited to the left of the center of the neck. The shooter was probably a step below Mr. Gimble and most likely taller, or the exit wound would be higher on the front side of the neck."

"Dr. O'Shaunessy, I've completed the photos of the exit wound," said Ian.

"Thanks, Ian. Would you help me turn the victim to his left side?"

Jack had followed her and was next to Claire at the table. "Can I offer a hand?"

"That would be great. Grab some gloves first." She noticed Patrick had approached the table to help and took a pair Jack held out to him. "Okay on the count of three we'll turn him to his left side. One, two, three," Claire called out.

Claire repositioned the head block under the victim's head. Carefully, she undid the victim's tie then walked around to the back of the head. "It looks like a classic hard contact wound on the neck."

Patrick looked at the circular indentation of the entrance wound.

"Notice the seared and blackened edges. The muzzle flame released when the gun was fired. The material exits the muzzle and goes beneath the skin, due to the tight seal against the skin, causing a larger and irregular exit wound. The irregular edges were due to a deformed bullet."

Jack took his turn to view the wounds. "I hear the bullet was not recovered."

"That's correct. I assume this means the shooter thought to take it with him. He must be very cold and calculating to make sure the evidence wasn't left behind," Claire said. "He's probably killed before. This was business, not personal. Mr. Gimble didn't struggle. Perhaps the shooter threatened him. If you look at Mr. Gimble's suit jacket, there aren't any tears or wrinkled areas from being grabbed. The shooter had complete control over him with minimal physical handling. The few abrasions and hematomas on Gimble's face are a result of his face hitting the stairs."

Ian shot a set of photos of the entrance wound. "Should we

start to undress him?" he asked.

"Yes," Claire responded. "We'll start with his jacket and shirt since we have him on his side." For the next half hour, everyone helped Claire remove John Gimble's clothes and bag them for trace evidence.

"Claire, I think we've got something here," Patrick called out. With his gloved hand, he carefully shook out the right front pants pocket. A small cassette fell onto the table. "This must be from a recording device."

"Don't touch it," Claire stated. She inserted a hemostat in the center of one of the reels, picked it up and dropped the tape into the evidence bag. "Ian, please take this over to finger printing. When they are finished with it there, have them send it upstairs to Bruce. I'll give Bruce a heads-up. The tape looks in good condition. Bruce should be able to get a recording for us. Who knows if this tape is even related to the case?"

"Sis, I feel like I just found the prize in the box of Cracker Jack. If it is, I bet the killer didn't realize Gimble had it in the pocket he was lying on."

Claire smiled. Patrick was handling this autopsy much better than Dr. Parks' case. Of course, Mr. Gimble was found shortly after he was shot. Dr. Parks was discovered several days after the wild life had been snacking on him.

"Okay, I'm going to finish the external exam and take the fingerprints of our victim while Ian runs the tape over to the fingerprint department."

Claire methodically checked the body from head-to-toe for any other trace evidence. When she was certain there was nothing more to find, she clipped Gimble's fingernails and took a full set of prints. Ian returned to help her wash the body and repeat photographs of the entrance and exit wounds.

"I don't think I'm going to find anything different on the internal exam. The neck dissection should show exactly what we suspect from the external exam. If anything shows up differently I can call you." She looked up at Patrick.

Jack's cell phone rang. "Detective Miller." After a moment he hung up. "Captain Ramos sent a squad to pick up Gimble's brother. Apparently, John left more tapes and information. John must have felt threatened because he left a message on his brother's voice mail where they were hidden."

"Thanks, Sis. I'd give you a hug for all your efforts but you need to change your perfume first." Patrick threw her a salute as he and Jack headed out the door.

"Ian, I think we've been stood up." Claire picked up the scalpel. With precision, she made the 'Y' incision, the door to John Gimble's body.

Chapter 39

Captain Ramos stood outside the interview room. "Paul Gimble is pretty shook up about his brother's death. He said his brother, John, instructed him to bring an envelope to the police if anything happened to him."

"Do you believe his story?" asked Jack.

"The guy is upset. Let me know what you find out." Captain Ramos walked down the hallway towards his office.

Jack opened the door and entered the drab interview room. The only furnishings were the table with a chipped edge and three metal chairs. Paul Gimble barely looked up when Jack and Patrick stepped inside. His eyes were red and puffy.

"Good morning, Mr. Gimble. This is Detective O'Shaunessy and I'm Detective Miller. We are sorry for your loss," Jack said and extended his hand, before Patrick did the same. Mr. Gimble shook both. "May we call you Paul?" Jack asked as both he and Patrick sat across from him.

"Yes, that would be fine," Paul responded.

"We are investigating your brother John's death. We understand John left a message on your voice mail Monday directing you to a package he had hidden."

"Yes. I was out of town all weekend at a tool and die convention. When I arrived home Monday evening, there were two messages for me. The first was from John with this cryptic message. The next call was from John's wife. She had been visited by the police regarding John's death."

"What did John say?" Patrick had his pocket notebook out.

"You should know John and I are totally different." Paul clutched the large brown envelope in his hands. "He would prefer to read a book on the Civil War while I'm happiest at my tool bench. When John and his wife built their home, the builder included a workbench in his garage. I always teased John that the builder could have skipped the workbench and saved him some money. In the message, John told me if anything should happen to him, I should look in the one place he never would use. That's how I knew where to look."

"The workbench," Jack finished for Paul.

"Yes. I found this envelope stuck underneath the top of the workbench and behind a box. I opened it and read his letter." Paul handed the envelope over to Jack.

Jack read the outside of the envelope, "For Paul." Next, he pulled out several sheets of paper. The first sheet was a letter addressed to his brother. The contents of the letter were as Paul had said, *"If anything happens to me, take this envelope to the police."*

The next sheet of paper was a letter to John's wife and kids. The following sheets listed names, account numbers, dates of payments to the bank and collection agencies. The last piece explained his involvement with Dr. Arthur Rothschild. The final proof was the cassettes, the recorded conversations between John and Dr. Rothschild.

"I knew Dr. Rothschild was a slimy bastard the minute I met him," Patrick said.

Paul pulled out a small tape recorder from his pocket. "I brought this in case you wanted to listen to any of the tapes."

Jack leaned forward and spoke directly into his eyes. "Have you told anyone about this envelope or its contents?"

"No. No one," Paul said, his eyes widening.

"What about your wife or John's wife?" Jack asked.

"I'm divorced, the curse of being on the road too many hours and not at home. And I didn't tell John's wife. She was already upset, as you would imagine."

"Good," replied Jack. "Do you know how your brother died?"

"The police said he was shot in the neck and died instantly. They found him in a self-pay garage stairwell. This seemed strange because John never drove to work. His office was only a short walk from the train station."

"Did you read anything besides the letter addressed to you?" Jack asked.

"Yes," Paul admitted. "I didn't read the letter to John's family, but I read the rest. This Dr. Rothschild blackmailed my brother. John was always so honest. He was an Eagle Scout. This must have killed John to feel forced into doing what he did."

In more ways than John realized, thought Jack. Jack read the labels on the cassettes. They were dated going back about eleven years. Slowly he began putting them in order. They stopped a few weeks before John was killed. He bet the one Patrick found in John's pants pocket was the last one.

"Paul, I would like to make an inventory list of all the contents for you."

Patrick was already filling out the inventory sheet. "We'll have you sign as soon as I finish."

"Okay," was all he could say.

"Please don't mention this to your sister-in-law until we have had time to go over everything. She has enough to deal with right now, and so does John's children. Also, for your own safety, I encourage you not to mention this package to anyone. Please don't try to make contact with Dr. Rothschild. We're not sure who he is working with, but killing doesn't seem to bother them. We don't want you to be next," Jack stated.

"We believe your brother's death may be linked to several others," Patrick added. "It will take a little time to go through all of the tapes. We're hoping to be able to make an arrest soon. Can we rely on you to maintain silence?"

Paul's eyes were as wide as saucers. "What type of operation did my brother get trapped in? Was he involved in murder?"

"At this point, I think he was a victim in a blackmail scheme. We have no knowledge he was aware of the other murders," Jack said. "Our investigation is far from over. If John was the type of man you said he was, then he probably was a victim. Most likely, he was murdered to prevent the information you gave us from coming to our attention. We will have to go over every tape, but keep in mind, John has been preparing for this moment for a long time. These tapes go back at least eleven years. Let's hope the information John left for us will clear his name for you and his family."

Patrick's phone rang. He read the number. "Excuse me, but I have to take this call," he said as he left the room.

Paul got up and stretched his legs. "I can't believe this happened. I can't believe this has been going on for years, or that John never confided in me. Thank heavens our parents are gone. This would have destroyed them." He stopped and held on to the back of the metal chair. "What should I do now?"

Jack took the lead. "Go visit your brother's family. They need your support. And, you can make plans for John's services. His body should be released in a couple of days. Please keep this information to yourself. Should it fall into the wrong hands, we might not be able to catch the people responsible."

Patrick re-entered the interview room.

Paul reached over the table and shook Jack and Patrick's hands. "You have my word. Thank you."

"Detective O'Shaunessy or I will personally keep you abreast of the situation. Thank you for understanding the position we're in." Jack showed Paul where to sign on the inventory list and gave him a copy. He opened the door, and they said goodbye.

"What do you think?" Jack asked Patrick after Paul had left.

"My guess is he's tired, scared, depressed and in shock. How would you feel? He came home exhausted from a business trip and found the brother he admired dead and caught up in a blackmail scam. What a shitty way to end a grueling business trip. By the way, Dave called."

"What did he have to say?" Jack asked.

"Gladys and her husband, Hank, found the estate. The entrance wasn't marked and difficult to see. She researched the ownership through county land records. A small corporation out of Chicago owns the property. Gladys has been digging through the paperwork to see if she can connect it to Rothschild."

"Well, that sounds promising," answered Jack.

"While Gladys and Hank were pulling a bird watching stunt, they discovered cameras up in the trees and a heavy gate set in from the edge of the woods. Then the gate opened and our friend, Edwards, drove out in his Navigator. Gladys said the SUV was sporting Missouri license plates."

"Let me guess, the plates were stolen."

"Jack, my boy, you are learning fast. Dave has his deputies checking for all possible entrances into the estate. He also has the place under surveillance and had a chopper fly over once for pictures. Edwards can't leave without being followed."

"Let's update Captain Ramos and listen to the last few tapes. Maybe he can put a rush on the remaining tapes so they get transcribed before Christmas," Jack said. "Afterwards, I need to run an errand."

Patrick looked at Jack slightly puzzled. "What's up?"

"I contacted the Chicago Marathon race director and explained the situation. He has a couple tee shirts for Dr. Parks' sons. Charlie Barron said he would get the shirts to them."

"That's a nice touch. Perhaps this will help his sons believe their dad had cleaned up his life and was trying to get healthy."

"Maybe…"

Chapter 40

Patrick called Claire on his cell phone. "Hey, Sis, is there any word from your friend Bruce on the tape we found in Gimble's pants pocket?"

"Yes. He said the tape was in good condition."

"Could you get Bruce to make us a copy?" Patrick briefly explained his and Jack's meeting with John's brother.

"You have eleven years' worth of tapes? That's incredible. I'll call Bruce now. When can you swing by and pick it up?"

"Would an hour be okay?" asked Patrick.

"I'll call you back if it's not," answered Claire.

"Thanks."

Claire stared at the stack of case files she needed to complete. Where to start? Bruce.

She called Bruce and was able to arrange to have the tape ready for Patrick. The stack in front of her was the same height as before. How she hated all this paper work. "Okay Claire," she said to herself, "settle down and clear your desk." But even a promise to herself that she would deserve a cappuccino after work if the pile was completed before she went home wasn't working.

She opened the chart on the top of the file when her phone rang again. Frankie's cell number appeared on her caller ID. For a moment, she stopped breathing.

"Hey Gorgeous, I'm headed to the store. What do you want for dinner?"

"Frankie, don't scare me. Is Kelly all right?"

"Of course she is. I told you no one would be able to penetrate my perimeter. Now I need an answer about dinner."

"Sorry, what was your question?" Claire asked.

"Hey, are you okay?"

"I'm fine. It's crazy around here, that's all. How about hamburgers on the grill? I'm sure there's gas in the tank out on the balcony. Who's staying with Kelly?"

"Would Frankie leave Kelly stranded? I've got my brother Vince on his way up. Business is slow this week, so dad can spare him." She knew Frankie's family owned a car repair service.

"Vince is more of a ladies man than you. Will she be safe?" Claire couldn't make up her mind which of the four Biaggi brothers was the most dangerous when it came to the ladies.

"I have his word. What time do you think you'll be home?"

"I'm trying for six, but I'm drowning in paper work. If I don't make it on time, go ahead and eat."

"Okay, but I'm counting on seeing you at six."

"Bye Frankie."

Claire tried to focus on the charts, but everything else invaded her brain. It was Tuesday, and she wasn't sure how much longer she could keep Kelly cooped up in her apartment. At least Vince would provide a nice alternative to Frankie. Claire knew Frankie could have sent Vince to the store, but he probably needed to stretch his legs and check his backup. Frankie never left anything up to anyone else. He always checked and double-checked. And Vince would follow Frankie's orders to a 'T'.

The issue was Kelly. She wanted to go home, but understood the situation. Kelly asked her mother to pack a weekend bag for her and drop it off at Jimbo's for Frankie to bring over. She talked with her parents several times a day, but the separation from them was wearing on her. Hopefully, this would be over soon, if for no other reason than Claire was gaining weight from all of Frankie's cooking.

Claire finished the first chart and reached for the second one when her personal cell phone rang. The caller ID was blocked. Claire's heart skipped a beat. "Hello," she answered.

"Hello," the person on the other end of the line answered. "Is this Claire O'Reilly?"

Now Claire's heart really skipped a couple beats. "Yes, this is," she answered as relaxed as possible.

"This is Renata from Dr. Rothschild's office calling."

"Oh, he told me to expect your call." Claire tried to inject as much warmth into her response as possible while a sick feeling rolled in her stomach.

"Dr. Rothschild had a last minute cancellation and was wondering if you would be available this evening. I know this is short notice, so if you can't make it he would understand."

"Tonight would be great. I've nothing planned," Claire answered.

"When was the last time you ate?"

"About ten this morning." Claire knew this was a lie. She just finished her lunch, but with her experience she could calculate what the correct answer should be.

"The timing is perfect. Please don't eat or drink anything but occasional sips of water for the next few hours. If you become nauseous, the anesthesiologist can give you Zofran. Are you allergic to anything?" Renata asked.

"Nope. No allergies."

"Good. Our driver will pick you up in front of the Union Train Station at eight this evening. He'll be driving a black Lincoln Navigator."

Claire already knew what Edwards would be driving. "What is his name?"

"Oh," Renata answered, sounding a little off guard. "Robert."

"I'll be there. Thank you for calling."

"No problem. I'm sure everything will go smoothly for you."

"I've never had a problem before. I'm sure I'll be just fine," Claire lied.

"I'll call you tomorrow to see how you are doing. Goodnight." Renata hung up.

Claire just sat there. Her heart raced. This was actually going to happen. Of course, she could choose not to show up and change her cell phone number, but she thought of all the times Sarah helped her out of scrapes when they were kids. She owed Sarah. And there was Kelly and many other girls who could be Dr. Rothschild's next victim.

Like it or not, she was committed. "Dad," she silently prayed, *"please keep me safe."*

"Here's the copy of the tape you requested."

Startled, Claire jumped.

"Are you okay Claire? I didn't mean to scare you," said Bruce.

"Sorry Bruce. I must have been concentrating and didn't hear you come in. Thanks for making the copy."

"Hope this tape helps to get the bad guys."

"Patrick seems to think it will. Thanks again." Claire took a breath in, held it for a few seconds, and let it out slowly. This was the third time something rattled her in the last hour. *Relax*, she told herself. Patrick would be over soon, and he always picked up on the slightest change in people.

Claire turned her chair so she could see Patrick arrive. Good thing Vince was available to be with Kelly. Soon this would be over, and Kelly could return home.

For a brief moment, Claire thought of one alternative. She could tell Patrick, and after he blew off some steam, she could convince him to let her go. He could put a tracking device under the car's back bumper and follow at a safe distance. He could call Sheriff Wilson for help. Claire was sure Sheriff Wilson would be happy to close his end of the case. However, Captain Ramos would have Patrick's shield for risking the safety of a civilian's life even if it was Claire and she was willing. There was only one answer. Claire was going to have to enter the estate under false pretenses and pray she could get out before it was too late.

Now she was the one who needed a plan, and one which came with a safety net. She couldn't hide a gun in her purse or jacket, so she was going to have to rely on her own wits to get out of this. Her boots! It was the perfect spot, if she wasn't asked to take them off in the presence of staff. Claire grabbed her boots from under her desk and put them on to check for space. She scanned the top of her worktable. She spotted the letter opener sitting in a mug with pens and hemostats.

The letter opener was perfect. It was strong like a screwdriver, and there was enough space to hide it in her boot. The best part was she could stick it down inside her boot without cutting her foot. A straight knife could wound her. She took her boots off and replaced them under the worktable. She left the letter opener inside so she wouldn't forget to take it. She still had room in her remaining boot. She stuffed a straight hemostat in the boot. Like the letter opener, it slid in easily and wouldn't hurt her.

What else did she dare take? She had better write everything down. This was worse than cramming for an exam. Nobody died if she flunked a test. If she forgot something important, well, her mind wasn't going there.

For a moment, Claire wanted to laugh. What would Agent 007 put on his list? Claire was sure he would have a gun at the top of his list, maybe two. As much as a gun would be comforting, it just wasn't going to be possible.

She looked at the clock. She was running out of time. Besides preparing for tonight, she needed to complete these files on her desk today, and Patrick would be over soon. That was the real problem. Patrick. If she could just get past his visit, Claire knew she could get back to business.

"Hi Sis," Patrick called out as he entered her office.

If timing was everything, thought Claire, then Patrick's visit was perfect.

"Hi," said Claire. "Here's the tape you requested." She reached over and handed the tape to Patrick. "Where's Jack?"

"He's in the car. Tell Bruce thanks. Sorry I can't stay, but Jack and I are trying to get through all the tapes."

"I'm floored Gimble had eleven years' worth of tapes." Claire was relieved Patrick's visit would be short.

"I almost forgot to tell you. Do you remember Gladys from Sheriff Wilson's office?"

"She's the one who made the sticky bun cake you liked."

Patrick hid a smile. "Anyway, she researched several sites in LaSalle County, and on Saturday she and her husband disguised as birdwatchers went to check them out. On their third stop they believe they found the place where the clinic might be operating."

Claire leaned forward. "You're kidding me? What did they find?"

"The place had a gate set back off the road in a thick wooded area with cameras up in the trees. But the best part was a black SUV, now with Missouri plates, stopped them. The SUV was driven by none other than our suspect, Edwards."

"Can they go in after Edwards?" Claire couldn't believe they had found Edwards.

"Sheriff Wilson wants to wait until we have listened to the tapes and see if we can't bring down the entire operation along with Edwards and Dr. Rothschild. The land isn't listed in Rothschild's name, but Gladys is still digging.

"However, they located several entrances to the property and he has them under surveillance. I'll keep you posted. Sorry, but I have to run."

"No problem, Patrick. See you later." After Claire was certain Patrick was far down the hall, she breathed, "Yes, I have my safety net." She knew she wasn't out of the woods by any means, but thanks to Gladys, the area was under Sheriff Wilson's radar.

Suddenly, Patrick's information gave Claire the surge of energy she needed. She was focused. She wrote cell phone on her list. It would be an acceptable item, after all everyone carried them. This could double as a camera, too. However, there was one major problem. If the cell phone fell into the wrong hands, the personal information on it could be dangerous for her family and friends.

Quickly Claire copied the phone numbers down on a separate piece of paper. The only two numbers she left on speed dial with no names attached were Frankie's and Patrick's. It pained her to delete all the information. It only took seconds to erase it, and it would take forever to re-enter the numbers.

Next, she would need her Claire O'Reilly ID's Frankie had made for her. Claire would leave her work ID at home along with her wallet. She added bottled water, small flashlight, paper, pen, tissues, small mirror, lipstick and a small hairbrush to her list. All these items could be found in a woman's purse. Nothing anyone would be suspicious about, but any one of them might come in handy.

Claire read the list. Her list was pitiful, but it would have to do. Since Renata hadn't mentioned her credit card bill, she could claim she forgot it or didn't have time to go home for it after work.

This was all good, thought Claire, but it didn't save her tail. Her original plan was to photograph anything which would prove there was an illegal clinic operating on the grounds. Then she would escape out of a window or door and run to Frankie, who would be waiting for her. Thank heavens, Patrick stopped by and told her about the cameras and gate. He didn't mention dogs, so that was a plus. Now her best guess was to stay in the woods and follow the driveway to the main road. Frankie would have to wait there.

Claire rubbed her forehead. Small spurts of pain attacked her. There was only so much she could plan for and the rest was in the hands of fate. In spite of everything, the one thing for sure was the stack of charts in front of her that wasn't getting smaller. After filling her water bottle and taking a couple Ibuprofen, Claire dug in with earnest.

Chapter 41

"Arthur, I'm done. I'm not doing this again for you. You have bled me dry."

"John, I don't believe you are thinking clearly. You will handle this for me. I'm sure your wife..."

"You can stop threatening me."

Patrick turned the tape recorder off. He and Jack had played the tape through a couple of times, and this was the last entry. "Captain Ramos, what do you think?"

"This is incredible. The DA's office sent over the transcriptions for the last eighteen months. Both Dr. Arthur Rothschild and John Gimble use each other's first names. With voice recognition software, I'm sure the DA will be able to prove who's speaking. The last tape confirms John Gimble refused to be part of the blackmail scam any longer. This probably cost John his life. Now we have proof to connect Rothschild to Gimble. We know Edwards posed as Sarah's brother and Rothschild was Sarah's doctor. It shouldn't be long before we tie Edwards to Rothschild."

Patrick exchanged glances with Jack.

"Is there something I don't know?" Captain Ramos asked. "If not, I'm headed home for dinner."

"No, Captain. Patrick and I have been bouncing a couple of ideas around, and it sounds like we might have guessed right." Jack stretched his legs to divert his eyes away from the Captain's.

"Good. Keep me apprised. As soon as we connect the final dots, we'll issue the arrest warrant for Dr. Rothschild, and Sheriff Wilson can do the same for Edwards. I assume Sheriff Wilson and his people are keeping an eye on Edwards and the estate in LaSalle County."

"Yes, that's correct," Patrick answered as Captain Ramos left the room.

"When was the last time you won at poker?" Jack laughed. "Ramos knows we have information we haven't shared. Do you think he is giving us just enough rope to hang ourselves?"

Patrick tapped his pencil on the edge of the desk. He and

Ramos went way back, like to grade school. Their blue-collar families were from the old neighborhood where family and church were the center of people's lives. There was an unspoken code of trust. Ramos might be his captain, but he hadn't forgotten his roots. "Nah, Ramos just wants us to do our best. He's giving us the space to do our jobs."

"And Claire?" Jack looked straight at his partner.

Patrick stopped tapping his pencil. "Ramos grew up with Claire. He knows she can be unpredictable. But as long as Kelly is safe, I know he will have to call us on it, but nothing will go into our personnel jackets."

"Unpredictable, huh? Patrick, she's a loose cannon," Jack said. "I suppose having Kelly as a house guest isn't the worst thing she can do. When was the last time you checked on Kelly?"

"I saw Claire today," Patrick answered. "And as much as you won't like hearing me say this, I trust Frankie. We don't need to check up on Kelly."

"What about Ramos? What's his take on Frankie?"

"Professionally, Ramos would call him a wise guy. Off the record, he would trust Frankie with his mother's life."

"That was some neighborhood."

"Yeah, it was. I'm grateful it lasted through my childhood. Time has changed it. Most of my parents' generation has died, and the young people have moved to the suburbs."

"But you still live there and so do your sisters," said Jack, throwing a stack of folders in his desk drawer before locking it.

"It's still a great place to raise a family. Speaking of family, making it home on time for dinner would put me in Sylvia's good graces. Do you want to join us?" Patrick locked the transcript and tape in his desk.

"Thanks, but you deserve the evening alone with your family."

"You're family."

"Considering the number of dinners I have at your home, you should count me as a tax deduction." Jack grinned.

"Better yet, Sylvia and I are thinking about taking off for a long weekend and having Uncle Jack babysit." Patrick smiled at the idea of Jack keeping his daughters in line and the dog from digging up Sylvia's flowers.

Jack wadded up a piece of paper and threw it at his partner.

Patrick ducked. "Just kidding. Where do you think we should start on the case tomorrow?"

"I hate to say it, but I think it's time to bring Kelly in for an official statement," Jack said. "She's all we have to make the connection. She sent Sarah to Dr. Rothschild, and he had Edwards pick Sarah up for the procedure. That friend of Sheriff Wilson's daughter saw the driver of a black SUV in the cemetery dumping Sarah's body. Gladys and Hank saw Edwards in the SUV in LaSalle County. I would say we are one step away from connecting Edwards to Rothschild."

"I agree. I hate to do it to Kelly, but it's time. She's scared stiff. I'll call Sheriff Wilson tomorrow and see if Gladys was able to track down the owner of the property she saw Edwards on. If it's Rothschild's property, I bet we can get warrants for arrests. Once we have Rothschild and Edwards behind bars, Kelly will feel better and so will I."

Chapter 42

Claire dropped off the completed charts in Dr. Johnson's office for his final review before rushing home. She doubted she would get any sleep tonight. And, the last person she wanted to face tomorrow was Dr. Johnson. He was a great boss, but he expected his pathologists to complete the paperwork as soon as possible.

With everything on her mind, she had fallen behind. Families of the deceased wanted not only their loved one's remains released in a timely fashion, but they needed the death certificate for burial and insurance purposes.

A quick glance at her watch told her it was almost six when she parked her car in the building's underground garage. Frankie was waiting at the apartment door for her.

"Gorgeous, you are almost late. I'd hate to ground you for dinner curfew."

"Is Vince still here?"

"What no 'hi or hello' for your Frankie? All you want to know is if Vince is here? My feelings are crushed. He's flipping burgers on the balcony." Frankie put his hand to his forehead feigning distress.

Claire rolled her eyes at Frankie as she called out to Kelly. "How was your day?"

"Pretty nice, actually." Kelly's smile perked up. "Things are getting more interesting with the arrival of Vince. Frankie tells me he has two more brothers. I was wondering how long I have to stay to be able to meet them all."

"Well, I hope to spring you in a day or two, but I can arrange it so you can still meet the remaining Biaggi brothers."

Vince came in from the balcony with a platter of burgers. "Hi Claire, long time no see. Glad you moved back. Let's eat." He put the platter on the table which was already set and filled with side dishes and condiments.

"Good to see you, too. There's nothing better than burgers just off the grill. Thanks for cooking." Claire checked her watch as she dropped her purse and jacket on the couch. "Kelly, you have no idea how lucky we are to be dining with two of the most desirable men in Chicago."

"Cut the BS, O'Shaunessy, what's up?" Frankie asked, looking at her pointedly.

Frankie knew her too well. He never called her by her last name unless he was demanding answers. "I'll tell you over dinner. I don't have much time."

After he'd served everyone, Frankie hit Claire up for the answer. "Okay, let's have it."

Claire put her finger up to indicate 'just a minute' while she took a bite of her burger. She savored every morsel. "This is outstanding, Vince."

"Thank you," Vince answered as he served himself some of Kelly's potato salad.

"O'Shaunessy, out with it," Frankie demanded, "or I'll take your burger away."

Claire quickly took another bite just in case Frankie was serious. She was amazed how hungry she was. She would have thought the anticipation of tonight's mission would have had the opposite effect on her. "All right, here's the condensed version." Claire shared Patrick's news about Gimble, from his possibly involvement, the tapes, to his death.

After a quick sip of iced tea, Claire continued. "Meanwhile over the weekend, the LaSalle County Sheriff's Office was able to locate the property where they believe the illegal clinic is operating. Two of the sheriff's people pretended to be birdwatchers. They noticed security cameras up in the trees. The place was practically under lock down with a heavy iron gate." Claire stopped to take another bite while she let her friends digest what she had just said.

"Why do I have a feeling there's more?" Frankie helped himself to more chips.

"Hang on, Frankie. While the two birdwatchers were scanning the skies for cameras, the gate opened, and Edwards drove out in his black Lincoln Navigator. He told the birdwatchers to leave."

"They found Edwards?" Kelly exclaimed.

"Yes," answered Claire.

"Did they arrest him?"

"No, not yet." Claire hated telling Kelly this. She knew Kelly didn't understand the semantics of police investigations.

"What do you mean 'no'. How can they let him get away?" Tears formed in Kelly's eyes.

Vince got up and protectively put his hand on her shoulder. "I'm sure they had a good reason."

The way Vince looked directly at Claire told her she better provide a plausible reason, and soon.

"Sheriff Wilson is a good cop. I know he has the place under constant surveillance. Edwards won't get away. My guess is Sheriff Wilson is gathering enough ammunition to be able to obtain a search warrant for the estate. He wants to nail Edwards and the clinic, while at the same time Patrick and Jack will take down Dr. Rothschild. These men are not going to get away with what they did to Sarah."

"Are you sure they won't let Edwards escape?" Kelly wasn't convinced.

"I'm positive, but I need your help." Claire went over to her desk for paper and pencil.

"What do you mean?"

"You were at the estate a number of times. I know you were medicated, but each time you went, subconsciously you retained another scrap of information regarding the layout."

"I can't remember." Kelly shook her head back and forth and tears rolled down her cheeks.

Vince pulled his chair in closer next to Kelly and slid his arm around her shoulders, and then he pushed the dinner plates to the side. "Yes you can. I'll help you."

"Rothschild's office called me today," said Claire. "I'm scheduled to be picked up by Edwards at eight at the Union Train Station tonight."

"What?" Frankie yelled as he dropped his burger just before it met his mouth. "No, you're not going."

Frankie looked like he was going to lock Claire in her bedroom. Why was it all the men in her life reacted that way?

"We don't have another choice. Patrick and Jack need confirmation that Rothschild is operating an illegal clinic. Wilson's office has been researching ownership of the property, but they don't have it positively connected to Rothschild. I have the perfect 'in'. I can take pictures with my cell phone for them."

Kelly sat up and wiped her tears. "Do you need to do anything to get ready?" she asked Claire.

"Yes."

"Then do it while Vince helps me draw a picture for you."

Vince gave her a hug. "That's my girl."

Claire and Frankie exchanged glances. Vince was definitely a mover.

"Gorgeous, I still don't like this. I think we should call Patrick and let the professionals handle this," Frankie stated.

"They can't, Frankie. Rothschild's office took a photocopy of my driver's license. I'd bet any money Edwards has a copy. Either I do this, or Rothschild could get away. They can arrest Edwards for dumping Sarah's body, but we still don't know who killed Sarah, Dr. Parks or John Gimble. I put my money on Edwards for the two men."

"Do you have a plan? What about protection?" Frankie finished the last of his burger.

"I can't take a gun, but I've stuck a letter opener in one of my boots and a hemostat in the other."

"A what? Oh, never mind. Still that's not going to help you," replied Frankie. "I can't let you do this."

"Yes, you can. Frankie, besides having you as my backup, the LaSalle County Sheriff's office has the grounds under surveillance. They will be monitoring Edwards, even if he leaves the estate. Technically, we have help at our fingertips. It'll be okay."

"I still don't like this."

"I know, but I have to do this for Sarah. Try not to get arrested while I'm on the inside."

"Don't you worry; Frankie's got your back."

Claire filled her purse with the items on her list. She wrote down Patrick's cell and home numbers, along with Sheriff Wilson's cell number and gave them all to Frankie. She gave him strict instructions not to call anyone unless he had no other option.

In her bedroom, she dressed in a tee shirt and pulled a dark sweatshirt on. The legs on her jeans covered the tops of her boots. She stopped in front of her bedroom mirror. She stood there for a minute and stared at herself. "How many times did I sneak out with Sarah and not get caught?" she asked herself. "Well, I'm not getting caught this time either."

Back in the living room, she asked Frankie, "Can Vince stay with Kelly?"

"I don't think I could separate the two if I wanted to."

"I want you to drop me off a block from the train station, and I'll walk over. Then, pull around in front as if you were waiting for someone to arrive. After Edwards leaves, you could follow at a safe distance. My guess is he will take the Dan Ryan to Interstate 55, then go west on Interstate 80. I'm not sure which exit he'll use, but Sheriff Wilson said the estate was directly south off Route 178."

"When do I get to race in and rescue you?" Frankie took the last sip of his pop.

"You don't. There's too many cameras in the trees. If they see you, my cover might be blown. I'll come out to you." Claire could feel her pulse racing.

"And how do you plan to do that? It's not like you can just say goodbye and walk out."

"I know that. I'm hoping Kelly can remember a little bit about the layout. If I'm lucky, I'll be able to use my cell phone to photograph equipment, or something, to prove this is an illegal operation and email the pictures to Patrick's cell. I'll get out through a door or window and cut through the woods to your car. If I'm not back in twenty minutes, call Sheriff Wilson and Patrick. Let's see what Kelly has." Claire double-checked her boots and purse to make sure she had everything.

"Claire, I think I remembered enough to help you out." Kelly showed Claire the drawing. "Edwards parks behind the main building. That's the building they will take you to. I vaguely remember a long hallway before I went up a narrow set of stairs."

"That was probably the servants' stairs," noted Claire.

"I think I went in the second door on my right where I was told to change. The room wasn't very large. There was a narrow bed and a chair. I almost forgot. The room didn't have any windows, but there was a set of double doors that must lead outside." Kelly froze.

"Kelly, you're safe. It's okay." Vince reassured her.

"Sorry. Depending on how drugged I was, someone might stay with me before I was walked down to the procedure room."

"Was that on the same floor?" Claire asked.

"The procedure room must have been because I don't remember walking down or up stairs until it was time to leave. My drawing isn't very good." Kelly handed the picture over to Claire.

"It's fine. You told me the basic layout." Claire looked at her watch. It was time to go. "Take good care of Kelly for me, Vince."

"I intend to."

Claire wondered just how good of care Vince had in mind, but she couldn't think about it now. "Frankie, let's go."

Frankie came out of the kitchen on his cell. He hung up and said goodbye to Vince and Kelly.

"Do you want to take my car?" Claire asked.

"Gorgeous, no offense, but Edwards could spot your old Taurus a mile away. It's practically an antique."

"That's your fault. You and your dad simply service it too well. But what car are we taking?"

"We'll know when we get downstairs," answered Frankie.

Sure enough, a car was waiting outside in the drive. The doorman handed Frankie the keys as if it was their usual routine. The dark Ford Explorer was probably about five years old, but nothing about it said 'notice me'. Claire decided not to ask how the Explorer got there.

Chapter 43

Frankie didn't say a word on the ride to the train station. What could he say? Nothing short of tying Claire up was going to stop her. Her professional license may read M.D., but Frankie was convinced under her skin there was a police shield over her heart. There was just too much police blood in her veins. And he didn't like her plan.

While Claire was going over Kelly's drawing of the estate and floor plan, Frankie had called in backup, his brother Sol. This way, Edwards wouldn't notice him as the only car following him. The other vehicle was a Ford pick-up with a V-8 engine and a reinforced front bumper. He didn't ask, but he knew his brother would have more than a letter opener for protection. Frankie had his gun wrapped in a rag under his seat.

"You can pull over here," Claire directed.

"How much time do you have?" Frankie asked.

"About ten minutes."

"You can change your mind, you know." Frankie squeezed her left shoulder.

"Sarah was my best friend growing up. Somewhere along the way, life separated us. I feel partially responsible for her death. I should've been a better friend. I have to do this for her. You loved her, Frankie. You must want the bad guys to pay. I'll be all right. I've got you for backup, and I know you won't let anything happen to me." Claire bent over and kissed Frankie on the cheek then she was out of the Explorer.

"You better believe it Gorgeous."

***

Frankie watched Claire disappear around the corner of Union Train Station. He would give her a minute lead-time and that was all. He didn't trust Edwards. He may be there already, and Frankie wanted to see which vehicle Claire got into.

Frankie checked the clock on the dashboard. Two minutes had passed since Claire got out of his Explorer. Time to go, he thought.

He used all of his self-control to keep from peeling out and cutting the corner. He couldn't risk calling anyone's attention to him, especially Edwards or the cops.

He spotted Claire standing out front the second he came around the corner. Frankie pulled past her and parked. He turned his parking blinkers on and acted as if he was waiting for someone to come out of the station. He could see Claire in his right front side mirror. She didn't look his way. Good girl, he thought.

Five minutes later a black Lincoln Navigator pulled up a short distance behind him. Frankie could feel his blood pumping.

The SUV hit the horn once, and Claire walked over to the vehicle. Frankie was sure his heart would jump out of his body. This was a bad plan. Before he could get out of his Explorer to stop Claire, she got in the backseat of Edwards' car and they pulled into traffic.

A Ford pick-up pulled up behind his Explorer. Frankie followed, focused on the SUV as it headed for the expressway.

Claire had guessed right; the SUV turned south onto the Kennedy which ran into the Dan Ryan. Frankie knew Claire was in over her head. He didn't care what he had promised her, he was calling Patrick now before things got out of hand.

Frankie hit speed dial for Patrick's number. He had added Patrick's and Sheriff Wilson's numbers while Claire was going over the floor plans with Kelly. The number rang twice before Patrick answered.

"Hello, is that you Frankie?" Patrick asked.

"Patrick, Claire's in trouble." Frankie kept his eyes glued to the black SUV several cars ahead of him.

"What do you mean, Claire's in trouble?"

"She saw that Dr. Rothschild last Friday, and his office called for her to donate eggs tonight." His brother was right on the Lincoln's tail.

"She did what? Where is she now?" Patrick yelled.

"Claire's in Edward's SUV, a couple cars in front of me. We're headed south on the Dan Ryan. He just pulled into the lane for the St. Louis exit. I'm on him."

"Shit, when did she get this hare-brained idea? What does she plan to do?"

"Well, I think Claire plans to get inside this estate pretending to be an egg donor, take a couple pictures, then get out a door or window, sneak through the woods and meet me just south of the driveway."

"Why in the hell did you let her do this, Frankie?" Patrick was still yelling.

"Look Patrick, she didn't want me to even call you, but I made that decision. Are you goin' help or not?" Frankie made the turn for the St. Louis exit. Now Sol was behind him.

"Okay, can you stay on their tail?"

"Yep, plus I have backup behind me."

"Who's the backup?"

"My brother Sol, okay?" Frankie was becoming annoyed. He should have stopped Claire before she tried this crazy notion of hers.

"Good. My guess is Edwards will take Interstate 80 next. I'll call Sheriff Wilson out in LaSalle County. He has surveillance on the estate, so at least we know where Edwards should be taking Claire. He probably had coverage in case Edwards left the estate. For now, you keep with Claire's plan and I'll make sure Sheriff Wilson's people let you be. I have to call my Captain, then my partner and I'll be on the way. Do you have the sheriff's number?"

"Right on speed dial, next to yours. Claire gave it to me."

"Well at least three of her brain cells are working. Call me if anything changes, you understand? And where's Kelly?"

"My brother Vince is with her at Claire's."

Patrick disconnected.

Well Patrick hadn't changed much. He still had that take-charge attitude, and he still couldn't control Claire. But who could?

He phoned Sol, and asked him to take the lead until they took the Interstate 80 west ramp. No sense drawing Edwards' attention to him.

Frankie could make out the Navigator's taillights in the distance. Edwards was driving just below the speed limit to stay under the police radar. Sol's Ford pick-up kept a half a dozen car lengths behind Edwards while providing good cover for Frankie. By the time they passed Joliet, the only lighting was by exits and the skies were pitch-black.

Frankie allowed himself to relax. He couldn't do anything for Claire at the moment but follow. He was going to need all the energy he had to save her. "Gorgeous, I've got you in my sight. Nothing is going to happen," he prayed.

Chapter 44

Patrick hadn't even pulled into his driveway when Frankie called. He immediately turned around and headed for the station. He called Sylvia and explained there was an emergency, and he would be out very late. He didn't tell her that it was Claire. He couldn't. Next, he called Jack.

"I'm going to wring her neck when I get my hands on her," Jack said.

"Get in line," responded Patrick.

"Okay, what do you want me to do?" Jack asked.

"I'll make the call to Captain Ramos and fill him in. We need to make sure Rothschild doesn't flee. Could you call Dave Wilson and fill him in? Ask him to have his people leave Frankie and his brother Sol alone for now. Frankie is in an Explorer, and Sol is driving a Ford pick-up. I'll meet you at the station, and by the way, thanks."

"Hey, it's a nice night for a drive in the country. I'll call Dave. I'm about five minutes from the station." Jack hung up.

Patrick didn't know if he should say the Act of Contrition or do a lap around the beads before he called Captain Ramos. Ramos was going to be pissed, and he had every right to be. Hell, Patrick was already there. Damn it, he thought when Claire went into the medical field he had her in a safe place. In reality, Claire's profession as a forensic pathologist only made the situation worse. Any injustice inflicted on her patients became her personal war. But this was a whole different game, and if Claire lost, she could end up dead.

Patrick punched in the Captain's number.

"This is Captain Ramos."

"Captain, this is O'Shaunessy and I have a problem." For the next several minutes Patrick explained to the Captain what had taken place and requested surveillance for Rothschild. Then he proceeded to fill the Captain in on Claire's plan and all the players involved. He told the Captain that Jack was notifying Sheriff Wilson who already had surveillance on the property because his people had spotted Edwards there.

"Captain, I can't tell you how sorry I am for Claire's interference. Her hare-brained scheme just might get us the proof we need to nail Rothschild's operation."

"If she doesn't get herself killed first," said Ramos. "Patrick, I know you didn't encourage her. I'll have a stiff talk with her after the case is closed. I just hope she doesn't mess anything up for the DA. I'll send a car over to keep an eye on Rothschild. You and Jack head out to LaSalle County, and *please* be careful. If this goes down bad, the press will have a field day. I should have the State Police pull Edwards' car over and get Claire out," Captain Ramos stated. "Would you like me to do that?"

Patrick thought a moment. "I would like to say 'yes' to your offer, but if there is a chance we could close down the operation, then I think we're going to have to let Claire give this a try. I know she'll never go through with donating eggs."

"Okay, keep me informed."

"Thank you Captain." Patrick couldn't believe the Captain had given him this much leeway. But he was smart enough to know that if this went down bad or any of the good guys got hurt, there would be a price to pay. Ramos may be from the old neighborhood, but he only could stick his neck out so far.

Patrick pulled into the station on two wheels, then raced inside. Jack was already strapping an extra gun to his lower leg. Besides his shoulder holster, Jack had another weapon on his desk. "Jack, we're going after Claire, not the mafia."

Jack checked his revolver. "I have a feeling it would be easier to bring in the mafia than Claire."

"You got that right. I cleared this with the Captain. What about Dave?" Patrick checked his weapons and removed an extra clip of ammunition from his desk.

"Dave said he has a tail on Edwards, so he is aware Edwards had picked up another young woman at the train station. He just didn't know it was Claire. We're to call him when we get off Interstate 80 on to Route 178 south. He'll give us directions from there. In the meantime, he'll contact his people about the situation. That includes Frankie. Are you ready?" Jack slid the third weapon in his waistband.

"Yeah, we better get going. Once we're on the road I want to check in with Frankie and see how far they are." Patrick dropped the extra clip in his pocket.

"I'm driving. You're too close to the situation," Jack stated. "Because they have at least a thirty minute head start, we're going lights and sirens if we have to."

"Okay, let's roll," said Patrick. His mind was distracted. He would never forgive himself if anything happened to Claire.

Chapter 45

So far, everything Kelly had told Claire was accurate. Once she was in the back seat of the SUV, she noticed all the car doors locked. She wondered if Edwards had done this on purpose so she couldn't change her mind. On the seat beside her lay a blanket, pillow and an envelope with her name, Claire O'Reilly, printed across it.

There was a window separating the front seat from the back, like the dividers in cabs. Kelly hadn't mentioned the window. The window opened electronically. Edwards, or Robert as Renata had called him, spoke to her.

"Ms. O'Reilly, in the envelope is the medication the doctor told you about. You are to take it now. There is a water bottle in the pouch behind my seat if you need to wash the pill down. Please feel free to make yourself comfortable with the blanket and pillow."

"Thank you. I just opened a water bottle before you picked me up. But the blanket and pillow look inviting." Claire already knew from Kelly that Edwards would watch her take the pill and ask for the envelope back. She opened the envelope and shook the Valium into her left palm. In between her left fingers was the hidden aspirin. She picked up the aspirin and swallowed it, leaving the Valium in the aspirin's place. Claire then removed her water bottle from her bag with her left hand, allowing the Valium to fall to the bottom. She didn't trust that something might have been added to the water Edwards offered. She was grateful he didn't give her a hard time about drinking her own bottle.

"I'll take the envelope for you," Edwards offered.

"Why thank you." Claire smiled and handed him the envelope. "I had a long day. I think I will take a nap." Claire positioned herself so Edwards couldn't see her face in his rear view mirror. She prayed he didn't have any hidden cameras in the back. She faced out the right passenger's side so she could read the road signs.

Claire felt the SUV pull to the right not long after they were on the Dan Ryan. She barely opened her eyelashes, but she could see the sign for St. Louis. Now she had to stay awake for the rest of the ride. She tried to gage the speed of the SUV. The ride was smooth. Edwards was watching his speed, Claire thought. Good, that would make it easier for Frankie to follow.

She had turned the face of her watch to the inside of her wrist, but it was too dark in the back seat with the tinted windows to read it. Once they had passed the last vestiges of Chicago's sprawling suburbs with all the lights, Claire realized how truly dark the sky was away from the city. She needed to be very observant once they arrived at the estate, or she could get herself totally turned around, and she might end up walking away from Frankie instead of towards him.

Why didn't she look at a map or go on-line to Google Earth just to familiarize herself more with LaSalle County? Being there just once recently wasn't enough.

About the only thing Claire did remember about LaSalle County was that Ottawa, the County Seat, was almost in the center with Starved Rock State Park to the west. The Illinois River met with the Fox River and combined; they cut the town of Ottawa in half and then traveled along the north side of Starved Rock. *Well, that was a nice geography lesson*, thought Claire, but in the dark how was that going to help her? She would have to watch her position as they approached the estate without Edwards realizing what she was doing.

Claire almost dozed off when she felt the car pull to the right. Bright lights flashed everywhere as trucks whizzed by. The bold green sign for Iowa flashed through her eyelashes. Edwards must have turned on to Interstate 80. She said a silent prayer that Frankie had made the turn. Even though Claire had told Frankie she expected this would be the route, she worried that a truck would block his view. If he should miss the turn off, Frankie would be able to find his way back to the turn. The real question was would he be able to catch up with Edwards.

She guessed that ten minutes had passed when Edwards picked up speed. He probably knew where the State Troopers parked. Claire wanted to look out the back to make sure Frankie was there, but it was too risky. This whole plan was a crapshoot at best, but it was the only one she had. If Frankie had to call Patrick for help, she was dead meat. Patrick had raised Claire and her sisters after their dad died. She knew better than to put additional stress on him. Besides the fact that Patrick needed to take better care of himself, she could be compromising his position with the police department. Claire promised herself that if she got out of this situation alive, she was going to stay on the straight and narrow and stop adding more gray hairs to Patrick's head.

Suddenly Claire felt the SUV slow down and exit the expressway. At the top of the ramp she felt Edwards turn to the left as she slid slightly towards the passenger door. What little light she could see at the exit immediately vanished. Edwards obviously was familiar with the roads as he picked up speed. A short time later, he slowed down for a few quick turns in Utica. Claire was able to read her watch under the dim streetlights. They had been on the road ninety minutes. She prayed Frankie was close by.

Even though the estate was under surveillance, she suspected the deputies had no idea what was taking place.

Abruptly Edwards came to a stop before turning on to a rough country road. In spite of the darkness, Claire could see open fields on either side of the SUV before entering a heavily wooded area. Next, he pulled to a stop. Claire listened to the sound of metal grating against metal. The gates were opening.

A moment later, Edwards parked the vehicle in a dimly lit area. Claire heard the divider between the seats open.

"Ms. O'Reilly, we're here," he announced.

Claire sat up and rubbed her eyes. "Are we here already?" The passenger door opened, and Edwards offered to help her out. He grabbed her by the elbow as she stumbled on purpose to give him the illusion that the medication was working.

Chapter 46

Jack was grateful traffic on the Dan Ryan was low. There was only a handful of cars traveling south with a dozen trucks at this time of the night. He was able to use only the police lights to move around traffic. In no time, at all, he was exiting at the St. Louis entrance to Interstate 55. He didn't want to catch up to Frankie, but lag behind him enough so Edwards wouldn't see several sets of car lights on his tail. He overheard Patrick talking with Frankie.

"Where are they?" Jack asked Patrick as soon as he had hung up.

"They're approaching Interstate 80." Patrick held onto the door armrest.

"I'd expect them to be on 80 by now," Jack replied.

"Frankie figured Edwards has been driving close to the speed limit on purpose to stay below the state trooper radar. That might be our break to catch up to them."

"We can't catch up to Edwards, or he'll notice. We need to keep a safe distance back. Remember, he still has Claire. We don't want this to turn out like the Alamo." Jack passed the few cars on the expressway.

"What if this goes down bad?" Patrick asked.

"Claire's a tough woman. We should probably feel sorry for Edwards." Jack actually thought that there was a chance Edwards might come out on the short side.

"I know Frankie and his brother Sol will have weapons, but Frankie said Claire only had a letter opener and a hemostat on her."

"How many brothers does this character Frankie have?" Jack felt like there was an invasion of Biaggi brothers.

"Sol is a year older than Frankie. Vince is two years younger and Joey is in high school. All four were cut from the same mold. Are you worried about the competition?"

"What competition?"

"Man, you are asking for trouble. You've got the hots for Claire."

"I don't have any such thing for Claire." Jack felt the tips of his ears go red. Thank heavens Patrick couldn't see them in the dark. "All I see when I look at Claire is a warning sign, beware dangerous curve ahead." But he still didn't like this Frankie character. He seemed too slick, too smooth, too familiar with Claire, and Jack definitely wasn't comfortable with that. Frankie sounded like a street thug. Claire was too refined. No, that wasn't the right word.

Well, she was too educated for Frankie. He probably thought all he had to do was snap his Italian fingers, and the women would drop at his feet. After this was over, Jack would make sure Frankie returned to the old neighborhood and stayed put. How he was going to accomplish that he wasn't sure, but what if Claire had a thing for Frankie?

"Hey Jack, the ramp for Interstate 80 is coming up," Patrick called out.

"Thanks."

"Thinking about Claire?"

"No, not like you think," Jack lied. "I was wondering how she was holding up. Give Frankie a call and see where they are at." He had turned the flashing lights off when he turned on Interstate 80. They were making good time. The road was almost deserted. Their unmarked car had a powerful engine which they rarely ever had the chance to use in the city. But out here on the open roads they could practically fly if they needed to.

With his phone on speaker mode, Patrick hit Frankie's number. "Where are you now?"

"I just got off Interstate 80 at Route 178. Edwards made a left turn just as Claire suspected he would. I'm crossing over the Illinois River."

"Do you have Edwards in your sight?"

"Yes, but I'm staying back far enough for him to ignore me. Sol is in front of me, and he is going to take the next right turn then catch up with me down the road," Frankie answered.

"Okay. My partner, Jack, and I are on Interstate 80. If Edwards is off 80, we can use the police lights without worrying that he'd see us. I'll call Sheriff Wilson as soon as we turn off. He has informed his people not to interfere with Edwards' vehicle. They are expecting you and Sol. So don't be surprised if they approach your car after you park."

"Claire told me to give her twenty minutes before I was to come after her," Frankie announced.

"Claire isn't getting twenty minutes. Sheriff Wilson should have a subpoena by now to search the property for the kidnapped sister of a Chicago homicide detective."

"Pretty cool, Patrick. How did you pull that off?" Frankie asked.

"Simple, you went to pick Claire up at the train station and she was forced into a black Lincoln Navigator. You called me, while you continued to follow the SUV."

"If anyone asks, I've got my story straight. Call me when you are closer." Frankie hung up.

"You didn't tell me about the kidnapping scheme? When did you talk with Dave?" Jack was starting to feel left out of the loop.

"Dave called me after you spoke with him. He came up with the idea. The judge's daughter was on his park district soccer team last spring. Sorry I forgot to mention it."

"No problem," Jack said. "Is there anything else you forgot to tell me? I know you have been preoccupied."

"That's it. Let's gun it. I want to get this done." Patrick tightened his grip on the door's arm rest.

Jack turned the police lights back on and floored the engine. The weather was in their favor. No wind, no rain, and no moon. He wasn't sure what the layout of the estate was, but at least Dave's people had scouted it out. He figured Dave would know all the entrances. Patrick was going to have to break it to Frankie and his brother that they had to stay back. They weren't going to participate in the charge.

Claire may have told Frankie to come in after her, but it wasn't happening. They may have learned to fight on the streets, but they had no business being involved any further. This was a police matter.

Jack was surprised at his own line of thinking as he pushed the unmarked squad down the highway. He had a job to do. He would have to examine his thoughts later. Right now, he had to get to Claire. Patrick was looking incredibly stressed. Maybe Patrick should wait at the rear too, but he knew Patrick would never go for it.

Jack checked his watch. They should be approaching the turn off in a few minutes. Claire may want twenty minutes, but Jack hoped this would be over way before then.

Chapter 47

Claire kept her emotions in check even though she could feel rage building up inside. She couldn't imagine women agreeing to participate in such a venture, but she had never experienced that hopeless, desperate feeling either.

Claire's only motivation was to find Sarah's killer. For women to believe that they didn't have another choice was an awful situation to be in. She wondered how many women Dr. Rothschild had exploited over the years. If John Gimble had eleven years' worth of tapes, then this had been going on for a very long time.

As Edwards guided her down the long hallway Kelly had described, Claire made sure to lean on him just enough to let him think she was drugged. When they arrived at the foot of the narrow staircase, he put her hand on the railing and pushed her up the stairs.

"Watch your step. The stairs are narrow here. Just put one foot in front of the other. You're doing fine," Edwards said.

Claire wanted to turn around and kick him in the face, but she didn't. "I'm all right," she reassured Edwards in a pleasant tone. At the top of the stairs, Claire took a good look down the hallway in front of her while Edwards was behind her. There were two doors to her right and one at the end of the hallway where light shown at the base of the door just before the hallway turned to the left. Claire couldn't see around the corner. If she came up the back stairs then the hallway must lead around to other rooms and the main staircase.

When Edwards helped her out of the car, Claire had taken a brief moment to assess the mansion. She noted it was a large two-story building with a steep-pitched roof. She hadn't seen the front of the building, but the back appeared fairly plain. Across the open area from where they parked was another building which was probably a tackle barn. She doubted they had horses on the property now.

Edwards nudged her down the hallway. He stopped at the second door. "You can change in here. Everything you need is on the bed. A nurse will be in to see you in ten minutes. Do you have any questions?" He opened the door.

"No. Everything seems fine," Claire slurred her words a little before stepping in the small room. Edwards closed the door behind her. She was all too aware after growing up in a family with policemen, that there could be cameras watching her. She was going to have to be very careful of her movements. She sat for a moment on the edge of the bed, took out her brush and ran it through her hair.

After a yawn she stretched. Kelly had told her about the double doors. She wandered over to see if they opened. If anyone came in, she could claim she wanted a little fresh air. To her surprise, the right one opened out onto a balcony. For the benefit of any cameras, she stood in front of the door and took in a couple breaths before closing it.

Claire really needed to see the procedure room. Her next thought was to pretend she was looking for the bathroom. With her purse strap looped over her neck, she opened the door and walked into the hallway. She probably had only seconds before someone stopped her, so she better make it look good. With her hand on the wall for presumed support, Claire walked to the door where she had seen the light at the bottom. As she opened the door, her other hand reached for her cell phone inside her purse.

A Chinese man stood over a small table setting up equipment. "You shouldn't be in here yet."

"I'm sorry I was looking for the bathroom," Claire said in a sleepy voice. Her eyes caught a glimpse of the exam table with its stirrups. She may have found the procedure room, but there wasn't a prayer she would be able to take a picture without exposing herself. She held on to the doorway as if she needed the support.

"Go back to your room. I will send someone to help you."

"Okay, thank you," Claire said as she closed the door.

"Where are you going?" Edwards' voice was no longer pleasant.

"Oh, I was just looking for the bathroom. Sorry to bother you." Claire hoped he bought her act.

"Come this way," said Edwards. "I'll take you. We can't have you wandering around. We don't want you to fall." He grabbed her tightly by the elbow and directed Claire around the corner to the left. "Here's the bathroom. I'll wait for you."

Claire decided not to argue with him. She went in and locked the door. She banged the lid up on the toilet to make Edwards think she was using the facilities. Then she turned the water on as she took her cell phone out and texted Frankie. Please let him answer, she prayed.

After a few seconds Edwards banged on the door. "Are you done?"

"I'll be out in just a minute," she called out. Frankie didn't answer. Maybe there wasn't a cell tower close by. She tried again. This time he answered. "Come get me," she texted. She slipped the phone in her back jeans pocket and put her flashlight in the other rear pocket. She turned the water off and flushed the toilet before opening the door.

"Thank you for waiting," she said to Edwards.

"Right," he answered. With a voice was laced with annoyance, he returned her to the room with the double doors. "Now stay put until the nurse comes for you."

"Okay," she responded as if she didn't notice his irritation. This time Claire was sure she heard a lock click after Edwards closed the door. She knew she had to get out now. Cameras or no cameras, she was leaving.

First, she took the chair next to the bed and hooked it under the door handle. It won't hold forever, but it might buy her some time.

She opened the door to the balcony. She stepped out on it. Everything looked black in the darkness. She figured she only had minutes before the nurse appeared. She took her flashlight out and turned it on and off giving the classic SOS signal several times. She didn't have any idea if Frankie got her message or if he would see her signal, but she had to try. She stuck the flashlight back into her pocket.

Claire looked over the balcony railing. How many times had she scaled down the trellis back home to meet Sarah? She looked for a trellis, or anything she could climb down. There was a gutter on the right side.

Praying it would hold her weight; Claire reached with her left leg as she heard the bedroom door rattle. She could hear someone's voice arguing with Edwards as he busted into the room. Before Claire could even inch her way down the rusty gutter, Edwards was out on the balcony pulling her back over the railing.

"You stupid bitch," he yelled as he slapped her across her face.

Claire felt the power of his blow. He was too big for her. She raised her knee as hard as she could up towards Edwards' groin and screamed at the top of her lungs. He let go of her as he doubled over. This might get her killed, but Edwards had it coming for slapping her.

"You're dead, you bitch," he whispered in a deadly tone as he tried to grab her, but Claire was just out of his reach. She ran back through the small room into the hallway. She looked down both ends of the hallway. She couldn't hear anything. She knew there was a Chinese man in the procedure room and somewhere was the woman she had heard argue with Edwards. If she ran into the woman down the backstairs, there was nowhere for her to go but back up, and Edwards would be waiting. She ran towards the hallway around the corner from the treatment room. At the corner, she reached down and removed the letter opener from her boot.

Claire didn't see anyone as she turned the corner and ran. She heard Edwards shouting behind her. He was calling for Renata.

Oh my word, Claire thought. That's the woman from Dr. Rothschild's office. Claire's choices were limited. She could try for the front stairs and pray she could run out the front door, or she could hide in one of the other rooms.

Claire entered the next room on her right. The room was dark, but she could make out it was a bedroom. At least it was on the front side of the house.

She ran towards the window and opened it. An alarm immediately sounded as she pushed the window up. Claire kicked out the screen. She looked out. The drop was easily fifteen feet. A busted ankle would be the least of her injuries. She had no doubt the next time Edwards got his hands on her, he would kill her.

Chapter 48

"Dave, we're on Route 178 south. We just crossed the Illinois River. Where do you want us to meet you?" Patrick asked.

"You should see a sign for Matthiessen State Park on your right pretty soon. Right after the second state park entrance, you will see an open area, then the driveway for the Vermilion Quarry. We're right in front," answered Dave.

"How far away is Claire from you?"

"About a quarter of a mile. Don't worry, we have the place under surveillance, and I have the signed subpoena. This is the best place for us to meet and make our final plans," Dave informed Patrick.

"Okay, we should be there in a few minutes." Patrick closed his cell phone. "Did you hear?" he asked Jack.

"Yep, pull in at the quarry."

"We're definitely out of Chicago and probably out of our element out here." Patrick removed his tie and opened the top button of his shirt.

Jack rarely had seen Patrick remove his tie. He always followed the dress code even in sweltering weather. His partner was nervous. Jack knew there wasn't anything he could say to ease the tension for him so he said nothing. He was just as worried as Patrick. If they were right that this Edwards character had killed Dr. Parks and John Gimble, another body wouldn't matter one bit to him. The sooner they got to Claire the better.

"There's the sign for the quarry," Patrick called out.

"Okay wing man, I've got it." Jack slowed down and pulled in. Someone flagged him over. Patrick was out of the unmarked car before Jack finished putting it in park. He could see Dave walking towards them.

"You made good time," Dave extended his hand to Patrick and Jack. "Come over here, and we'll show you the map. I'll run the plan by you and see what you think."

"This is your territory, you tell us what works," Patrick responded.

"Okay," said Dave.

Jack was impressed with the team Dave had pulled together. On the map, he had marked three entrances to the property. Right now, he had one car at each spot. He pointed to the main entrance where the gate and cameras were spotted. Dave and a deputy would approach on the main driveway. They would announce themselves over the intercom and if that failed, they had a blow horn they could use to let the occupants know they were at the gate.

"Don't worry, this thing is loud enough to wake up half the county. I'm sending a second car to each of the other two entrances, which are more like country back roads. We've discovered the front gate is only linked to a false fence that runs about a half a block on either side. I'll take a backup squad with me. I'd like the rest of the men to break up into two teams and enter the perimeter on either sides of the fence."

"Where do you want us?" Jack asked.

"Could I put the two of you on one of the teams going around the fence?"

"That's fine with me," Jack answered. "What do you think, Patrick?"

"Okay with me, whatever we can do to get Claire out of there," he said.

"Maybe you should stay at the back, in case things don't go according to plan," Dave offered.

"No, I want to get this son of a bitch." Patrick glared.

"Okay, here's a radio for you."

"Thanks." Before Jack could ask any questions, one of the deputy's ran over to Dave.

"Sheriff, Jed just radioed that Frankie insists he saw several flashes of light through the woods like a SOS signal. Jed couldn't stop them. They took off through the woods."

"Okay everyone, you have your orders. Remember, we have two civilians in the woods. Please be careful. I want all of you at the barbeque next weekend. That includes both of you," he said, nodding to Jack and Patrick. "Let's go."

"Are you sure you want to go through with this?" Jack asked his partner.

"Let's go," was Patrick's only answer.

Jack led the way. He stayed just to the left of the main driveway. The woods were thick with trees and underbrush. He wondered if there was any buckthorn out this way. That was the plant that had gotten them into this mess in the first place.

When they came across the fence, they walked the short distance around it. Jack turned to see how Patrick was holding up. Since it was dark, he couldn't see him, but had heard his partner's labored breathing. "Why don't you rest and I'll go ahead?"

"No."

"Then, let me have your cell phone. I want to find out where Frankie is?" It killed Jack to rely on Frankie's help, but this wasn't a time for his pride to get in the way.

Patrick hit the number and handed Jack his phone.

"Yes," Frankie answered.

"This is Patrick's partner. Where are you?"

"Sol and I are just in the woods before the front yard."

"Can you see Claire?" Jack asked as he kept moving between the trees.

"No, but right after I saw the light flash I thought I heard a scream. I'm behind a large oak tree. Sol is a few feet away. Wait, I think I see Claire pushing out a screen. No, she's gone."

"Hold your position. We're right behind you. I'll keep the line open. You might hear the sheriff on the bull horn."

Just then, Jack heard Dave's voice penetrate the silent night air. Seconds later he heard a couple of spurts of gunfire from the direction of the gate, followed by the voices of the men pushing open the gate.

"I guess Dave means business," he said to Patrick as he turned to see how he was doing. Using his flashlight, he saw his partner was bent over, grabbing a tree for support with one hand as he clutched the left side of his chest.

"Shit, Patrick!" Jack watched his partner collapse to the ground. "Patrick can you hear me?"

"Just leave me. I'll be okay. Get, Claire!" Patrick was gasping.

Jack hit the radio, "Mayday, Detective O'Shaunessy is having a heart attack. We are left of the driveway, between the fence and the house. I'm not leaving you. Help is coming."

Patrick grabbed Jack's tie. "If anything happens to Claire because you stayed with me, I'll..." He couldn't finish his statement.

"Okay, I hear you. Try to slow your breathing down. I hear

someone coming. Stay alive, will you?"

Jack raced through the woods as fast as he could. If anything happened to Patrick, he would never forgive himself for leaving him. Patrick may be his partner, but he was so much more. He was the father and brother he never had. The man had saved him from a depression that Jack thought he would never be able to crawl out of. Patrick was his mentor. Jack couldn't stand it if he lost one more person close to him.

What would he say to Sylvia, the angel who had opened up her heart and home, and showed him how to live again?

How would he face Patrick if anything happened to Claire? That redhead could drive him crazy, but he admired her commitment to her work. Please don't let me be too late, he prayed.

Chapter 49

Claire heard Renata yell at Edwards that she was leaving and going out one of the back entrances because the police were coming in the front gate.

Thank heavens, thought Claire, but her relief was short lived.

"I'll be gone as soon as I take care of that little bitch. She's not getting away." Edwards said loudly. He was closer than she expected him to be.

Claire's heart sank. The cavalry wasn't going to make it in time.

She heard Edwards opening all the doors in the hallway. Claire looked around. Now that her eyes had adjusted to the dark, she saw an antique bed with a long bed skirt to the floor. Quickly she squirmed under the bed and moved back as far as she could, just as the door opened.

Edwards immediately went to the window and looked out. He spent a moment looking out into the night. "Damn," he said as he tore out of the room.

Claire stayed put. Her heart pounded so hard she was surprised Edwards hadn't heard it. Her hand was clasped tightly around the letter opener. She strained to listen to his footsteps to hear which way Edwards had gone, but she couldn't tell. She had no idea what happened to the Chinese man she had seen in the procedure room.

Although muffled, Claire thought she heard someone speaking on a loud speaker. That had to be Sheriff Wilson. She vaguely heard the word subpoena.

There was no sound from the hallway. She couldn't believe Edwards was waiting just to seek revenge. He wouldn't risk arrest. He wasn't that stupid, or was he? If the sheriff comes through the front gate she thought, it would only make sense that Edwards was right behind Renata. Claire had to warn the sheriff so Edwards couldn't escape.

Quietly Claire moved an inch at a time to the edge of the bed.

Whatever she did now, she knew she would only have one chance if Edwards was lurking in the house. As she saw it, she had three choices. She could wait to be rescued, but might have to live with the fact that she let Edwards escape. As a result, the next time someone died at his hands, it would be her fault because she hadn't stepped up. Patrick wanted her safe, but he wasn't fond of cowards. Neither was her dad.

She could go out the window; but if she broke a leg, then she still couldn't stop Edwards. That left the worse choice. Claire could still fail, but at least she would have tried.

The last choice was what it had to be. The only issue remained, should she go down the back stairs or head for the front of the house?

Claire peaked out from under the bed skirt. She didn't see Edwards. Slowly she began inching herself out from under the bed. She desperately wanted to sneeze from all the dust on the floor. She bit down on her sweatshirt and pinched her nose. Somehow, she swallowed the sneeze.

Claire rolled over on her knees and gently eased herself up. Okay, so far so good.

Watching her step, she returned to the window. The fresh air smelled so good after lying in ten years of dust.

She took her flashlight out and sent another SOS. She repeated the signal several times. Suddenly her phone vibrated in her pocket. The number was Frankie's. She answered with barely a "yes." Her heart pounded with relief.

"Don't say anything. Sol and I can see you in the window. If you are alone flash once," Frankie directed.

Claire didn't answer.

"Flash twice if you think someone might be there."

Claire flashed twice.

"Okay, flash once if you think you could climb out the window and twice if you can't."

Claire flashed once.

"Okay, on the count of three you are going to climb out and jump. Sol and I will catch you. We are almost under the window now. Can you see us?"

"Yes," she whispered.

"Ready? Okay," Frankie directed. "One, two and three."

Claire swung her right leg through the window. Holding on to the window frame she brought her left leg though the window. She moved out onto the ledge and was about to jump when

Edwards grabbed her from behind. She hadn't even heard him return to the room.

Claire jammed the letter opener in her right hand as hard as she could into Edwards' ribs as he tightened his grip around her chest.

"Bitch," he yelled, "you're dead."

Claire screamed and tried to bite him. With all her weight, she attempted to throw herself forward as Edwards tried to pull her back into the room.

As she bent forward, she heard gunfire. Suddenly she was falling. Frankie and Sol broke her fall as they all tumbled to the ground. They looked to see where the shot had come from.

Jack stood where the woods met the front lawn with his weapon still drawn. Quickly he holstered his gun and sprinted towards Claire.

Within seconds, the whole place was swarming with officers. Dave ran over to them. "Is everyone all right?"

"Thanks to Detective Miller," answered Frankie as he brushed the fall leaves off himself. "Sol, you okay? Gorgeous, you got to lose some weight. Was that Edwards you took out up there?"

"I believe so," Jack replied trying to catch his breath. "Dave, how's Patrick?"

"What happened to Patrick? Jack, tell me." Claire thought she felt panic before, but this was much worse.

"We were coming through the woods when he started to have chest pain," said Jack.

"You left him?" Claire yelled.

"He insisted I go after you, Claire. What was I supposed to do? Dave, where is he?" Jack asked.

"He's in the ambulance down the driveway. He's okay, Claire. The paramedics have him on oxygen. They started an IV and gave him some meds. Come on, I'll take you to him. He'll be taken to Illinois Valley Community Hospital in nearby Peru. After he's stable, we can airlift him back to Chicago. You can ride with Patrick to the hospital." Dave led them down the driveway.

Claire wanted to cry. This was all her fault. If she just hadn't decided to get Edwards for Sarah's death, Patrick wouldn't have had a heart attack. The only good thing was Jack had taken out Edwards.

"Dave, did anyone check to make sure Edwards is dead?"

"My team is in the house. They found an Asian man with his throat slit in a procedure room and Edwards' brains all over the next room. This should keep the crime scene investigators up all night," Dave informed them. "Also, one of my men found a couple in a guest house near the river. According to their story, they are clients of Dr. Rothschild."

"There's one more person involved, Renata, Dr. Rothschild's assistant. I heard her say she was going down a back road," Claire explained as they approached the ambulance. Frankie and Sol were following her and Jack.

"Well, I didn't know her name, but Gladys took out a woman's tires with a couple rounds. The car hit a tree, and Hank has her cuffed to the steering wheel. I heard she was pissed."

"Patrick is going to like that part of the story," remarked Jack.

"Hey Gorgeous, do you think I could call Kelly and give her the good news about Edwards?" Frankie asked.

"I'm not talking to you, Frankie," Claire said.

"What do you mean?"

"It's your fault I gained weight."

Everyone stopped abruptly.

"Did he touch you?" Jack turned towards Frankie.

Claire laughed, "Nothing like a little male testosterone to liven up the night. Frankie happens to be one of the best cooks I know. I've been eating very well these past few days."

Jack looked sheepishly at the ground as they arrived at the ambulance. "You go in first," he said to Claire.

"Thanks." Claire accepted his hand to help her up into the ambulance.

"Well, Detective Miller, I guess you didn't know I had such culinary expertise? Sheriff, do you need Sol or me any longer?"

"Not tonight. I'll have one of my deputies call you for your statements tomorrow. Thanks for your help." Dave extended his hand to Frankie and Sol.

"Frankie, thanks for taking care of Claire." Jack offered his hand.

"Come on Sol, this place is getting too mushy. Besides, I left Vince with Kelly. I'm sure they need checking on. Goodnight, everybody." Frankie and Sol high-fived each other down the driveway.

"I think you'll want this," Jack handed Dave the weapon he had shot Edwards with.

"Thanks. I'll get it back to you as soon as I can," Dave offered.

"This isn't my service weapon, but I have a license to carry it."

"I understand." Dave took a deep breath. "Jack, we aren't in Chicago. Go ahead and ride with Patrick to the hospital. I'll have one of my deputies bring your car to the hospital. They usually have a couple guest rooms. Stay overnight and stop in and see me in the office before you head back tomorrow. We'll get all the paper work straightened out then."

Claire stuck her head out of the back of the ambulance. "Patrick's asking for you."

"Thanks for everything, Dave. Catch you tomorrow."

"No problem."

"Come on Jack," Claire called out again. "Patrick's not too patient."

***

"Heads up everyone, the cab driver is on board with our plan. Okay, the doorman waved. Dr. Rothschild should be coming out just about now," Sergeant Perchowski called over his radio. "That's him. Go!"

Dr. Rothschild ran from the building to the waiting cab, grabbed the back door handle, but it wouldn't budge. "What the…?"

"Dr. Rothschild, please step aside," Sgt. Perchowski ordered as several officers blocked him on either side.

"Do you know who I am? I have a patient to attend to. Get out of my way." Rothschild tried the cab door again, then pounded on the glass. "What's the matter with you, open the door now."

"Dr. Rothschild, the only place you are going is to jail." Perchowski stood with his feet slightly apart and his hands firmly on his hips. "Cuff him."

Dr. Rothschild swung his briefcase at an officer, but another one intercepted the case as cuffs were being applied. "I'll have your badge for this."

"Dr. Rothschild, I have a message for you from Detectives O'Shaunessy and Miller. You're under arrest as an accomplice in the deaths of Sarah Morgan and Dr. Parks, and for running an illegal infertility clinic. Also, I believe check fraud for a deceased Alice Monroe will be included. I'm sure the DA will have more charges. Okay officer, read the doctor his rights and take him to booking."

"I want my lawyer," Rothschild demanded, attempting to yank his arms out of the officer's grasp.

"I'm sure you do," Perchowski said. "All in good time, Dr. Rothschild, all in good time." It felt good to arrest someone who thought he was above the law. Captain Ramos had filled him in on all the details of the two homicide cases.

Perchowski pulled out his cell phone and hit Captain Ramos' number. His superior answered on the first ring. "Mission accomplished, Sir. How did O'Shaunessy and Miller make out?"

Ramos relayed the LaSalle take down to Perchowski. "O'Shaunessy will be transported back to Chicago General tomorrow. He'll be on desk duty when he returns."

Perchowski let out a laugh which was loud enough to wake half of Chicago. "Patrick will be pissed!" He'd known Patrick since their days in the Police Academy and he knew his old friend couldn't sit still for five minutes. "Good luck with that, Captain."

Chapter 50

Jack was drained. He had been up half the night notifying Sylvia and the Captain about Patrick's condition and the events at the LaSalle estate. What sleep he got was in small segments as a result of the constant noise in the hospital corridors. No wonder patients complained they couldn't sleep. The other half of the truth was he was too wired to sleep.

He didn't know which emotion to feel first as he worked on his statement for Dave at the station. He was damn grateful Patrick had suffered only a mild heart attack. He knew he was lucky he hit Edwards, and there weren't two O'Shaunessys in hospital beds. His mind didn't want to acknowledge that he could have easily hit Claire instead of Edwards.

Jack had never killed anyone before. He had shot the bad guys, but not killed them. He didn't know what to do with that feeling. Edwards was about as evil as they came. If a judge gave Edwards the death penalty, then that would have been okay. But it was a job he hadn't wanted.

Jack hated to admit it, but perhaps the department regulation requiring officers involved in a shooting to see a shrink was a good thing. Was Edwards the real issue, or was it Tad? The two monsters that had killed his best friend walked the streets free because of a technicality. They had no problem killing Tad, like Jack had had no problem killing Edwards. Was he no better than the next killer?

"I brought you some fresh coffee. How's your statement coming along?" Dave asked.

"Slow," Jack said. "Nothing a couple of days off wouldn't cure."

"Was this the first time you ever took someone out?" Dave sat on the edge of his desk.

"Yes."

"Even if the shoot is justifiable, it's never a good feeling to end someone's life. I've been there. I won't say you will feel better about killing Edwards down the road, but you will be more accepting of the fact that he didn't leave you any choice. I'm sure you weren't going to forfeit Claire for Edwards."

"Thanks, you're right about all of it."

Dave got off his desk. "I'll check on Claire while you finish."

"What about Patrick's statement?" Jack asked.

"I sent a deputy with a court reporter over to see Patrick earlier this morning. As soon as the statement is typed, the deputy will run it over for him to sign." Dave walked to the door and stopped. "If I forgot to mention it, thanks for helping us close the case on Sarah Morgan. Expect a call from Gladys next week. We are postponing our annual barbeque until Patrick feels up to making the trip out here."

"It was nice seeing team work between the two departments. Thanks for including us. If we can ever return the favor, don't hesitate to call."

Jack bent over the paper in front of him. Even though he took the scenario from beginning to end, he felt so much was left unsaid. His statement was simply about the facts, no more, no less. There was nothing in his statement about how the damage Rothschild and Edwards inflicted on others would affect their victims and families for years.

John Gimble's family was the perfect example, a husband and father gone. His family would experience all life's special events from now on without him. This didn't even include the emotional trauma John had suffered under Rothschild's thumb.

Kelly was safe, but she wouldn't get a free pass. Jack was sure at some point she would have trouble coping because she sent Sarah to Rothschild. Claire blamed herself for not staying in better touch with Sarah. However, even if Claire had, she may not have noticed Sarah's gambling problem in time to prevent her death.

The reality was Rothschild and Edwards had destroyed dreams and ended lives. They were just as evil as the two young men who robbed Tad of his life.

"Are you done?" Claire popped her head in.

"Yeah, I guess so," said Jack.

"I can wait, if you need more time?"

Jack picked up his statement and stared at it. "I don't think time could make it better. Let's get out of here."

"Can I bum a ride back to Chicago with you? After you say yes, could we drive over to the hospital and see Patrick before we leave. Gladys baked him a sticky bun cake, but I think I'll give it to Sylvia. I have a feeling it's no longer on his diet."

"Yes to everything, but I want a slice of Gladys' cake. Can you believe Gladys and Hank both qualified at the range last week? I hope I qualify at their age." Jack held the door as they left the Sheriff's Office.

"Patrick did get a kick out of how they took down Renata. I heard she was singing for her supper with the DA. She claims Edwards killed Dr. Logan, who was responsible for Sarah's death. Apparently, Edwards cremated Logan and spread his remains in a cornfield. What about Rothschild?" Claire asked.

"Captain Ramos said Perchowski arrested Rothschild outside his penthouse. He was hailing a cab for the airport. I have a feeling the accommodations at the state prison are not going to meet with his standards."

Claire laughed as they drove over to see Patrick. "So his Champagne taste has been reduced to a tap water budget."

"Something like that."

***

Claire gave her brother a big hug as they entered his hospital room.

Patrick smiled at seeing Claire and Jack. "The doctor insists I be officially transferred back to Chicago General. I told him I was just fine and could ride with you two. Help me get this IV out and the monitor leads off so I can escape."

"Not a chance in the world, partner," said Jack. "Even Captain Ramos said this was to be an official transfer. I think he also said something to the effect that if you didn't go along for the ride, he might suspend you a month without pay. I wouldn't want to be the one to have to face Sylvia if that happened. If I were you, I'd take the complimentary ride home." Jack stood there with his hands in his pockets smiling.

"What a fine partner you turned out to be. Claire, come on, you're a doctor, help me out of this crap."

"I happen to agree with Jack. Besides, I'm not a cardiologist. I cut up dead people, as Frankie would say." Claire kept her distance. "If you remove those leads, half the staff will respond to the alarms. Don't piss off the staff, Patrick. They're nice people."

"Detective O'Shaunessy, the team is here to transport you," the nurse announced from the door.

"Bye Patrick. See you in Chicago." Claire smiled smugly and waved as she and Jack left.

Chapter 51

Claire felt like she was in Mother Superior's office again. The experience had been repeated often during grade school, and more frequently in high school. The usual infractions were anything from talking in class, to smoking in the john or running in the hallway. Most of the time, the nuns took pity on her because she hadn't had a mother to teach her manners, and the social graces like her older sisters had. Mother Superior knew Patrick was doing the best he could raising his sisters after their father died.

Even though the nuns would write personal comments regarding her deplorable behavior on her report cards, Claire had never once been suspended. Usually she received detention, which worked in her favor. Since her butt was glued to a desk for an additional hour several times a week, she continued to maintain a high grade point average. Now she looked back on those years and thought of how the nuns had probably saved her from herself.

But the death of her father had stunned her. She couldn't believe God would take her only parent away from her, but He did. Sister Theresa had told Claire, God was challenging her faith. Claire told the nun to go to hell. Until that moment, she had played ice hockey for fun. After that, she played for blood, which had landed her in the penalty box plenty of times. The coach ignored her because she was his leading scorer and the reason the team went to state her senior year in high school. If she could get through high school, she could get through this interview with Captain Ramos.

"Claire, thank you for coming in." Captain Ramos stood behind his desk chair, his elbows resting on the back of it.

"You didn't make it sound like I had a choice." Claire wasn't going to give him an inch.

Captain Ramos went over and closed the door to his office. "Please sit down."

"Thanks, but I'll stand," Claire said defiantly.

"I'm not asking, I'm telling you. Now sit down," he said in a firm tone.

Claire sat in the chair opposite his desk. She wondered how

many times Patrick had been in the 'hot' seat himself.

Captain Ramos sat down at his desk. "The reason I asked you here today was to discuss a little problem we seem to be having."

"But..."

The Captain put up his hand and stopped her dead in her tracks.

"Claire, you need to understand something. I'm going to talk and you are going to keep your mouth shut if it kills you. Do we have an understanding?" Captain Ramos placed his hands on the desk and leaned slightly forward.

"Yes, sir." Claire wanted to call him Mother Superior but decided being flippant with Patrick's Captain was only going to make things worse for Patrick. Right now, she felt guilty enough about her brother's condition

"Good. I'm glad that's settled.

"I know you are a bright forensic pathologist, but I don't remember you passing the police exam or graduating from the academy. Nor do I remember the Department hiring you on as a specialist in any capacity. Do you agree with me so far?" he asked her directly.

"Yes sir." Claire didn't think he could bring any charges against her, but now she wasn't so sure.

"Good. I'm glad we are on the same page. It was very nice of you to invite Kelly Davis to stay with you for a few days. Since you have a generous nature, I'm going to overlook the fact that you interfered in a police investigation. This was not your intention, correct?"

"Correct, Captain Ramos."

"Good. I do believe you have the right to seek medical care from any physician you see fit, but not under an assumed name. I don't want to know where you got the fake ID. Frankie takes good care of my wife's car. I would hate for him to have to be a guest of the state and have my wife's car fall apart. Don't you agree?"

"Yes sir." *Shit*, Claire thought, now she had put Frankie in harms' way. She had a problem with not always thinking things through before she took action. She was going to get detention for sure.

"In the future, I suggest you verify with the state if a clinic has been licensed or not before you sign up for a procedure. You never know when a raid might occur and catch you in a compromising position."

"I wasn't going to go through with the procedure, I..."

"Claire, I really don't want to know. Since everything turned out well, I'm going to turn a blind eye to your transgressions. Stopping the operation may have been a wakeup call for Patrick to do something about his health. He's my best detective. I need him alive. Of course, if you ever repeat what I just said to him, I will deny it. Do we have an understanding?" Captain Ramos eased back in his chair.

"Yes sir." Claire was afraid to breathe.

"Good. Then you will only practice your skills as a forensic pathologist, while Patrick will remain the only policeman in your family. Do you agree with me?"

Claire breathed a heavy sigh. "Yes sir."

"Good. Consider this your one 'get out of jail free card'. I rarely hand out a second. Do you understand?"

"Yes sir." Somehow she had a feeling Captain Ramos was enjoying himself a little too much at her expense.

Captain Ramos rose and opened his office door. "I'm glad we had this chat. Please give my best to Patrick. Tell him I said he is to take whatever time off he needs. Goodbye, Claire."

Hurray! I didn't get detention was Claire's first thought. Captain Ramos opened the door, so she must be free. "Thank you Captain," was all Claire could say as she left.

"So he didn't give you five to ten for interfering with a police investigation?" Jack laughed.

Claire turned to see Jack resting against his desk with his arms folded over his chest and a big smile spread across his face. "You enjoyed the whole thing, didn't you?" she asked.

"Wish Patrick could have been here." Jack laughed. "You're lucky the Captain didn't throw the book at you or write Patrick up. I'm headed over to see him, do you want a lift?"

"As long as you never tell Patrick about Captain Ramos, or I might have to do your autopsy before you're dead." Claire didn't need Patrick aware of Ramos' reprimand.

"Claire, you are a hard woman. Is this the thanks I get for saving your life?"

A cold rush washed over Claire. Suddenly she felt ice cold, and the air seemed short on oxygen. The words 'bitch you're dead' boomed in her ears as her knees buckled beneath her.

"Perchowski, get me some water. I think Claire's passing out." Jack grabbed her before she hit the ground and lifted her into a chair. He pushed her head between her knees. "Take some slow, deep breaths." Jack kept his hands on her.

"Here's the water. Claire, are you okay?" Perchowski held it out to her.

Captain Ramos came out of his office. "What happened?" he asked Jack.

"You must have scared her, Captain," Jack said.

"Claire? That's not possible." He walked back into his office and slammed the door.

Claire lifted her head and accepted the water from Perchowski. "Thanks."

"Just sit here a while longer, then we'll go," Jack told her.

"I forgot to eat today, that's all." She didn't want to tell him about the memories. She hadn't been able to get the sound of Edwards' voice out of her head, or the thought of him trying to pull her back into that room out of her mind.

"I can fix that," offered Jack. He unlocked Patrick's desk and took out a candy bar.

"Why am I not surprised?" Claire laughed. "I think you better clean out his desk before he returns to work." The chocolate bar fed her blood sugar level.

"Think you can walk?" Jack asked a few minutes later.

"Sure, let's go." Claire stood up slowly just to make sure her legs were under her. She took a step to test out her knees before continuing.

"All right, but we're stopping to eat. Besides, I missed lunch. You can think about where you want to eat on the way to the car."

Claire's exhaustion made it too difficult to argue with Jack. She wouldn't be any good to Patrick if she couldn't hold her own. "Any place we can pick up a quick burger and a shake will be great."

"I thought Frankie said you needed to lose weight." Jack ducked before Claire could hit him.

Chapter 52

"Take the elevator to the third floor and turn right. The patient's room will be half way down the hall on your left across from the nurses' station."

Claire thanked the receptionist. She never liked hospitals. This was where a family's last thread of hope for their loved one was often destroyed.

Minutes later, she stepped into the empty elevator with Jack.

"Why does Frankie always call you 'Gorgeous'?" said Jack as he turned to face the doors.

"When I was a scrawny kid, my arms and legs seemed too long for my body, and I was the last one on the block to get boobs. All my sisters took after my mother. They got the curves and were well endowed at an early age. I didn't blossom until the end of high school. Sarah had all the curves, *and* all the guys. I think Frankie started calling me Gorgeous to make me feel better. The nickname stuck, but if he's pissed at me, he calls me O'Shaunessy," Claire explained as they left the elevator on Patrick's floor.

Claire didn't need a room number to find her brother's room. The noise and people spilled out of Patrick's room into the hall.

"Claire," her sister Chevoun called out. "Patrick said you jumped out of a two story window into Frankie's arms." Her sister gave her a big hug. "Hi Jack. We hear you were the one who saved Claire's life."

"I have a feeling Claire could've taken care of herself," Jack replied. "The deputies said they found a letter opener jammed in Edwards' rib cage." Jack stood comfortably in the middle of the chaos.

"So I *didn't* miss?" Claire asked.

"You stabbed him?" Her sister Colleen had come from inside Patrick's room. She looked Claire up and down then wrapped her arms around her sister.

"Well, I did what I had to do. No big deal," she told her sisters.

"You better not let Caitlin or Callie hear you say that. They think you're this nice doctor, except for the cutting up of dead people part," Chevoun stated.

"They're called autopsies, Chevoun. Now all of you sound like Frankie."

"Hey, did I hear my name?" Frankie said as he came out of Patrick's room. "Hey Gorgeous, how are you doing?" Frankie planted a smacker of a kiss on Claire's lips and squeezed her butt. He looked straight at Jack. "I always greet all the O'Shaunessy women who aren't married like that."

"How many aren't married?" Jack asked with a slight hard tone to his voice.

"Just Claire. Come on in. Patrick has been asking for you. Claire, next week do you think we could plan a small memorial service for Sarah? Kelly offered to help."

"Of course, Frankie. I'd like that." Claire knew in spite of all the craziness lately, this was something they all needed to do. Say goodbye to Sarah.

"Are you going with him or something?" Jack whispered in Claire's ear.

"No. We're just old friends. Frankie likes to rattle your cage because you let him." Claire whispered back as the party moved back into Patrick's room.

The room was wall-to wall people with Patrick in the center. Claire squeezed through the relatives and friends and gave Patrick a hug.

"Can you spring me from this riot?" asked Patrick, referring to the noise in his room.

"Not a chance big brother. Seriously, how do you feel?" Claire couldn't hide the worry. She knew Patrick could read her like a book.

"I feel just fine, but if I don't get out of here soon, I *will* have a heart attack."

Claire glanced at the cardiac monitor at Patrick's bedside. "How about I get the nurse to play bad cop and send everyone home except Sylvia and the kids. Your readings on the monitor look great, but you do look tired."

"You know patients can't sleep at night with all the carts going up and down the halls," Patrick complained.

"Let me get Jack while I sneak out for the nurse." Claire found Jack with Sylvia in the doorway.

"How are you doing?" Claire asked her sister-in-law.

"I've been warning him for years to slow down, or he was going to make me a beautiful widow. But does he listen to me? No. And, I hear you were involved in his latest caper?" Sylvia gave Claire a big hug.

"Well, not officially. I'll tell you about it someday. Right now Patrick wants to see Jack, and I'm going to see what I can do to reduce the noise level in here."

A short Asian man Claire recognized as Patrick's physician appeared in the doorway. Jack and Sylvia stepped aside so he could enter.

"Patrick, I'm sure this wasn't what I meant when I said you needed peace and quiet. You can hear the party from the main entrance," boomed Dr. Ben Wong's voice over the noise. Everyone stopped talking at once.

"Hi, Doc," said Patrick. "I think everyone will be leaving soon."

"It is just as well they're here. I can save myself some time and give everyone your discharge instructions now," announced Dr. Wong.

"What about patient privacy?" Patrick frowned.

"Consider your friends and family part of your support team." Dr. Wong smiled.

"Are you letting me out now?" Patrick asked.

"No. If you have an uneventful night, then tomorrow will be soon enough," answered Dr. Wong. "Okay, here are some of the basic rules. Sylvia, this especially applies to you. No more bread saturated in buttery garlic or second servings of lasagna. Lean meats broiled or grilled with healthy salads. This does not include croutons or cheese. And donuts and fast food are absolutely out of the question."

"Doc, you're killing me," Patrick moaned.

"Which one of you is his partner?" Dr. Wong asked.

"I am sir. Jack Miller's the name." Jack extended his hand to the doctor.

"Just as I expected. Patrick, your young partner's the picture of health. Okay Mr. Miller, you've been assigned to drag Patrick down to the gym, the bike paths, whatever you want, but get him moving and no rewards of food afterwards. Water will work just fine. The rest of you are to help him make this work. Is that understood? I don't especially enjoy funerals. Besides, loosing patients is bad for business."

Claire noticed everyone was trying to hide their smiles. She knew it was going to take an act of God or Congress to get Patrick to change his life style.

"Patrick, I'll see you in the morning. The rest of you get out of here and let the poor guy get some rest." Dr. Wong waved as he left.

"Thanks, Doc," Patrick called after him.

"Hey partner, how do you feel?" Jack asked, moving to stand next to his bed.

"Like the gowns are too short. Any word on the case yet?"

"Yes. Dave called just before I left the office. The LaSalle County crime scene guys brought Edwards' SUV in for inspection. I hear it's quite the car. Edwards had secret compartments built in about every free space you could think of in it. Even the inside of the driver's door was used to store guns and ammunition."

"Wow. Where did he get that type of work done? That had to cost him a pretty penny. Did Dr. Rothschild pay that well?"

Claire noticed that Patrick was starting to look alive again. The apple doesn't fall far from the tree. He was definitely their father's son.

"I don't know, but here's the grand prize," said Jack. "In one of the compartments, they found various sets of driver's licenses and plates from all over the Midwest. That accounts for the different plates he used. And, there was a phone number with the name Dirk," Jack explained.

"Who's Dirk?" Patrick asked.

"Within minutes of Gladys researching the phone number, she got a call from one of her old friends at the Bureau. They've been investigating this Dirk character. Has something to do with a mercenary ring," said Jack. "You know Gladys, if she told me any more information, she would have to kill me. But she was able to research the LaSalle estate back to Dr. Rothschild. Even the best lawyers shouldn't be able to set him free."

"At least we have prevented more women from being harmed by Dr. Rothschild," Patrick said.

"This Dr. Logan, who Renata claimed Edwards had killed, came from the same rehab clinic that our Dr. Parks attended. Both were working on suspended licenses," Jack said. "Can you imagine what our department could accomplish if we had both Gladys and Finch working for us?"

Claire watched the last of Patrick's energy drain out of his face as his eyelids drooped. "I think it's time to end the party before our guest of honor falls asleep on us."

Patrick sighed in relief. "Thanks everyone for coming, but for once, and only once, I agree with Claire."

Claire caught his smile as she felt her cell phone vibrate in her pocket. She read her boss' number on the caller ID. "O'Shaunessy here," she answered.

"Claire, this is Dr. Johnson. How's your brother doing?" he asked.

"He's doing well. Looks like if he behaves tonight, the doc will spring him tomorrow," Claire answered.

"That's good. I hate to bother you, but I need you to come in for an autopsy."

"I'm not on call. I think Dr. Shah is." Claire looked up to see everyone's eyes pinned on her. They were used to her leaving in the middle of family gatherings for work, but this time she was sticking to her guns. Dr. Shah could take his own call.

"You don't understand Claire, I need you to come in and do *this* autopsy," Dr. Johnson's voice was firm.

"But I'm not on call, and Dr. Shah does a great job," she insisted. Besides, I'm at the hospital with Patrick."

"You don't understand, Claire, you have been requested."

"What do you mean '*requested*'? When the patient is alive it is one thing, but how does one do this from the afterlife?" Claire knew her last comment was uncalled for, but this was crazy.

"The mayor has requested you."

"The *mayor* of Chicago has requested *me*?" Claire could hear Jack's phone ring. She looked him straight in the eyes.

"It's the mayor's sister, Claire. She's dead."

Dr. Johnson had dropped a bomb. "I'll be right there, Dr. Johnson." Claire hung up and looked at her family. She hated to leave them, but she had no other option. Dr. Johnson's call trumped family tonight.

"Captain Ramos said I'm to drive you."

Claire gave Patrick a big hug and whispered the issue in his ear. She knew he would be pissed if she didn't share, especially since Jack had been called in, too.

"Are you ready?" Jack asked.

She nodded, then turned and kissed her brother's cheek. "Duty calls."

"Love you sis," said Patrick with a crooked grin.

"I love you more." she said, repeating her dad's phrase as she followed Jack out of the room.

"Is one ever ready for the media circus this will cause?" Claire asked.

"No, but I think you can handle it," said Jack, pushing the elevator button. "Look what you just pulled off. You potentially just saved more women from Sarah's fate. That's impressive in my book."

"Right, but the toll it took on Patrick wasn't fair. Almost getting myself killed was one thing. I'll never forgive myself for putting Patrick's life at risk," said Claire as the elevator doors opened and they stepped inside.

"You have it all wrong, Claire. Patrick's health was an issue long before you moved back to Chicago because of the choices he made. Now, he can choose to make healthy changes."

"I'll think about what you said, but we both know I didn't help matters."

In the parking lot, Jack opened the car door for her and said, "Well, then, let me give you something to think about." Then he gently squeezed her butt.

"Why Detective Miller," she said, grinning at him over her shoulder, "you give me plenty to think about." Then she slipped into her seat and he winked at her before he shut the door.

About the Author

Sue (Schreck) Myers was raised in Libertyville, Illinois, and lives in the next town over with her husband, Gene, their cats, and a backyard full of birds and squirrels. Her first encounter with a dead body was in third grade. Whenever a classmate lost a relative, the nuns would march them up to the funeral home to say prayers over the deceased. Sue would stare at them, daring them to wink. Lucky for her, none did.

In her twenties, Sue worked as an ER Tech in a Chicago hospital between Rush Street and the projects. Because of the ER's interesting cliental, she was exposed to a whole array of situations involving the 18th District Police. Years later, Sue became a registered nurse, but her experiences in the ER never left her. She spent her nursing career in Labor and Delivery, Neonatal ICU and infertility. Her career in the medical field fueled stories which begged to be told. When Sue isn't writing, she can be found in her garden or quilting.

Made in the USA
Lexington, KY
17 October 2014